**Sara w... S...ish ...ome... ... first,
but sh...** ... **in
Jason...**

His mouth ... on hers, so... at first, then
picking up a heat and fierceness and intensity that
she felt helpless to do anything about but respond
in kind

No. S... never felt helpless. This was exactly what
she w...nted, precisely where she wanted to be: in
Jason's strong, sexy embrace. Kissing him as if
there was nothing, no one, in the world but them.

But as her hands raced under his clothes and up his
back to clutch his heated flesh, she heard, in the
distance, the sound of conversation.

"I--I'm sorry," she gasped. "This wasn't right."

"Oh, I'd say it was very right," Jason muttered.

UNTAMED WOLF

LINDA O. JOHNSTON

Linda O. Johnston loves to write. More than one genre at a time? That's part of the fun. While honing her writing skills, she started working in advertising and public relations, then became a lawyer…and still enjoys writing contracts. Linda's first published fiction novel appeared in *Ellery Queen's Mystery Magazine* and won a Robert L. Fish Memorial Award for Best First Mystery Short Story of the Year. It was the beginning of her versatile fiction-writing career. Linda now spends most of her time creating memorable tales of paranormal romance and mystery.

Linda lives in the Hollywood Hills with her husband and two Cavalier King Charles spaniels. Visit her at her website, www.lindaojohnston.com.

Untamed Wolf is dedicated to wolves, real and shape-shifters. It's also dedicated to our military, covert and otherwise. It's dedicated to Maryland, including the Eastern Shore and the area south of Baltimore, where we visit often. Plus, it's dedicated to my friends and my readers…and, of course, to my husband, Fred.

And it's especially dedicated to Harlequin and the Nocturne series, its editors and most particularly my wonderful editor Allison Lyons. And last but definitely not least, it's dedicated to my excellent agent, Paige Wheeler of Folio Literary Management.

Chapter 1

Sara pulled her car up to the formidable black wrought-iron gate at Ft. Lukman. She had been driving her small hybrid for more than an hour from D.C. to this out-of-the-way military installation on Maryland's Eastern Shore.

Stopping at the security kiosk, she pulled her ID from the purse on the passenger seat. "Lieutenant Sara McLinder, reporting for duty," she told the guard, a tall man, wearing a standard camouflage uniform similar to the one Sara had on.

So far, nothing here looked different or surprising, no matter what Sara's superior officer, General Greg Yarrow, had suggested. Of course not.

Even so, maybe she should have waited until tomorrow, as the general had said. It was early evening already, and she wouldn't have much time to get settled.

On the other hand, it hadn't been an order, and Sara didn't like to delay. Facing new situations quickly and immediately was more to her liking than waiting.

"Is General Yarrow behind you, ma'am?" asked the soldier.

"The general will be here tomorrow," she said.

"Very good, ma'am." He looked over her identification and passed it back. "Everything looks in order. Welcome

to Ft. Lukman, Lieutenant." The private saluted and the
gate slid open, away from the car.

Sara saluted back. "Thank you," she said, then drove
onto the base.

The general had provided her the layout in advance. She
knew that the building comprising the Bachelor Officers'
Quarters where she was to stay was to the right once she
entered the base. That was where she headed. She was also
aware that the cafeteria, not far from the living quarters,
should be open late—a good thing. She hadn't stopped to
eat on the way and was hungry.

Rather than pulling into the small enclosed garage, she
parked in the open-air lot closest to the BOQ, finding a
space at the far end, near a wall. She removed her suitcase
on wheels from the trunk of her car. She had already been
given a set of keys, so she had no problem either getting
inside the functional-looking concrete building or into her
apartment after taking the elevator up one floor.

Interestingly, or not, she didn't run into any other people. Also a good thing, since she didn't really want to have
a gabfest. Not now.

She didn't spend much time assessing the quarters where
she would stay as long as the general kept them at this base.
The place resembled a tiny one-bedroom apartment. That
was good enough.

She was back outside in only a few minutes, walking
in the remaining daylight along a sidewalk toward the cafeteria. As she neared it, she began to see people—others
also in camo fatigues and thick-soled shoes similar to hers.

She wondered if she would be able to discern any differences between the two main units now present at Ft.
Lukman. That was one of the reasons General Yarrow intended to station himself for a while at this base. He was
in charge of Alpha Force, the special-ops unit that had

been headquartered here for a few years. A new special-ops group, the Ultra Special Forces Team, had only been assigned here about a month ago to prepare for a highly classified and critically important team assignment with Alpha Force, and the general had heard about some friction between the two units.

He wanted to observe it—and, if necessary, make some changes.

Sara, as the primary aide assigned to General Yarrow, would be his eyes and ears and, if necessary, his mouth.

A group of four enlisted personnel—two men and two women—stood by the building's entrance. They stopped their conversation and saluted her, and she saluted back.

Interesting, since the general had said that things were fairly low-key and informal here at Ft. Lukman. These soldiers were therefore probably among the new arrivals.

The general had also hinted at a lot of other things about what went on at Ft. Lukman, none of which could be real. He liked to joke. His sense of humor was obviously quite different from hers. But she always admired how serious he appeared, even while jesting.

Inside an entry hall, Sara saw people going in and out through an open doorway in the middle—obviously the way into the cafeteria. The aroma of grilled meat grew stronger the closer she got, confirming her assumption.

The place was smaller than she'd anticipated for a base this size—a long room crowded with occupied tables. She headed toward the food line and picked out a hamburger and fries, then got a soft drink.

Once she paid, she looked around for an empty spot and saw none. She could get the meal to go, but for now was carrying a tray.

"Hi," said a female voice beside her. "You look lost."
Sara turned and saw a woman in camo uniform with lay-

ered tawny hair and a big smile—another lieutenant, like her. "You wouldn't happen to be General Yarrow's aide, would you? We were told you'd be here tomorrow, but I don't think anyone else is expected right now."

Sara smiled. "Good guess. I'm Sara McLinder." She saw that her new companion's name tag read Hodell.

"I'm Colleen Hodell. Welcome. Here, we'll make room at our table for you." She gestured across the room where some other soldiers were seated around a table. "They're all Alpha Force members."

"Thanks," Sara said, and followed Colleen.

By the time they got there, someone had pulled an empty chair up to the table. Eight people were already seated around it. Sara smiled and nodded through the introductions. Interestingly, officers and enlisted personnel were all eating together.

Alpha Force protocol might be stronger around here than that of the regular military. Well, the general had warned her to expect things to be different from what she was used to, and some of it had to be real. If this fraternization made her uncomfortable, she wouldn't show it. Just being friendly wasn't prohibited under military regulations.

She placed her tray on the table and sat down.

"Welcome to Ft. Lukman," said the man seated beside her. According to his insignia, he was a sergeant. It wasn't the first time she'd heard a welcome, but this soldier's deep voice resonated with what sounded like irony. She looked at him, planning to maintain her rank and dignity.

"Thank you, Sergeant," she said brusquely, then looked away after noting what appeared to be sexual interest in his flashing golden eyes.

She must have imagined it. That would be the kind of fraternizing that was definitely forbidden under military regulations.

Although…well, she wasn't supposed to notice such things, but that sergeant was one handsome guy. He looked fairly young, maybe late twenties like her, but his short, black hair was flecked with silver. His features were sharp, his smile gorgeous and challenging—and she couldn't help noticing how broad his shoulders appeared beneath his camo shirt.

"Are you a new member of Alpha Force?" asked the sergeant, whose ID tag said his last name was Connell.

"Not exactly," she said. "I'm General Yarrow's aide, and I'll be here as long as he is. He is planning some exercises for Alpha Force while he's here."

"Then you're not—" The female sergeant across the table, whose name tag said Jessop, stopped speaking when Colleen elbowed her in the ribs.

"Has the general told you much about Alpha Force?" asked another man at the other side of the table. Sara nearly rose and saluted as she noticed his brass. He was a major. But the informality around here stopped her. Members of this unit might act all military elsewhere, but while eating dinner in this cafeteria they were all, apparently, just people.

"No, sir," Sara said. "Not really." Greg Yarrow had implied that things around here were quite different from the rest of the military without giving any credible explanation. He had even suggested that some of the members of Alpha Force went beyond any military skill she could ever imagine—because they were shapeshifters. Hah! She had worked with him long enough to anticipate and deal with that offbeat sense of humor of his. Despite his straight face, he knew better. He couldn't actually imagine she was a gullible subordinate who'd buy into that. Even so, he hadn't told her anything genuinely distinctive about the remote and covert unit. She figured she would learn the real differences here on the job.

She took a bite of her hamburger. Not bad for cafeteria food.

"Interesting," said the sergeant beside her. "Maybe I should show you around. Teach you what you need to know."

"Back off, Jason." That was the major. She squinted slightly to see his name tag.

It read Connell just like the sergeant's. Jason's.

Talk about interesting… Were the noncom and officer related?

That would be unusual—not that relatives had joined the military, but that both men would be in the same unit.

Was that somehow part of the reason that Alpha Force was considered different from other special-ops units?

Doubtful, but— Well, it made more sense than imagining that any of these very real-looking people could be shapeshifters, despite the general's teasing insinuations that they were. But just being related didn't make these soldiers distinctive, unless, perhaps, their family members had taught one another useful skills from youth that other people might not have. She couldn't think of a good example, though.

Maybe they really had taught one another how to shapeshift.

Not!

She took a sip of her drink and another bite of hamburger, then glanced back toward the sergeant to see whether he was, in fact, backing off.

The expression in his eyes was now filled with what looked like irony—even as he seemed to assess her from head to toe as she sat there. Oh, yes. He was a real man.

The gaze heated her insides. Made her sexually aware of the guy all over again.

Forget that, she cautioned herself. She was entirely military. Obeyed all orders and loved it.

No way would she allow herself even to notice if this soldier decided to play games with her.

Although, she realized, she already had noticed...and somehow liked it too much.

The rumors had been correct, Jason thought. Not that Major Drew Connell—no, not just major, but also Doctor Drew Connell, his cousin—told him much of anything around here.

Jason was just a peon. At least, because of his very special background that had led him to Alpha Force, he had been promoted to sergeant quickly and wasn't just a private.

In any event, Jason took a sip of soda water and continued to watch the gorgeous, hot—and unapproachable—lieutenant who had only arrived at Ft. Lukman that night. She obviously wasn't armed with the knowledge she needed to fit in here.

Those rumors said she was a very important aide to General Yarrow. So why hadn't her boss informed her about what she was in for at this base?

"So tell us something about yourself, Lieutenant," he said, addressing her. She was slender, with short, blond hair, a pale but perfect complexion, and high cheekbones that underscored eyes of an unusual blue-green shade. "Have you worked with General Yarrow long?" Those were nice, neutral, friendly questions, weren't they?

Jason was still on probation here. Probably would be for the rest of his life unless he figured out a workable way to resign.

On the other hand, he would be leaving behind some

stuff he really liked along with the military regimen he despised. Some stuff he'd grown used to and didn't want to do without.

So he'd made his decision. He was staying—for the time being, at least.

He glanced at his cousin to make sure there was no angry scowl on his face, the result of every misstep Jason made in Drew's presence.

Fortunately, Drew just regarded the lovely lieutenant expectantly, as if awaiting her answer, too. So were all other Alpha Force members here—those who were like him, and those who weren't.

That was something damned special about this unit. They all worked together—and those who weren't like him were actually assigned to help those with the same characteristics as he had.

What would the lovely lieutenant think if she knew that half the members of Alpha Force were shapeshifters?

Oh, yeah, real dogs and other appropriate animals were kept on base as covers for them. Jason had even started helping to train the dogs in his spare time. But the reality was that Jason, and a lot of others, would be changing tonight under the full moon. By choice these days, which was especially cool.

"I've been in the army for nearly two years," the pretty officer was saying.

She was Lieutenant McLinder. Sara, she'd said during introductions. She didn't look as if she'd be thrilled for a mere sergeant to address her by her first name, even here.

"I've been an aide to General Yarrow for about five months," she continued.

Jason knew that the general had obligations in addition to being the commanding officer of Alpha Force. This lieutenant really could be as ignorant about the unit as she seemed.

Jason smiled. Wouldn't it be fun to see her expression when she finally realized the true nature of Alpha Force?

Maybe he could figure out a way to do that—although he would not be in a position, he was sure, to comfort the beautiful officer.

Not then, at least.

Would she run away screaming?

Somehow, he didn't think so. His first impression was that she was no-nonsense, all by the book. Her duty was to help the general, no matter what.

But Jason would bet she'd never anticipated this.

Perhaps he could help to educate her. Really educate her about what Alpha Force was about.

He would definitely try.

"Time for us all to go." That was the major talking, and clearly no one was about to contradict him.

Sara watched as everyone at the table rose almost in unison. She did the same.

So did the sergeant beside her. "Are you staying in the BOQ?" he asked.

Why? Did he want to accompany her there? Tear off her clothes the way his suggestive looks seemed to do, never mind the rules?

The idea made her private areas react in ways she hadn't felt in a long time—even as she shoved the very idea out of her mind.

"That's right. I assume you're not." She kept her tone brusque, not unfriendly but not anything but professional, either.

"Right. But…well, you'd better stay in your quarters tonight, Lieutenant."

Was he presuming to give her, a superior officer, orders? She glared—but at that moment his look wasn't sexy or suggestive... It seemed concerned.

Odd.

Although it was the night of a full moon. Maybe the general hadn't been playing her completely and this unit's members spread the word that they were shapeshifters to hide what they really did. But would anyone sane actually accept that?

"We'll walk you there." Colleen Hodell gestured toward a couple of other lieutenants who'd been sitting with them.

In a short while, Sara was walking toward the BOQ with Colleen, and with Lieutenants Marshall Vincenzo and Jock Larabey. Marshall was the tallest of the group, with a shock of dark brown hair and thin but surprisingly sensual lips. Jock looked as if he might live up to his name. He seemed quite muscular, judging by the way his uniform hugged his arms and chest.

"So tell me something about Alpha Force," Sara said lightly as they trod the path toward their residence. Something real, she hoped.

"I think that's up to the general," Colleen said.

"In fact," Marshall added, "I think Jason—Sergeant Connell—was right. You should just stay in your quarters tonight. It's safer."

"The base is safe," Jock contradicted. "But if you're not familiar with it, you'd be better off not wandering around at night, and definitely not tonight."

Okay, they did seem to be playing the general's game. But did they all really want her to hide in her BOQ unit tonight, maybe put her head under a pillow and pretend she wasn't here? Were they going to put on some kind of act tonight? If so, she wanted to see it.

Or maybe this was completely a sham, so they could actually do something else under cover of darkness.

They all separated at the elevators. "Good night," Sara said, wondering what each of the others was thinking.

When she reached the second floor, she noticed a female captain and male lieutenant down the hall. She went to greet them.

Neither was part of Alpha Force, they told her. They were Captain Samantha Everly and Lieutenant Cal Brown. Did she want to hang out in Samantha's unit with them?

Had they, too, been directed to stay indoors that night? If so, what story had they been told? But she didn't ask.

"Thanks," Sara said. "I just got here today and I'm really tired. I'll take a rain check, though."

She used her key to enter her apartment. There, she unpacked the scant clothing and other things she had brought, then sat down in front of the television.

She sat there for maybe an hour, but she was bored. And curious. She rose and walked to the window.

Lights illuminated the part of the base that she could see. So did a full moon that had just risen above the trees that surrounded the back portion of the base.

She saw no movement. No Alpha Force members or otherwise.

Hell, she was used to following orders, but the cautions she had been given didn't amount to orders, did they?

She wouldn't stay out long, and she would remain where the base was well lighted.

Would she need a weapon? Hardly. No matter what those Alpha Force members really did that night, they surely wouldn't hurt anyone, least of all the aide to the unit's officer in charge.

She stayed as quiet as she could, locking her apartment

door behind her and taking the stairs rather than the elevator. She exited through the BOQ's front door.

The spring air was brisk but pleasant. She moved out of the artificial lights toward the shadow of the nearest building, in case anyone was watching her.

Hell, she'd already determined that she wasn't disobeying orders. She was just outside for…for health purposes. The night air would help her sleep.

She walked around for twenty minutes, seeing nothing. Hearing—well, she wasn't sure what she heard. There were noises in the distance that she couldn't identify. Were there some kinds of wild animals living in the woods surrounding the base? Sometimes she thought she heard a howl.

Or was this all piped-in sound effects to make the gullible think there were werewolves out there? She wasn't about to buy that.

She drew closer to the edge of the woods, just to peek, not that she would get close. Had they really loosed some kind of wildlife, something feral, on the base?

Not likely. Not animals they couldn't control. Well, five more minutes out here and she would return to her quarters. It did feel a bit eerie after all, being alone at such a large facility.

What was that? She heard something—not howls, but a growl. There was no breeze that night, but she also heard crunching of leaves, as if something was walking in the woods.

Okay. Her imagination really was working overtime. Or maybe there were some kinds of animals out there. She'd better go back—

She stopped dead as something emerged from the woods. Not just one creature, but maybe half a dozen.

Wolves.

Should she freeze? Should she run?

An African-American man she hadn't met before suddenly appeared from behind them. He wore camos like her and didn't seem frightened by the wolves.

"What are you doing here?" he demanded. "Everyone was told to stay inside tonight. Go back to your quarters. Now."

"But are you safe with—?"

In unison, several of the wolves leaped toward Sara.

"Run!" called the man.

And Sara did.

Chapter 2

*H*e wanted to chase after her, that foolish woman who hadn't listened to him or anyone else.

Didn't she know how dangerous it could be, wandering around on the night of a full moon in an area where shapeshifters prowled?

If he had been in his human form, he would have laughed.

But Jason was in his wolfen form, loving it. Especially because the time of his shift tonight had actually been his choice.

He stood in the midst of his also-shifted comrades. None chased Lieutenant Sara McLinder from where she had confronted them here, at the edge of the woods surrounding Ft. Lukman. Most of them had leaped in unison to scare her off.

Soon, though, since she was an aide to the general, she would be told, and shown, the truth.

Jason looked sideways. The wolf beside him was Drew, his cousin, who had coerced him to enlist in the military, to join Alpha Force, for his own good.

At this moment, despite his misgivings about the future, Jason couldn't thank Drew enough.

His cousin nodded his canine head and turned. He began walking into the woods. So did the other shifters.

They were followed by their single human aide for the

night, Captain Jonas Truro, who was a medical doctor like Drew.

He was not, however, a shifter, but as a member of Alpha Force he was an expert at helping them, including assisting in perfecting the Alpha Force elixir.

All shifters here would continue to prowl until dawn. That was when they normally would change back on nights of the full moon anyway, even if they didn't have access to that very special Alpha Force elixir. His family had started to experiment with it, at least Drew had, and now, with the help of other Alpha Force members including Jonas Truro, he had developed some sophisticated and amazing formulas.

That elixir was one reason Jason's thoughts were so clear now, while he was shifted.

Why he could wonder, so precisely, exactly what lovely Lieutenant McLinder thought about her recent confrontation by an entire pack of wolves.

Oh, yes. He would laugh, if he could.

But since he couldn't for now, he would wait and look forward to a conversation, sometime soon, with pretty Sara.

Sara lay on her back in the dark, on the uncomfortable bed in her new apartment, willing herself to fall asleep.

She had closed the blinds, but a soft glow still penetrated between the slats. The light from the full moon.

Hell, she had trained her body as much as she had trained her mind. She never had trouble getting to sleep.

Except tonight.

Her thoughts kept returning to the pack of wolves she'd seen. They were wolves, weren't they? They didn't look like any breed of domesticated dog she knew of.

On the other hand, they had been so calm at first. Even

when a few had moved quickly toward her, none had acted as if it intended to attack.

And then there'd been that soldier who shooed her away. What was this?

Was the mysterious Alpha Force really composed of shapeshifters? Somehow, that didn't seem as nonsensical now as it had before.

Of course it could still all be some kind of ruse that the military was attempting to impose on enemy forces— couldn't it? That was the logical assumption. But if so, how had they tamed those wolves that way?

Sara turned over, trying to get comfortable. Maybe she should pull up a training manual on her laptop. Read something, at least.

But she knew that if she did boot up her computer, she would instead search for something else entirely.

Werewolves.

She had gone to bed in her usual sleeping attire—a T-shirt and matching shorts. She was comfortable in them. She kept telling herself that the room's warm temperature was fine. So was what she was wearing. So was everything except for the outrageousness of her thoughts.

She needed sleep, but it wouldn't come.

What time was it, anyway? She turned over and pulled her smartphone from the nightstand beside the bed where it was charging.

Really? Was it actually almost five o'clock? The night was nearly over.

And she clearly wasn't going to sleep a wink.

Throwing the covers off, she flipped the light switch at the side of the bed.

She had an idea what to do next.

She was going to track down those damned wolves.

* * *

She had dressed in her camo fatigues. She once more used the stairs to get to the first floor of the BOQ, then slipped out the side door again.

This time, she was armed—with a camera. She had shoved it into her pocket.

Since this Alpha Force was supposed to be so covert, she suspected that if she took any pictures of the wolves she might be considered in breach of military protocol—at the least. She might even be doing something illegal. Certainly, it could be contrary to her security clearance.

But she didn't intend to show anything to the world. No, if she found those wolves again, she would take pictures only for herself.

Darkness still hovered over the base—the darkness before dawn, since the moon was setting behind the trees. Soon, the sun would rise.

For now, Sara kept in shadows as she crossed the paths toward the woods where the wolves had emerged from among the trees.

She stayed just outside the foliage. Canines, whatever their nature, had keen hearing. They'd hear her anyway, but she didn't want to make it any easier by tromping on dry, fallen leaves.

She found the base interesting in its layout. From where she was, most buildings—nearly all low and two- or three-story—were to the left, and the woods were to her right. It wasn't hard to stay in shadows, but that was changing with almost every minute.

Dawn was breaking.

She— What was that?

She heard a noise in the woods, as if someone else stepped on those dry leaves. Was it the man who had shooed her back inside before?

Or was it an animal?

A wolf?

Okay, if she was going to have any chance at all of seeing what she sought, of taking pictures, it was time to move. Slowly, so she didn't make any more noise than absolutely necessary, she slid between the trees.

It was darker here than in the open, but the fact that sunrise was beginning made it easier to see.

There. She heard something again.

A howl?

No…it sounded more like a moan. A human moan.

Was someone hurt? Had those damned wolves attacked someone?

Less inclined to be protective of herself when someone might need her help, she walked faster in the direction of the noise.

The moans sounded louder, accompanied by other noise, as if something thrashed in the underbrush. Was it a person being attacked?

Damn, she really should have brought a weapon. She had her phone in another pocket and could call for help if necessary, but the first minutes during an attack could be critical. She needed to find out fast exactly what was going on.

She started running in the direction of the sounds.

She emerged into a clearing among the trees where daylight was beginning to glimmer.

Sara blinked in confusion and disbelief as she looked at the source of the sound.

Only one being was present in the clearing. It definitely wasn't a fight but—what was it?

That wasn't one of the wolves. Or at least the furry being didn't look like one—not exactly. It was larger, more elongated, and as Sara watched, the hair on its body appeared to be sucked in until only flesh remained except on the head—and in certain private areas where humans also had hair.

Male humans—and hair wasn't all that was private that Sara observed.

This couldn't be. And yet, it was.

As she watched—and, fortunately, had the consciousness to start shooting pictures, including a video—the wolf-like creature disappeared, replaced by the form of a man.

Not just any man.

She realized quickly that it was Sergeant Jason Connell she watched, changing from a wolf back into a human.

She couldn't stop staring at him, and not just because of the incredible metamorphosis she had just observed.

Jason Connell stood there, breathing hard as if shedding final discomfort at what he had gone through. He flexed his body—his arms, his chest and yes, his most private areas, riveting Sara's gaze there as she, too, started breathing a bit harder. Lord, was he generously endowed there. Was that a factor of who, or what, he was?

She continued to shoot pictures, but only for a moment.

Jason grinned then and looked straight at her. He flexed once more, and she swallowed hard. How long had he recognized that she was there?

He certainly did now.

"Good morning, Sara…er, Lieutenant," he said. "Like what you see? I'd be glad to demonstrate some more."

With a strangled cry, Sara turned and ran back the way she had come.

Jason considered just letting her go.

She wasn't supposed to be out here, anyway. But he didn't have any clothes here to slip on.

He had purposely separated from the rest of his pack a while ago. He had wondered if the lovely lieutenant would return to the area where she had found them to follow up on what she thought she had seen.

Sure enough, she had appeared where he had anticipated. Just by running into the pack last night, though, she really hadn't seen much of anything...then.

If he went after her now, he would only emphasize what she had seen this morning. Him.

Not that he minded. But even if he wanted to, he doubted he'd be able to slip into the BOQ nude to do—whatever.

He found the lieutenant hot. Presumably, she now found him hot, too. He hoped so. He hated to think all that moving and flexing, purposely giving her an eyeful, had been in vain. Not that either of them ever could, or would, act on it.

No, he would head back to his own quarters first. He would run into her casually on the base, anyway.

Hanging out with Alpha Force was why she was here.

"Hey, where've you been, Jason?" Jonas Truro slipped out of the woods. He held out a T-shirt and jeans toward him. "Not a good thing to wander around here like that, especially now." He nodded toward Jason's crotch.

At the moment, his private parts were at ease. He'd been alone there long enough, in the somewhat cool morning air, to chill out.

"Not with that new unit here," Jason agreed, taking the clothes and slipping them on. "Thanks." He wasn't about to mention that he'd been seen—especially considering who it had been.

Although it probably would have been worse had someone from the new special-ops group stationed here seen him. Though everyone was pretending cordiality, there'd been friction between Alpha Force members and the new unit, the Ultra Special Forces Team. They were here to engage, eventually, in some mutual training with Alpha Force for a so-far undisclosed covert assignment overseas. The team's unique skills still remained secret from Alpha Force. No one outside their group was supposed to ask questions about their nature.

And no one in the Ultra Special Forces Team was supposed to ask questions about Alpha Force.

"Everyone else back in their quarters?" Jason asked. All the other shifters were brass—officers, from lieutenants up through Major Connell. That was partly thanks to General Yarrow, he'd been told. Although their nature was revealed only on a need-to-know basis, the shifters in Alpha Force were regarded with esteem, and their special abilities were to be recognized by the military, at least by their ranks.

Everyone but him.

"They sure are. Drew said we should all get a couple of hours' sleep, then we'll meet up in the lab to compare notes about last night." Jonas yawned. "You okay on your own now?"

"Sure am." Jason gave him an exaggerated salute. "I'm off to my quarters. See you later, Captain."

Jason pivoted as if he felt like genuine, by-the-book military and headed in the growing light of dawn toward the better-than-barracks apartment building that housed a group of enlisted members of Alpha Force, not too far from the BOQ.

Jason was the only shifter in that building—the only Alpha Force shifter who wasn't a commissioned officer.

Most shifters in Alpha Force had individual aides to help them, primarily enlisted personnel quartered in the same building as Jason. For the exercises tonight, though, the decision had been that only one aide was needed, and Captain Jonas Truro had been it.

Jason didn't have his own personal aide, anyway. The only perk he'd been given was that he had been promoted to the rank of sergeant nearly immediately. Being a noncommissioned officer was better than just being a private, but he'd have liked the recognition given to the other shifters.

Of course he didn't have a college education—yet—like the rest of them.

And then there was the reason his cousin Drew had twisted some arms to get him accepted into the military, and Alpha Force, in the first place....

He still had a lot to overcome, damn it.

But having gotten a figurative taste of Alpha Force and how it worked, and a literal taste of the elixir that helped to make Alpha Force what it was...well, like it or not, he'd probably stay with this unit for a nice, long time.

Which meant that disobeying what Jonas Truro might consider to be an order wasn't in the cards. Not this morning, at least.

Instead of attempting to confront Lieutenant Sara McLinder after what they had—sort of—shared that night, Jason continued toward his small apartment.

The next time he'd see her would probably be at the upcoming meeting in the main building housing Alpha Force labs and offices.

There would be plenty of time then to embarrass even further the woman who'd watched him change that morning.

Chapter 3

Sara didn't even try to get more sleep.

Each time she sat down, or stood, or did nearly anything, her mind kept returning to that scene near the woods.

And so she spent the next hour sitting on the uncomfortable brown sofa in her quarters, trying to read a book on military history to distract her—and failing dismally.

She remained dressed in the camos she had donned earlier to go look for those damned wolves that had confronted her last night—and what a mistake that had been.

Had she imagined it? Was she nuts? She had, after all, performed some absurd research on her own earlier, about shapeshifters, after seeing the wolves. Had the general's strange attempt at humor and the innuendos about the unusual nature of Alpha Force left her susceptible to a really wild kind of joke?

But why would anyone here play a joke on her, especially Jason Connell? He didn't know her. No one here knew her.

Whatever Jason's reason, he'd at a minimum bared his very hot body to her. He had also somehow changed from a wolf to a man.

Impossible.

Yet... Her mind kept circling that impossible scenario over and over, which oddly gave it more credence.

She had never before hallucinated anything, let alone something so bizarre.

Yet somehow alluring…

She'd taken pictures. She looked at them again. Then put her digital camera away, hidden deeply in a drawer. It provided more questions than answers.

Once more she tried in vain to focus on the large volume she held on her lap. She barely got through the first ten pages.

At six-thirty, she headed for the cafeteria.

The temperature outside remained cool but comfortable. Once again, others in camo fatigues also strode across the base, a few heading in the same direction she was.

But no one she recognized.

Would she see Jason in the cafeteria this morning? If so, what would she say to him?

Heck, he was the one who owed her an explanation. Maybe even an apology for playing games with her that way.

Unless it was real….

No, she wouldn't go there.

She was soon immersed in the crowd entering the cafeteria, then stood in line. Though not especially hungry, she decided that comfort food wouldn't be a bad idea. Never mind that she usually scorned pampering herself in any manner.

She paid for her pancakes, bacon and coffee then scanned the compact eating area.

And saw no one she recognized.

She shoved away the pang of regret that Jason wasn't there. She wasn't looking forward to their inevitable confrontation—was she?

Well, maybe a little.

Maybe he would be kind enough to provide an explanation, one she could buy—and one that wouldn't make her feel like an utter fool.

No Alpha Force members were eating here at the moment, at least none she'd met. Did that have some significance?

She would find out. She'd learn all she needed to restore her sense of sanity and well-being.

For now she headed, tray in hand, toward a small table where the folks eating there all wore lieutenants' insignias. Were any of them members of the Ultra Special Forces Team, or could they be Alpha Force people she hadn't yet run into?

"May I join you?" she asked, stopping at an unoccupied chair.

"Sure," said a female lieutenant whose name tag read Swainey. She held out her hand as Sara sat down. "Vera Swainey." She looked at Sara expectantly.

"I'm Sara McLinder," she said.

The others at the table introduced themselves, too—three men and another woman.

"Are you all stationed here?" Sara asked.

"That's right," said Lieutenant Manning Breman. "You?"

"I just got here yesterday. I'm aide to General Greg Yarrow, who'll be stationed here on temporary duty for a few months."

The friendly atmosphere at the table suddenly seemed to freeze into icicles of stares.

"You're with Alpha Force?" Manning asked, his tone stiff.

"That's right." It wasn't exactly true, but she hated the antagonism that seemed to waft around her. Maybe they'd explain if she pressed. "Tell me what's going on here. I get the impression that your unit and Alpha Force aren't exactly buddies."

"You could say that." Vera's voice was also chill. "We were recently assigned here and assumed that— Oh, wait. I see the person we were saving that spot for. Cal, come over here." She sounded relieved as Cal Brown, the lieutenant whom Sara had met on her floor in their BOQ yesterday, approached with a tray of food.

There were plenty of empty chairs at nearby tables that Cal could pull up to their table. But all eyes of those seated there remained on Sara, as if demonstrating that she had outstayed her welcome.

"Here," she said to Cal as she stood abruptly, picking up her tray. "Have fun with this group. I certainly didn't."

She strode away, chose a small table near the door and sat down by herself.

She glanced at her watch. It was seven o'clock. She would phone General Yarrow soon. Warn him about the extent of the friction between the two primary units stationed here at Ft. Lukman.

Find out when he was planning on arriving that day.

She wouldn't, of course, mention what she had seen, or thought she had, earlier that morning.

But when he arrived, she would talk to him as soon as possible. Maybe even show pictures.

He could tell her more about Alpha Force. He had, after all, warned her to expect a different atmosphere and different kind of unit. Had even hinted at what she'd seen.

He knew what Alpha Force was about. She had just preferred not to imagine that what he hinted at could be real.

Now she knew better—and she hoped he would explain it to her.

Jason sat back on the uncomfortable folding chair, surrounded by colleagues, both shifters and not. He looked around the small basement office in the main Alpha Force building at the far end of Ft. Lukman.

This was where they always met on the morning after

a full moon. Other meetings were also held here for Alpha Force members in the secured laboratory area.

On the first floor, dogs were housed—those used as the cover, when necessary, for wolf shifters. Jason had a dog assigned to him: Shadow. He also enjoyed helping to train them in his spare time, although not today.

All the dogs had remained in their nice, well-maintained kennels last night—unlike the shapeshifters of Alpha Force.

"We need your report first this time, Jonas." Major Drew Connell, Jason's oh-so-perfect cousin, stood at the front of the room. He looked worried.

He'd really worry if Jason told him what he'd done that morning. Therefore, Jason wouldn't mention it.

"Everything started out fine," Jonas Truro responded as he stood up from his seat in the first row of four. He glanced around the group of shifters and aides who were present. "All our wolf shifters chose not to take the version of the elixir that would keep them in human form. Instead, everyone drank the kind that helped with human cognition while shifted but didn't stop them from changing. Our cougar shifter Colleen did the same." He nodded toward the woman who sat in the same row as Jason, a few people over.

The elixir was good stuff. Both formulas were. Jason gave the unit, and especially Drew, a lot of credit for that.

Now premixed bottles of both kinds were stored in a special refrigerated room nearby, even as Drew continued to upgrade the formulas for each.

Jason listened with interest as Jonas described everyone's change in the clearing in the woods that had been previously selected, then how he stayed with the wolf pack as they roved areas also designated in advance. With the Ultra Special Forces Team there for the last month, it had become impossible to have the run of the entire base while in shifted form when the moon wasn't full. At least last night, with the moon full, the USFT personnel had been told to stay in their quarters...without being told why.

Jason had no doubt that some, if not all, of that unit already suspected the true nature of Alpha Force. They probably scorned it—or feared it. But the official position for both units, at least for now, was to stay separate in all training exercises and otherwise. No joint exercises yet, although that was intended for the future. When? Peons like him weren't kept informed about such important matters.

"There was one incident," Jonas said. "Minor, but everyone should be aware of it. Lieutenant McLinder was wandering around outside around midnight and saw the pack. I shooed her back inside, but maybe someone should talk to her about maintaining silence about what she saw."

And about what she saw around five in the morning? Yeah, she definitely should stay silent about that, Jason thought. And probably would, even without being cautioned. He strongly suspected she wasn't about to announce to the world, *her* world, what she had observed. Even though he'd seen her taking pictures.

She might talk to him about it, though.

If so, he was ready. Very ready.

"Our next exercise will probably be later this week," Drew was saying. "We'll decide who'll shift and who won't. That will also dictate which of our aides and cover dogs— and cat—are needed."

He talked a while longer. Jason had started to tune his cousin out when a knock sounded on the office door.

It startled Jason, and probably everyone else in the room. They exchanged glances.

Before Drew could look outside to see who it was, the door opened.

Lieutenant Sara McLinder walked in.

Though she wasn't extremely tall, her straight stance

and the glare in her blue-green eyes had her dominating the room in that instant.

She was definitely a good-looking woman. Or maybe his opinion was colored by what he knew she'd seen…and, perhaps, enjoyed.

"Sorry," she said. "I'm obviously interrupting something. But you all should know that General Yarrow will arrive here at Ft. Lukman around ten o'clock this morning."

Sara wasn't sorry at all about interrupting this meeting, whatever it was about. It clearly involved Alpha Force, since she recognized most of the people who sat staring at her.

Including Sergeant Jason Connell. He was as great-looking as she recalled, of course—even with his clothes on. Seeing him in person again only stressed that she couldn't have imagined what she'd observed…could she? Under his camos, his shoulders were broad. His face was incredibly handsome, and the small streaks of silver in his dark hair only added to the appeal of the package.

She met his amused golden eyes only briefly, then turned back to the major.

The family relationship was apparent between the two men. Major Connell also had gold eyes and flecks of silver running through his dark hair. He was nice-looking, too. Maybe a little older than Jason. But not nearly as handsome.

More quietly than her earlier pronouncement, she said to him, "Major Connell, you know I'm here representing General Yarrow. He even gave me his card keys to get into this building and the lab area on his behalf. If this is an Alpha Force meeting, I should have been invited."

"I know your assignment, Lieutenant. You'll be invited to all meetings necessary to what the general, and you, are here to accomplish. This was a recap of some prior exercises and I didn't think it appropriate for you to waste your time."

"I'll let the general decide what's appropriate for me." She kept her expression neutral, though her words weren't.

"I understand." The major turned back to the group. "I think we're through here," he said. "Everyone is dismissed."

Especially me, Sara thought. But she didn't complain. Not yet. Nor did she ask any questions.

She had contacted the general, though, and she was really glad that he would arrive in only a couple of hours.

She would be there waiting for him.

For now, she scanned the group until her eyes lit again on Jason Connell, who was approaching the major.

Did Major Connell know what Sara had seen last night? Had Jason told him what he had done?

Surely the major knew who, or what, his own cousin was...assuming Sara hadn't imagined it all.

Should she simply ask the major? Maybe, but she wanted to talk to General Yarrow first.

And preferably to Jason even before that, to gauge his position about the incident.

Not now, though. He was engaged in a conversation with the major. Time for Sara to leave, along with the rest of the group.

Outside the door she feigned answering her cell phone but hung up as Jason came through.

"I'd like to talk with you, Sergeant," she said, inserting her most formal military quality to her voice.

"I'll bet you would, Lieutenant." There was humor in his tone and a suggestive smile on his face. "Would you like to go someplace where we could...talk alone?"

She felt her face flush. "No, thank you. But I would like for you to give me an official tour of this facility."

"I can only do that on the major's orders, Lieutenant."
This time, he sounded serious.

Which suggested further to Sara that she was being kept
outside the Alpha Force loop for now. She was a superior
officer, yet he was refusing to obey her while giving a good
excuse. That would surely change when the general got here
and ordered everyone to cooperate with her as well as him.

"Then come with me, please. There's something I'd like
to show you." Not really, but she decided to lead him back
to the area where he had shown *her*...a lot.

"Yes, ma'am." His tone again suggested he was thinking about exactly what she was.

He didn't comment as they walked up the stairs to the
main floor of the building. There, she stopped in the kennel area to look at the dogs she had been told were there.

They were all of moderate size, and most resembled the
animals she had seen last night: wolves.

"I like dogs," she said casually. "Do you, Sergeant?"

"Yes, ma'am," he responded, smiling. "Especially those
guys. My favorite is Shadow."

He reached inside the chain-link fencing of a nearby kennel and stroked the head of the closest dog inside, whom
he introduced as Shadow. Sara couldn't help thinking that
this dog in particular bore a strong resemblance to Jason
in wolf form. Could he somehow have pulled a prank on
her after all? But how?

"Any kinds of dogs you like better than others?" Jason
asked.

He probably wanted her to say something like the kind
she'd seen last night—and especially that morning. But that
wasn't something she intended to admit.

"Small ones," she said. "These guys are cute, but they
look difficult to walk and control. I like dogs that I can train
and manage." Oh, Lord. She knew she was stepping into

a nasty mess that had nothing to do with dog excrement. He could read a lot into her words if he chose. Maybe that was a good thing, if he really was what she suspected. But there was no way she would ever admit to him that what she had seen had touched her libido, gotten her most intimate parts simmering.

"Sounds like a very interesting way to treat your...dogs," he said. "I'd be glad to teach you how to work with these guys—or any others."

She'd had enough. They were outside the building on a walkway that led toward the woods in one direction, or toward the BOQ in the other. "I've got someplace I need to go now," she said. "See you later, Sergeant." She stood straight, looking at him, until he saluted her. She saluted back.

"Yes, ma'am," he said so officially that it sounded facetious, then he whirled on his heels and strutted off.

Sara headed back toward her quarters. She would find something productive to do until it was time to go meet the general.

At around nine-thirty, Sara realized she had actually gotten something accomplished in a short time, although not what she had intended.

For one thing, she had thoroughly searched Google on her laptop to see if she could find any information to suggest that shapeshifters could be real.

Of course there was. The authors could all have been credulous fools who wanted to believe, so they did. Nothing stood out to her as proof.

There were also a lot of websites ridiculing the whole idea.

She logged off the computer and left it on the small table in the kitchenette in her quarters. Then she checked herself in the mirror. Almost time to go wait for the general.

She'd decided to meet him right away, before he had time to talk with anyone else.

Soon she headed down the stairs in the BOQ and out the door. She walked toward the front gate.

And got waylaid by Jason. What was he doing out here?

He soon told her. "Hello, Lieutenant. I'm the general's unofficial greeter from Alpha Force. Is that why you're out here? I'm supposed to call Drew—er, Major Connell—and let him know when the general arrives."

"Won't the security guys notify the major?" Sara asked.

"Probably. But those were my orders."

"Okay. We'll both wait for him, then." She didn't want to wait with Jason. He would be a big distraction. He would keep her from asking the general questions right away, too. But she nevertheless walked with Jason toward the base's front gate.

She saw a few other soldiers walking around and some cars cruising the nearby roads. But she was extremely aware of Jason's tall, masculine presence beside her.

Especially when he said in a voice tinged with suggestiveness, "How are you enjoying Ft. Lukman so far, Lieutenant?"

"It's fine, Sergeant. I intend to get a lot accomplished here. Learn a lot, too."

"About Alpha Force?"

"That's right," she said. "I have some ideas already about how it can be improved, and I intend to let the general know."

She sensed Jason's hesitation beside her, but she wiped the grin off her face before she turned to him. His expression now was grim, not suggestive of anything but worry.

Good.

She looked again toward the guard gate, just in time to see the general's old, classic Jeep stopping. His ID was apparently approved right away, since the large gate opened inward and the general drove through.

Continuing to drive slowly, he approached the area where Sara and Jason stood.

And then Sara spotted smoke pouring out of the car's back end.

Chapter 4

What the hell? Jason didn't need Sara's frantic shouts of fear, magnified by his canine senses, to spur him to dash to the burning vehicle that suddenly veered off to the side.

He assessed the situation as he ran toward the front of the car. He kept all assumptions and fears, all emotions, in check. Now was only a time for action.

He had worked on the general's Jeep a couple of times when the old man had come to Ft. Lukman for meetings since Jason's recent enlistment. It was an early 1990s model Jeep, not quite old enough to be a classic, but still an admirable aging vehicle.

The gasoline tank was in the back—near where the smoke was pouring from, but down low, beneath the axle. That model's gas tank was built well, to prevent catching fire from sparks off the road or otherwise. Everything should be fine.

Except that the tires were flammable. So were the seats, the carpeting, the safety belts...

And right now, there was plenty of smoke. What remained of the canvas cover could confine a lot of it inside, enhancing the danger of smoke inhalation by the general.

Plus, depending on the location and intensity of the fire...well, despite the built-in precautions, there were no guarantees that the gas tank wouldn't explode.

Jason aimed for the driver's door, shoving his hands in his pockets as he ran to check for anything useful. Despite his dedication to working on cars, he didn't coincidentally happen to carry tools that people were supposed to keep in their glove compartments to shatter windows in emergencies. All he had were keys. A pocket knife. His cell phone.

Nothing likely to be helpful.

Was the general still conscious? The haphazard way the car now progressed suggested otherwise. Yet if he was, maybe Jason could get him to turn off the engine and take the thing out of gear. Push the button to unlock the driver's door.

For now, he would assume the commanding officer remained alive. He had no evidence he wasn't...at least not yet.

The stench of burning rubber and more grew even ranker as he arrived at the vehicle, but Jason ignored it. He also ignored the shouts of other people. All behind him? He saw no one closer to the car than he was.

Unsure what was searing hot and what wasn't, he yanked off his camo shirt and wrapped it around his right hand.

He reached the door and looked in. Smoke. Lots of it. But in the middle of it all, Jason could see that the general appeared conscious—barely. His eyes were open. His hands? Moving, but not in the right direction to get him out of there.

Jason first tried to yank the door open, to no avail. He pounded on the window to get the general's attention. "It's locked!" he shouted as Yarrow's head jerked toward him. Had he heard? Was he aware enough to understand?

Yarrow, one hand at his mouth as he coughed, turned toward the door. In a moment, Jason heard a click that probably wouldn't be audible to someone with normal human hearing, but with his acute senses it sounded nice and loud. He again tried the door.

This time it opened.

He coughed, too, as smoke smothered his face and his ability to breathe. But it didn't completely mask visibility.

"Let me help," said a familiar female voice from behind him. Sara McLinder. The lieutenant had kept up with him.

"Stay back," he said as he leaned inside.

But she apparently wasn't used to obeying orders from lower-ranking soldiers. As Jason leaned in and grasped the now-limp body of the general, he was suddenly glad that was so.

He needed to get the CO out of there fast. In moments, as he thrust his hands under the general's armpits and heaved him out, he found Sara, despite also coughing, grabbing the legs and swinging Yarrow even farther from the frying car.

Others who'd caught up with them, Lieutenants Seth Ambers and Grace Andreas-Parran, also helped to form a stretcher of human—well, somewhat human—arms.

Grace was a doctor as well as a shifting member of Alpha Force. It was still too soon to have her check the general's condition, though. Awkwardly but quickly, Jason helped the group maneuver the general's barely conscious body far from the car and within a parking area near the base's entry kiosk.

The harsh smell of the fire suddenly multiplied, and so did the background odor of oil as the flames apparently reached the engine. How secure was the gas tank now?

Jason swiftly noticed that he wasn't the only Alpha Force member helping here whose eyes had widened as their noses lifted.

And then, *kaboom!* As loudly and completely as any explosion in an action movie, the general's car detonated.

* * *

"Sir? Are you okay? Greg?" Sara wasn't certain where the tarp had come from on which they gently laid the general down on the hard parking lot surface. Maybe from one of the vehicles parked nearby. It didn't matter.

What did matter was how her boss, commanding officer to many of those present at Ft. Lukman, was doing.

Was he still alive?

He hadn't responded to her queries, which she knew sounded pitifully plaintive. Maybe he couldn't hear her. She wasn't right beside him now. Not the way things had worked out as the group of them had laid him down gently.

She therefore maneuvered around on the periphery of the tarp to be nearer to his head, not exactly elbowing others out of her way but coming close to it.

She prayed she didn't imagine it, but the general's chest seemed to be moving slowly, indicating he was breathing.

"General Yarrow? Sir?" she said, louder this time and definitely closer to his ears, not caring that her voice broke as she addressed him.

He was her mentor. Her friend.

And he might be dying.

Sure, she was a soldier. She had joined the military prepared to go into combat. To lose comrades in arms, if necessary.

But not here, on U.S. soil.

And not this very kind, very wonderful man.

She moved even closer, only to find her way blocked by Jason. "You probably haven't met Lieutenant Grace Andreas-Parran yet," he said to Sara, gesturing to the woman in camo uniform, like all of them, who knelt at the general's other side. "She's a medical doctor as well as a member of Alpha Force."

"Oh." Sara knew what Jason wasn't saying. She needed to back off. Let the doctor do what she could for the general.

Grace was slim and attractive, with blond hair so pale that it almost looked silver.

More important, her luminous brown eyes were narrowed as she concentrated on scanning the general's body. From what Sara could see, his camo uniform was intact. Unsinged. Maybe he hadn't been burned.

That didn't mean he would survive. Smoke inhalation could kill people. And so far Sara didn't know if he'd suffered any other kinds of injuries.

"Was he hurt?" she asked Grace. "I mean, besides being in a burning vehicle."

"Not sure yet." The doctor's long fingers moved rapidly along General Yarrow's prone body, clearly checking for injuries along with her concentrated gaze. "You're his aide, aren't you?"

"That's right," Sara said.

"Are you aware of any medical conditions he may have—heart related or otherwise? It'll help diagnose and treat him if we have all his information."

"I don't know of any. He's not exactly forthcoming with that kind of stuff, but I've made him occasional appointments for checkups at Bethesda Medical Center. I can call there."

"Just get me the contact information. With privacy issues, they're more likely to let me know matters like that."

Which peeved Sara. She was almost like family to the general. But Grace was right. She was the doctor. She was the one they'd talk to about anything needed to save Greg Yarrow.

Sara was aware of Jason's presence right behind her. He must have heard the conversation. He rested his hand firmly on her shoulder. To warn her to back off? But the contact seemed more comforting than cautionary.

Under other circumstances, Sara wouldn't allow him to touch her at all. She was his superior officer. They were on duty.

But at the moment his touch somehow helped her to survive this horrendous situation.

She heard a lot of voices near them, too, and looked around to see other soldiers she had already met here. Some, like Seth Ambers, Colleen Hodell, Rainey Jessop and Jock Larabey, were members of Alpha Force. Others, including Lieutenants Cal Brown, Manning Breman and Samantha Everly, were members of the Ultra Special Forces Team.

All circled the general's vulnerable body, staying respectfully back.

"Hey. What the hell happened?" That was Major Drew Connell, who maneuvered his way through the crowd.

"He's a doctor, too," said Jason into Sara's ear. "A damned good one."

She already knew that Drew, CO of the unit, was also a physician. "Great." She turned to look toward Jason. His expression was bland, but his gaze, as he looked at her, seemed surprisingly sympathetic and she felt tears rush to her eyes. "Two Alpha Force doctors right here?" she continued, needing to say something else to demonstrate that she wasn't some emotional wimp. "The general's in good hands." Sara prayed that was so.

A siren sounded in the distance. "Good," stated Drew Connell. "I called 911 immediately."

"I did, too," Grace said. "The general needs to be checked out by EMTs with appropriate equipment, then transported immediately to the nearest emergency facility. That's at the Memorial Hospital in Easton, isn't it?"

"That's right," said Drew.

"What…" The word was soft but interjected into the conversation from below them.

The general!

It was all Sara could do not to push her way through all people, doctors or not, to get closer, to hear what Greg had to say.

Only…was it good for him to expend energy trying to talk?

The wail of the siren grew closer. It would be even more difficult to hear him, anyway.

But his eyes opened. They looked around, cloudy and dazed—not at all the usual strong expression conveyed by the powerful and confident CO.

"What happened?" he said. His voice was loud enough now to be heard. He began moving, as if wanting to sit up.

"We're not certain yet, sir." Drew held him gently on the ground. "Please stay still for now till we can check you better for injuries. Your car caught fire and we're going to get you to the nearest hospital for an examination as soon as possible."

Which was a good thing. Sara had learned, from the general's initial description of Ft. Lukman, that it held an infirmary with high-tech equipment. But that couldn't compare with a genuine medical facility staffed by specialists and nurses. Greg Yarrow was entitled to the best care possible.

"Fire?" The general's look somehow hardened, despite the overall laxness and pain in his features. "Hell." That apparently cost him a lot of effort, since he grew silent again.

The siren was extremely loud now. Sara saw the ambulance screech up to the entry kiosk that, only a few minutes earlier, had admitted the general's now-destroyed car.

The EMTs were allowed in immediately. They quickly gave the general an initial exam, and then loaded him into their vehicle. Lieutenant Grace Andreas-Parran and her

husband, Lieutenant Simon Parran, who had just joined
the group around the accident site, got into the ambulance
with him. Jason also let Sara know who the newly arrived
man was—and that he was a doctor, too.

"There are a lot of medical doctors in this unit," Sara
said. Did that have something to do with their apparently
woo-woo nature, or did their backgrounds somehow help
to mask what Alpha Force was really about?

"Yeah, there are," Jason responded. "In case you're wondering, those two are especially appropriate to go with the
general. They recently returned here after dealing with an
ordeal of their own." Sara had heard about that from the
general. "They'll take good care of him."

Major Drew Connell stood beside Sara and Jason, along
with some Alpha Force members Sara recognized and other
people she didn't. As the ambulance pulled out of the gate,
Drew turned toward them.

"So, cuz," he said to Jason, then gestured toward the
smoldering hulk of the destroyed car. An emergency truck
with a Ft. Lukman sign on the side had pulled up and was
spraying the wreck with chemicals, presumably to put out
the fire. "I doubt there'll be much left to examine, but when
those guys are done I want you to take a lot of pictures.
We'll need to secure the wreck where it is temporarily, but
I want you to move it ASAP into a secure part of the main
parking structure and cordon it off so no one can reach it
till I get a good forensics team here to check it out. I need
to know exactly what happened. Vehicles like that don't
just catch fire for no reason. You okay with that?"

"Is that an order, Major?"

"It sure is, Sergeant."

Jason offered up a halfhearted salute along with his grim
smile that looked right at home on his sharp-featured, too-
handsome face. "You've got it, cuz. Er, sir."

Sara didn't smile, even though she recognized the lightness in the exchange between the two cousins as most likely their way of dealing with this terrible event.

At least the general had survived. But now, as Drew had suggested, they had to figure out what had happened.

She wasn't certain how, but she intended to help.

She would do all that she could to bring to justice anyone involved with endangering her CO.

One of the first things Jason had done after enlisting in the military, and showing up at Ft. Lukman for a very specialized form of basic training, was to check out the closest auto-repair and maintenance facilities.

Jason understood from even before he enlisted that his primary official assignment would be to take care of Ft. Lukman's vehicles, which was what he knew best...besides shapeshifting. Oh, and stealing cars—but that would remain in his past. Like it or not, he'd started over here, as a member of Alpha Force.

The base didn't have much in the way of auto-repair equipment for him to use, though. He'd bought some of the basics. But he had also needed to figure out where he could rent what he'd need only occasionally.

As a result, he had an immediate answer when Drew asked, "Any idea how you're going to move that thing?"

They both watched the base security guys who'd finished spraying the damaged vehicle with foam to end its smoldering.

"Sure do," Jason said. "There's a well-equipped service station in Mary Glen that has a car-carrier tow truck to haul in wrecks or whatever. I'll see if I can rent it. If not, I'll get the owner to bring it here and move the carcass for us."

"Sounds good. Meantime, I'll keep an eye on that hulk to make sure no one plays with it. We don't want any further destruction of evidence of what caused the fire, especially if it was somehow deliberately set."

Jason turned to walk through the substantial group of onlookers still hanging out despite dissipation of the excitement. Sara McLinder remained among them. In fact, the lieutenant hadn't moved, and he couldn't read the expression on her beautiful but clearly sad face as she continued to stare in the direction where the general's ambulance had departed. But it held more than sorrow. Anger? Determination?

Hell, he wanted to find out what she was thinking. He approached her and asked impulsively, "Hey, Lieutenant, you haven't been here long enough to visit our nearest town, Mary Glen, have you?"

She turned toward him and blinked her amazing blue-green eyes as if she'd just been brought back to awareness from some kind of dream. "No," she said slowly, as if wondering why he asked, "I haven't."

"Okay, then, come with me while I pick up a truck to move that thing. We won't stay long, but at least you'll get a sense of the place." He paused then drew nearer and said in a confidential tone too soft for nearby members of the Ultra Special Forces Team to hear. "Oh, and by the way, some of the townsfolk even believe in shapeshifters. I'll tell you all about them on the way."

Sara was fascinated.

First of all, she liked that, riding beside Jason in his souped-up, old, red Mustang, she could pay much more attention to the road leading away from Ft. Lukman. It was surrounded by gorgeous, thick woodlands composed of trees including mature oaks as well as evergreens.

The road was basically two-lane—barely. They made a

sharp left turn at the edge of the base, and Jason swerved to avoid some stones on the pavement.

Sara was definitely an urbanite, but she still found the area charming and attractive. Definitely worth visiting.

But not under these circumstances.

"How far is Mary Glen from here?" she asked Jason.

"Not far in mileage." He glanced toward her from the driver's seat for only an instant before redirecting his eyes back to the risky road. "Light years away in attitude."

"I suppose you're going to explain," she said.

"I suppose I am." He grinned. And then he began telling her an utterly wild tale about Mary Glen and some murders that had been committed there over several years. "I don't have firsthand knowledge of this," Jason said, "But my cuz Drew told me about it. It's how he met his wife, Melanie, in fact. Now they even have a kid—little Emily."

"Really?" Sara said. "Now I'm getting interested."

"Okay, I'll tell you about it. First of all, he said a lot of townsfolk bought into the legend of shapeshifters living in the area. I don't go to town a lot, but I gather some of its citizens still believe the story. If nothing else, they liked the legend because it brought tourists—and, in fact, it's one reason Ft. Lukman was established so near Mary Glen, as only loonies like them would buy into the rumor that anyone had seen shifters in the area. Other people here, though, hated both the idea and shapeshifters."

He explained how the parents of Lieutenant Patrick Worley, one of the members of Alpha Force, had been killed by silver bullets, about a year apart, theoretically because they were werewolves.

"And in fact, Dr. Worley, senior, was a shifter. After he died, Patrick sold his dad's veterinary practice to Dr. Melanie Harding—Melanie Harding-Connell now, my cousin-in-law. Drew's wife."

It seemed that a cult of shapeshifting groupies used to hang out in Mary Glen hoping to see, and perhaps dispose of, some shapeshifters by shooting them with silver bullets. Maybe some still did.

"That's an absolute myth, though," Jason added. "Shapeshifters can be killed just like regular people, by any normal kind of ammunition."

Sara just rolled her eyes but didn't comment.

In any event, back then someone had shot Drew's cover dog, Grunge, who was found injured by Melanie, and, excellent vet that she was, she had saved the dog's life—while endangering her own as an apparent shapeshifter lover. She'd proven to the town that Grunge was not Drew in shifted form. Drew, of course, never admitted to shapeshifting—especially not to that wacko group of people.

Eventually, after more killings, the perpetrator was finally caught. Things around Mary Glen—and around Ft. Lukman—had settled down to a relatively peaceful existence.

Until now.

"Do you suppose anyone from town could have sabotaged the general's car?" Sara asked.

"Possibly, but that all happened a while ago. I'd bet instead that it was a member of our new best friends, the USFT."

"But why?" said Sara.

"When we figure that out," Jason replied, "we'll probably know who it was, too."

Their discussion was enough of a diversion for Sara that the drive to the main street of Mary Glen, Maryland, went quickly.

So shapeshifting was real. Jason certainly sounded convincing.

He had looked even more convincing….

* * *

The car-carrier truck was definitely available for rent. At the right price. At the right *high* price.

But hell, Jason thought. Uncle Sam would be footing the bill, not him.

And the vehicle, with its black, shining cab in front and car-size, ramplike bed in back—along with a hookup to pull a car onto it—was exactly what he needed.

Sara didn't seem impressed, but he figured she wasn't a vehicle aficionado, at least not the way he was. He haggled for a few minutes with the owner of the service station that owned the truck, though, so she'd figure he was a good military guy who wanted to save his employer, and his country, some money.

After more discussion, he locked his beloved Mustang in a relatively secure-looking garage area.

He then returned to the truck, opened the passenger door and took Sara's hand, helping her climb inside.

He liked touching her warm hand, feeling her firm grip.

Wondering what it might feel like elsewhere on his body...

Hell, what was he thinking? Why had he even taken this woman along with him? It wasn't in his nature to feel sorry for someone who was apparently suffering in sympathy for a downed friend—in this case, a superior officer.

But he had enjoyed her company. Too much.

"This thing rides amazingly well," Sara said as they headed back toward Ft. Lukman. Then she paused. "But I really like your Mustang."

Okay. If he hadn't already been attracted to her, Jason knew he would be now.

But, he told himself, just because she was beautiful and sexy and fun to tease—and talk to—and he'd inhaled her light and appealing citrus scent on their entire ride to town, and even though she liked his car, that didn't mean he could let himself get involved with her.

She was an officer—a non-Alpha Force one at that. She seemed completely by the book. Ready to obey all orders of her commanding officer, the injured general.

Horrified that she'd seen Jason shapeshift and now trying to ignore it.

And he was just a military peon.

One who happened to be a shapeshifter, and proud of it.

Their ride back from Mary Glen wasn't as enjoyable to Sara as going the other direction.

Surprisingly, she had been enthralled by Jason's glib tale about the quaint small town and its foibles. Not that she'd liked hearing about murders and strange shapeshifter groupies, but the way Jason had described the amazingly squirrely people had captured her interest.

But on the way back, it seemed as though he'd exhausted his interest in the town—and her.

Even so, their being cooped up in the small cab of that truck hadn't seemed uncomfortable.

Sara hadn't let it.

Her verbal encouragement hadn't spurred Jason to tell more stories about Mary Glen, or even himself. Maybe he didn't want to talk to her about his shapeshifting. Maybe then he would have had to explain what Alpha Force was really about.

And Sara would have enjoyed hearing it. Been relieved, in fact, to learn the secrets.

She had other questions about him, too. Why had he joined the military at all? He didn't seem enthralled by it. Was it simply to join this team of military shapeshifters?

But he was a noncommissioned officer, and many other

members of Alpha Force whom she'd met so far were lieutenants and above. Why was he different?

She didn't ask. Not now. And when Jason stayed quiet, Sara had started talking about herself—and how she had become General Yarrow's aide. She'd first gotten her undergraduate degree in political science at Kent State University, where she'd also joined ROTC. She'd always wanted to give back to her country, plus she loved the order of the military. She'd planned early on to make it her career.

She didn't mention, though, that Alan, her college boyfriend, had thought her nuts and kept trying to get her to do things outside the box. All he did was make her feel uncomfortable.

One night she'd joined Alan at a party and found him drinking, indulging in "recreational" drugs—and making out with another woman. That ended their relationship. And Sara hadn't been seriously interested in another man since then.

Which was a good thing, especially now. She would never get involved with someone like Jason. She was superior in rank to him. She had the honor of being an aide to a general, and Jason fixed cars.

And, worst of all, he was an amazingly genuine shapeshifter.

His sexy, amusing demeanor didn't make up for any of that.

"I'd really like to know more about Alpha Force," she finally finished. "And what makes it tick. General Yarrow is really proud to be the unit's commanding officer and always hinted broadly at its...unusual characteristics. One thing I do like is the camaraderie among its members." Although she knew she'd have to remind herself more than once that it was okay to call other members here by their first names instead of their ranks, as she did sometimes in private with her mentor, Greg Yarrow. She'd slipped, though, out of fear for him earlier today, but she wouldn't do it again.

Alpha Force was military, but its members clearly were less formal than any other unit she had associated with.

Jason shot a quick glance at her then—just as he flipped on the truck's turn signal.

They were back at Ft. Lukman, and he was about to enter the part of the road nearest the entry—just beyond where they'd first seen General Yarrow's car on fire.

Jason slowed down again, as if seeking clues. Or avoiding those stones on the road. Or both.

Sara couldn't help it. She looked around, too. The area was surrounded by trees similar to those they'd passed all along the drive. Could someone have shot something from the cover of the forest that set the Jeep's canvas on fire?

But wouldn't the guard in the kiosk have seen it?

Maybe it had been completely accidental. Maybe the people studying what was left of the vehicle would find an indication of what the general had been storing in the back that caught fire. Or maybe he was a closet smoker—though she'd been around him a lot over the past months and had seen, and smelled, no indication of that. And surely the vehicle would have been designed, for safety, for its canvas cover to withstand being hit by a lit butt, just in case.

Still, it seemed awfully coincidental for it to start burning in earnest, however it caught fire, just when the general entered Ft. Lukman.

Jason stopped at the kiosk. As he showed credentials to the guard who greeted them, Sara jumped as she heard a rapping on the passenger window beside her. She looked over.

It was Major Connell. She immediately pressed the button to roll the window down.

"Good," said the major. "You're back."

Sara felt herself quiver in anticipation. Had something else bad happened? Before asking, she looked around.

The hulk of General Yarrow's car was still there in the spot ahead of them. A couple of soldiers stood by it, rifles at their shoulders, obviously guarding the vehicle's corpse.

With the truck she rode in, there was a means of moving it to an out-of-the-way spot for further study before official disposal.

For now, though, Jason would have to steer around it.

But not immediately.

Sara stared back out the window toward Drew. "Is the general—" she began.

"He's doing okay. He wants to see you and me at the hospital ASAP."

"Fine." But Sara darted a glance toward Jason. "Only—"

"I'll get some of the guys to help me move the damaged car onto the ramp back there," he said, casually gesturing toward the back of the truck. He didn't seem at all perturbed that she'd be deserting him this quickly.

Which shot a bolt of unanticipated sorrow through Sara.

She hadn't planned on being with Jason for this amount of time.

She certainly hadn't planned on enjoying it.

But this just might be the only opportunity she would ever have to spend time with this appealing, sexy—and unattainable—man.

Ever.

And now it was over.

Chapter 5

General Yarrow's hospital room didn't impress Sara as looking any more exciting than any other hospital room she'd ever visited, except for its privacy. It was compact, with a single bed—which the general occupied—and two windows along one wall where the blinds had been opened, spilling light inside. The illumination struck the small chest of drawers where patients or their families could stow belongings. A TV hung overhead on the far wall. There were chairs—four of them, occupied now, including the one where Sara sat nearest to the general's right hand.

Appropriate, she realized.

It was all she could do to prevent herself from taking that hand in hers. To reassure him that everything would be okay.

Ridiculous. He was the one used to dictating the status of how whatever was happening each day played out. Plus, he was still her commanding officer. He would be shocked if she treated him like her friend or relative, no matter how fondly she thought of him.

Major Drew Connell and Sara had arrived only a couple of minutes ago. They'd entered the room and sat down in the seats as the general directed. The other two were occupied by Lieutenant Simon Parran and his wife, Lieutenant Grace Andreas-Parran, who'd obviously done a good job of accompanying the general here and ensuring that he was seen quickly in the emergency room.

Fortunately, his injuries were not life threatening. Grace had met them at the door and briefly informed them that General Yarrow had suffered a substantial amount of smoke inhalation. He'd been coughing and complained of a headache and shortness of breath. He was currently being treated with oxygen that he inhaled via tubes placed in his nose. Otherwise, he was fine.

He looked ashen, though, as his head rested on a pillow at the top of the raised back of the bed. His paleness was emphasized by the unmitigated blackness of his full head of hair—now more askew than Sara had ever seen it before.

But his light brown eyes were flashing, as always—ensuring that anyone on whom he directed his gaze knew exactly who was in charge.

"So where is the shell of my car now?" he demanded of Major Connell. The general, in his blue-plaid hospital gown, was the only one not dressed in camo attire. Sara wasn't used to seeing him in anything but his casual uniform, jeans and T-shirt during off hours, or, occasionally, something more formal.

"By now it should be secured in an area within the base's main parking garage, sir," Drew said, leaning toward him. "Lieutenant McLinder went with Sergeant Connell to rent a special flatbed vehicle to move it, and they arrived back at the base just in time for the lieutenant to accompany me here."

The general nodded his approval toward Sara. The gingerness of the movement might not have been obvious to the others in this room who didn't work with him daily, but Sara could tell that he was in real discomfort—and trying to hide it. They all were doctors but she knew the general better than any of them.

She was his primary aide and hoped she would continue in that position for a long time to come.

But maybe not where he had intended, most recently, to station himself—Ft. Lukman.

An image of Sergeant Jason Connell flashed through Sara's mind, and she willed it away. If they didn't return to the base housing Alpha Force, then she would never see the gorgeous, devil-may-care noncom again. In either of his forms.

Either of his forms? Heck, the fire in the general's car had taken precedence in her mind over all else—even pondering how strange, and outrageous, the reality of shapeshifting was.

Not seeing Jason again would definitely be for the best.

"What's the next step, then?" the general asked. "I presume you're having the remains examined by someone who'll be able to tell me what happened to the damned thing."

"I will, sir," Drew said. "I'm just having a little difficulty deciding on the right kind of forensics team for this. I of course don't want to use a civilian team, and because of the…well, delicate nature of the units stationed at Ft. Lukman and their relationship, I want to be sure I get the right kind of expertise in place, with complete discretion. And honesty."

"In other words," Simon said drily from his seat on the opposite side of the general's bed, "you want to bring in someone who won't either be ready to reveal any unusual things he may see—like shapeshifting—or afraid to point fingers at our new best friends, the Ultra Special Forces Team."

Simon was a tall man, whose straight, dark eyebrows matched his wavy, thick hair. Sara had noticed how often he shot glances toward his wife. She knew they were newlyweds, and had also heard, as a result of the general's grumblings, some of the awful details of their kidnapping while on their honeymoon.

Fortunately, other members of Alpha Force, primarily Simon's brother, Lieutenant Quinn Parran, and Grace's aide, Sergeant Kristine Norwood, had helped to bring them home—although their involvement hadn't been strictly in accordance with military protocol. That hadn't pleased the general—but Sara thought his irritation had been more for show in his position as commanding officer of Alpha Force than his real feelings.

What Simon had just said worried Sara, who liked everything military to be by the book. That included all units being…well, ordinary—even if she already knew that Alpha Force was anything but.

Plus, all military units should unquestionably keep any rivalry under control for the good of the country.

Assuming rivalry was what was going on at Ft. Lukman. If so, it was way out of hand in the event it had been the reason for General Yarrow's injury.

"You think they're responsible for this?" Sara demanded, recalling how Jason and she had already discussed that possibility. Her initial experiences with members of the USFT unit, in the cafeteria, in the BOQ and otherwise, hadn't been especially cordial. In fact, she'd sensed a lot of animosity from that team without understanding why… although maybe they simply mistrusted another military unit alleged to have woo-woo stuff affiliated with it, like shapeshifters. She could understand that. But all military troops had to act for the good of the country, not in accordance with their own suspicions or misgivings.

Surely no one within the USFT would intentionally do something to harm the commanding officer of another unit…would they?

Simon appeared ready to say something affirmative in response to Sara's question, but the general waved his hand dismissively. "Unknown, at least for now. That's why we have to be sure to handle the investigation appropriately."

"Do you have any suggestions about who should investigate your car, then, General?" asked Grace, who was seated beside her husband, opposite Sara.

Before he responded, Sara broke in. "I have an idea, sir. At least for starters. We can keep it low-key at first, but there's someone stationed at Ft. Lukman who apparently has an excellent background in working with cars. If we get him to do more than just move the vehicle—"

"You're talking about Sergeant Jason Connell, aren't you?" Simon's tone was neutral, but there was something troubling about the way he avoided looking toward Drew— cousin to the soldier under discussion.

"That's right," Sara agreed. "I understand he's an expert in fixing automobiles. As long as he doesn't do anything to obscure any evidence needed to be confirmed by a neutral third party, why not have him start the investigation? Major Connell already directed that he take a lot of confirming photographs while the car was still at the scene of the event. They can be shown to whoever conducts the official investigation later, too." She didn't call what had happened an accident. With that intense a fire, she suspected it was anything but.

"I don't mean to insult your cousin, Drew," cut in Grace, her gaze now on the major, "or offend you, but—"

"But you're going to, anyway." Drew turned to Sara. "You're probably not aware of the full situation with Jason, Sara, but—"

"But he's a car thief," broke in Simon.

"*Was* a car thief." Drew's expression darkened as he turned toward the lieutenant. "He enlisted in the military and joined Alpha Force as part of his penance for past misconduct."

"Right. It didn't hurt that joining up kept him out of prison." Simon was smiling now. "Hey, we understand. Far as we know, he's now a model soldier. A fine member of Alpha Force. We've seen him do great things with the unit's automobiles that need servicing. But—"

"I assume you're not suggesting that he could have been the one to somehow booby-trap my car, are you?" asked the general drily. "Why would he?"

"Why did anyone?" countered Simon. "Assuming it wasn't just spontaneous combustion."

Sara tuned out of the discussion for a moment, digesting what she had just learned. Sergeant Jason Connell wasn't merely a car lover and outstanding mechanic. He had apparently been arrested, and maybe convicted, of being a car thief. He must have agreed to join Alpha Force and throw himself under the scrutiny of his well-regarded cousin Major Drew Connell, a commissioned officer and a medical doctor to boot, to keep himself out of prison.

And this was the guy Sara had found so sexually exciting?

Hell, even if he was sexually exciting, everything she learned about him made him even more of a wrong choice for involvement.

Even so... "General, sir, I didn't know all that about Sergeant Connell. But he is a member of Alpha Force, and you're its commanding officer. He has a good reputation for working with cars, and he obviously isn't going to steal what remains of your Jeep. Sir—" Sara turned to Drew "—as I said, you've already ordered that photos be taken. You've also said that the remains should be kept in a protected area. You can additionally order that some of the other soldiers on base, maybe more security team members who aren't part of Alpha Force or USFT, assist Sergeant Connell, and be there the whole time he's conducting his investigation. Although—" She looked back at the general. "If he was involved, and there was anything he could steal off the damaged car and hide, he'll have done that already."

"True," said General Yarrow. "And I wouldn't have approved acceptance of the sergeant into Alpha Force if I'd thought he was still any kind of risk. Although having someone watching to confirm he doesn't do anything wrong with my former vehicle now is a good idea. In fact—"

Uh-oh. Sara didn't like the general's smile. She had seen it before when he was about to give an order that he knew the recipient would hate.

He was looking at her.

"Lieutenant McLinder, I hereby order you to work with Sergeant Connell to find out what the hell happened to my car—and to make sure he does a good job of checking it out."

Her shock must have shown on her face, since, for the first time that she'd seen after the explosion, General Yarrow actually laughed. So did the other three Alpha Force members in the room.

Then the general grew serious. "One thing, though. I'm pretty sure you already know it, that you've seen some things you didn't expect despite my warning before you preceded me to Ft. Lukman."

"Are you about to tell me that Sergeant Connell is a shapeshifter, sir?" Sara tried to put levity and nonchalance into her voice, but knew she failed miserably. She looked, one by one, at the three Alpha Force members now in her presence, all medical doctors and commissioned officers. "I don't know if everyone in Alpha Force is a shapeshifter," she said, "but I now believe that some of you are. And that includes Jason Connell. So if you—"

General Yarrow raised his hand in a sudden gesture that she recognized was intended to command. She immediately shut up.

Which was a good thing, since a voice sounded from behind her. "General Yarrow. Greg. We just heard and had to come here to make sure you were all right."

Sara turned. In the doorway were a couple of the USFT members she had seen in the cafeteria. They were preceded by a short, stocky man also in camos, his insignias indicating that he was a general. He'd been the one to speak.

"I'm fine, Hugo. Everyone—" General Yarrow's gaze took in the Alpha Force group around him as he gestured toward the newcomers "—this is General Hugo Myars, commanding officer of the Ultra Special Forces Team. I'm sure you've met some of his team members." He nodded toward the not especially friendly officers Sara had previously spoken with.

Myars maneuvered his way around the representatives of Alpha Force, while his backup remained near the door, their caps respectfully doffed and in their hands. "I know our people aren't merging as well as we'd initially hoped, so the exercises we planned are on hold, and now this. But I'm here to let you know, Greg, that the USFT and all its team members wish you a speedy recovery, and we're ready to work with Alpha Force as soon as we can start conducting joint training sessions."

Nice gesture, Sara thought.

Unless, of course, this was just General Myars's way to try to disguise the fact that he, or some of his subordinates, were the ones who'd set fire to General Yarrow's car.

But if so, why?

And did this unanticipated get-well visit make what

Jason would find in the Jeep's remains even more critical…because it would point right to these apparently kind-hearted fellow soldiers?

Jason couldn't help it.

At the moment, he stood alone on the hard concrete of Ft. Lukman's main parking garage, arms crossed, enjoying the rare and temporary solitude. Thinking.

He was in the military now. That usually meant having too many people around.

Although there were some people—one in particular at the moment—who he admitted to himself weren't so difficult to be near. But not just now.

He loved cars. They had a purpose, were understandable and followed logical rules.

They were indifferent to the fact that he was a shape-shifter, didn't care that he had made some mistakes when he was younger—well, except that he'd occasionally taken some cars away from their real, and possibly abusive or ignorant, owners.

He particularly loved those cars that could be considered classics.

That didn't necessarily include General Yarrow's aging Jeep, but Jason had seen, when he had serviced it before, how the general had babied it. Kept it in excellent condition.

Let experts—like Jason—work on it.

Now, though, it was gone—a pile of mostly metal debris. Smelly, fire-scarred, isolated wreckage that Jason was currently examining, all by himself.

He had done as ordered and found a rare location within the main garage that contained only a few spaces, an area on the third floor where only the top brass were authorized to park. A secure enough area that, by closing a garage door and erecting a barrier comprised of excess metal and wood from recent construction on the base, he'd been able to jerry-rig a portion into a pretty secure area after hauling the wreckage there in the truck he'd rented.

He'd been there for a while now, initially just staring at what was left of the deceased Jeep.

As he'd been told, he had found some security guys who were not members of either Alpha Force or that damned Ultra Special Forces Team, and given them orders to show up in about an hour to guard the general's former car.

That was one good thing about being a sergeant. Even though he was a noncommissioned officer, there were some folks who were of inferior ranks, and he could give them orders.

On the other hand, there were plenty of people of higher rank than him.

Like that gorgeous, sexy lieutenant. He hadn't wanted to think about her now, but she had insinuated herself into his mind, anyway.

And that stirred some of his most sensitive body parts. Bad time to allow her into his thoughts.

No, right now he ached to dig into the mess and figure out exactly what had happened. And not just because the senior commanding officer of his very special military unit had been in the vehicle when it caught fire.

No, it was even more because he gave a damn.

But Drew wanted a completely unbiased review, by non-Alpha Force investigators, of what was left, in case it contained evidence that pointed to someone's having caused the damage.

Someone like one of the members of that other major unit at Ft. Lukman, whose members had decided to look down their snooty human noses at their rival team here that they didn't understand at all, except to believe it inferior.

Little did they know.

But would they have tried to kill the superior officer of that unit? If so, why? And how had they set that fire?

Jason had changed into a well-worn T-shirt and jeans so he wouldn't appear to be doing anything official. Plus, he didn't want to mess up his uniform.

As he'd intended all along, he now approached the charred mass from the rear.

That was where the smoke had first appeared, or at least that was what it had looked like while watching the general drive through the gate.

He studied it first, then drew closer, knowing he'd better not touch it or move anything around. He wasn't an expert in finding evidence, and he might ruin any that happened to be there.

But he knew cars, damn it. And he particularly wanted—

"Hello, Sergeant Connell."

He forced himself not to jump out of his skin—his human skin—despite being startled by the familiar, strong female voice from behind him.

Instead, he pivoted to see Sara McLinder walk through the only door to this area that he had left accessible.

"Lieutenant." He nodded in acknowledgment but didn't want her here. Did he? The sight of her slim body, sexy even in her unisex camo uniform, made him want to approach her and do a lot more than salute.

He stayed where he was.

Especially because he anticipated that she was there to give him orders—like, get away from the damn wreck. Go somewhere else. Obey what she said, just because she could tell him what to do.

"Sergeant—Jason," she said. "Do you have a camera with you?"

He nodded. "I took a lot of photos before having this

thing moved here, like my cuz said." He'd have done it, anyway.

He'd wanted the reminder of how this poor vehicle had ended up immediately after its destruction.

"Good. Let's take some more right here before we start."

"Start what?" He didn't even attempt to hide the suspicion from his tone.

But that only brought a smile to her lovely, smooth features. A smile that emphasized the natural pinkness of her lips that wasn't enhanced by any lipstick.

Lord, how he'd love to taste them...right now.

"Drew knows a lot better than I do about your skill in working with cars, but I've been impressed with what I've seen and heard. You should pretty much only look, and touch only what you have to—and take a lot more photos so that, when any experts are brought in, they won't say that any evidence has become so tainted that they can't draw any logical conclusions. But even unbiased investigators might miss something a car expert wouldn't. So I've gotten your cousin's approval to ask you to conduct an initial investigation."

"You did that for me?" Jason's look was smug and sexy as he aimed a smile at her. "I didn't know you cared."

Sara shouldn't have told him she'd been the one to convince Drew. The guy obviously assumed that she'd done it because she was attracted to him.

Not that she'd admit it to him...but she was.

She raised her chin as she shook her head in a slowly skeptical denial, staring him straight in those gorgeous golden eyes. "I don't—not about you. But I do care about General Yarrow, and I want to make sure we get all the answers in case this wasn't simply a terrible accident."

"So you think his car was sabotaged." Jason's words

sounded more like a statement than a question, even as his expression grew serious.

"I believe it's a real possibility, so I want to know the truth." She pulled her own camera and some rubber gloves from the tote bag she had carried, then set the bag on the concrete beside her. "Besides, I'm here to observe…and help."

His turn to look skeptical. She didn't like that at all. "Just how do you plan to help?"

She wasn't about to tell him she was under orders to supervise him—not unless that became necessary because he looked about to screw things up. With his apparent ego, it would be better to let him think he was in control. *Think* being the operative word.

"Observation is the main thing. And taking pictures, too. In fact, since you've already taken some, I can be in charge of the rest, at least for now. Plus—well, if you need assistance I'll see what I can do. I can at least hold things out of the way, act as a second pair of eyes, whatever."

He nodded. "That sounds doable."

"Fine. Let's get started. Put these on first." She handed him one pair of the rubber gloves, keeping a second for herself. Then, drawing her gaze abruptly away from Jason, she strode toward the pile of metal remains, aiming her camera and snapping initial pictures.

This was the same camera she'd used to take pictures of his shift. She had already downloaded them onto her laptop computer and made a backup copy, password protected both files, then erased them from the camera.

Alpha Force's cover would not be blown by her.

Taking closer pictures of the Jeep now would be better, though. "Why don't you do this in a narrative?" she suggested. "I have a lot of memory left on the card in this camera and can take videos."

"Good idea."

Great. They seemed to be in agreement. For the moment, at least. And the division of labor seemed reasonable.

Sara considered herself fairly competent with a camera, but less so with a car.

Even so, she wanted to do a damned good job of supervising Jason as he conducted his preliminary analysis of what had happened to the Jeep to cause it to catch on fire.

Maybe even help with it herself.

Assuming, of course, that the fire hadn't destroyed all indications of its initial cause.

Jason began at the rear of the hulk. There was nothing left of the canvas that had once been the removable exterior covering, but the metal framework, blackened and curled in places from the heat, remained mostly intact.

"Is it cool enough for you to touch anything?" she asked.

"Yeah, it's fine now." He was already bending over the back of the thing, mostly looking. But then he probed a few places with his fingers.

For the next few minutes, Sara mostly recorded and listened as Jason used his knowledge of cars to study every centimeter of what he was able to see and described what he was doing.

At first, he apparently saw nothing that he seemed to think was out of place in the remains of a burned-out Jeep.

At one point he asked, "Do you happen to know if General Yarrow was carrying anything in the bed here?"

"He didn't mention anything."

"Well, we'll need to check with him. I see a few things that are definitely not part of the car, but they don't look especially dangerous, either."

Without moving them, he pointed them out to her. One was the burned carcass of what appeared to be a battery, and the other was a small piece of metal that could have

Untamed Wolf

been from a child's toy, maybe even a model of the Jeep, judging by its angles.

Then there was what was probably the remains of a steel fishing rod and a lure box containing what once had probably been hooks but were now just melted puddles of metal. Some additional small, melted clumps of metal. Nothing useful or conclusive. In the passenger seat were the remains of what must have been the general's overnight bag, still partially intact.

Sara dutifully continued to shoot the video, recording Jason's mention of each item and exactly where it lay in the midst of ashes and other debris.

She was impressed with Jason's meticulousness and attention to detail in the ruined Jeep. He pointed out the parts he recognized, those that were no longer recognizable but had qualities that allowed him to make assumptions, and more.

He occasionally asked for her to gently touch something, holding it out of the way so he could pry even farther into some inside area. She shot more pictures of each of those areas when her assignment was complete.

Eventually, after more than an hour, Jason was through.

"I know it'll all be speculation," Sara said, holding the camera on Jason, "but do you have any initial opinion about the origin of the fire?"

His handsome features grew even sharper as his expression hardened. "Nothing conclusive, nothing I can point to that proves it was anything but some odd mechanical failure or spontaneous combustion or unavoidable accident," he said, "but despite finding nothing obvious during this first examination, I knew this Jeep well after servicing it for General Yarrow. I believe this was somehow deliberately sabotaged, set on fire. And I'll do anything I can to find proof."

Sara turned off the camera and looked at him, seeing the frustration and sorrow on his face. She wanted to do something to comfort him, but all she could do was to acknowledge her agreement. "That's my belief, too," she said quietly. "But since you didn't see anything to hang that opinion on—"

"I will," he said grimly. "Count on it."

Chapter 6

Jason used his cell phone to call the head of the small base security team. Time for them to guard the car's remains. It was getting late on this very busy day.

Sara waited with him, concern furrowing her brow beneath her short cap of blond hair. He'd never thought frowning sexy before. But, as unfortunate as it was, everything about Lieutenant Sara McLinder made him ache to touch her.

Everything including her light citrus scent.

And the way she'd jumped in to help him study the Jeep. Concentrated on taking videos. Essentially interviewed him to preserve his thoughts and actions in case they helped lead to what the hell had caused the vehicle to catch fire.

Everything including the way she now pulled her phone from her pocket often to check the time.

Yes, even that was sexy and taunted him to get up close and personal with her, encourage her to relax...and more.

Not that he'd ever give in to those urges. She wasn't exactly the kind to appreciate them.

Soon, three men on security detail—all privates, none a member of either of the primary units at Ft. Lukman, and all vetted to be trustworthy—arrived.

No chances were to be taken with the Jeep's carcass, even though Jason felt certain he'd done a pretty good job checking it over. There just wasn't anything useful to be found.

But the general would want to see it once he was feeling well enough to return here. Maybe he'd examine the remains himself. And, most likely, he would call in his own most trusted military forensics experts to confirm Jason's conclusions—or at least he'd have to consent to whoever was given the assignment.

"Let's go report to my cuz," he finally said to Sara as they left the garage. "We can show him the photos, see what he wants us to do with them." He kept his tone casual, sergeant to lieutenant.

"Fine," she responded in her characteristic clipped tone. Why did he find that sexy, too?

Sara kept pace with his long strides across sidewalks toward the building near the entry gate that housed the offices of the base's commanding officers.

That included General Yarrow's. Jason had seen his specially furnished office here on the senior CO's earlier visits.

Drew had an office there, too. It was down the hall of the building's second floor. That's where Jason headed now, along with Sara.

But he hated having nothing conclusive to report. Especially since Drew had initially put him in charge of moving the damaged vehicle, but also agreed that he should start the investigation into the fire's cause. Thanks to Sara.

Of course Jason wasn't sure why she'd promoted the idea of having him check out the Jeep first. She clearly was uncomfortable with who, and what, he was.

They passed other soldiers on Ft. Lukman's sidewalks, some from Alpha Force, some from the Ultra Special Forces Team and others among the few miscellaneous soldiers with high security clearances who also happened to be stationed there. Jason saluted appropriately. So did Sara.

Jason recalled his first days after enlisting, getting used to such stringent protocol. He'd wanted to rebel, but knew that being there, following the rules, would be all that could keep him out of prison. He'd kept telling himself it would eventually be second nature to him.

Even now, it wasn't entirely, but he'd gotten used to it. He'd even gotten used to his own ambivalence about being in the military. Sort of.

Sara said nothing, not at first. But as they reached the building, she stopped and turned toward him. Her expression appeared troubled. He wondered again why such an unsexy look on her face made his downstairs body parts want to stand up and salute.

She shook her head then and tossed him a smile that seemed anything but happy. "You know, as we walked here, I kept looking at everyone I didn't yet know, wondering if he or she was part of Alpha Force, and, if so, whether they were shifters. And you know I'd been fighting any belief in people…like you. Even though, having seen you, I now know the truth."

He realized how much that stuff that she considered woo-woo, yet real, must really bother the by-the-book officer. Growing up the way he did, knowing that his kind needed to hide from most of the world to stay alive, he should have despised her.

He didn't. Instead, he kind of understood. And wanted to help.

"A lot of Alpha Force members are away right now, either on missions or vacation, so you've probably met everyone in our unit who's here at the moment. Tell you what, one of these days maybe we'll have a little talk not only about Alpha Force but shapeshifting in general. It's always been fascinating to me, even though I'm part of it. Maybe learning more will make it easier for you to deal with, too."

She sucked in her full lips pensively. He wished for a moment that he could do the same…in a nice, hot, endless kiss. But he just waited for her response.

"I'd like that," she said, then pivoted and headed toward the building's front entrance.

They walked up the stairway to the second floor. General Yarrow's office was right there, and Jason noticed Sara's glance toward its closed door, with the CO's name on it, before she accompanied him down the hall to Drew's office. His cuz, too, had his name on the outside door. Jason knew that this office, a new one for Drew, was mostly for show and convenience.

Drew spent most of his time when present at Ft. Lukman in the downstairs lab area of the building near the outer edge of the base. His primary office was a small one there, too—the one where the recent Alpha Force meeting had been held.

Sara, who had slightly preceded Jason, knocked on the door, but he didn't wait for a response. He opened it and walked inside, holding the door open for the lovely lieutenant.

She blinked at him in irritation but he turned immediately toward the standard-issue desk at the far side of the room. Drew sat behind it, also glaring at him.

"Come in," Drew said through clenched teeth.

Jason just smiled. "Don't mind if I do." Again without waiting, he approached Drew's desk and pulled out one of the two chairs facing it, both with gray tweed upholstery attached to a light wood frame, and motioned for Sara to sit.

She hesitated, as if not comfortable with the gesture, but then complied without comment.

"Okay, you two," Drew said, and Jason was glad to see that Sara didn't cringe at being grouped with him in Drew's upcoming inquiry. "I gather you didn't find anything particularly helpful, but give me a rundown."

Jason did, starting with the photos he'd shot before relocating the charred remains, then annotating the narration they presented when Sara ran her videos.

Drew was silent for a moment when they finished. "Maybe I am trying to make a bigger deal of this than it warrants. General Yarrow was injured, but he's okay. In fact, I understand he'll be well enough to return here as early as tomorrow. If there's no evidence that the fire was deliberately set—"

"Then someone was damned good at setting it," Jason interrupted. From the corner of his eye he saw Sara glance toward him. He caught her gaze, and they both gave slight nods.

"Then that's what you think, too, Sara?" Drew asked.

"Until someone proves that it was just some stupid little thing like the sun shining on a piece of glass inside and heating a spot on the canvas cover till it ignited, or the general just unfortunately passed a smoker who happened to flick a butt at just the wrong angle—and, yes, I can see from your expression that you're as dubious as I am about those—then I'm going to assume the worst. We're not experts, but I'm sure you and the general can find some guys who do this all the time. I'd just request that you keep me informed about anything they find."

"Me, too," Jason said, wanting not only to support Sara but to hug her, as well.

She had expressed everything he'd wanted to, and then some.

If she let herself, Sara knew she would feel depressed as she left the major's office with Jason.

They headed back toward the stairway that had taken

them to this floor, then down the steps. Jason's footfalls were light, sounded carefree as he took those steps a couple at a time.

Their discussion with Drew must have pleased him more than it did Sara.

The good news was that General Yarrow was improving, might even be there, at Ft. Lukman, tomorrow.

The bad? Well, nothing that she didn't already know. No news wasn't necessarily good news.

And now it was very late in the afternoon. Sara hadn't yet formed any friendships with other officers at the base. She wanted to, at least with members of Alpha Force, and might be able to call on one or two and invite them for coffee or whatever to get to know them better.

She didn't even want to try with any members of the Ultra Special Forces Team. She might have a lot more in common with them than with Alpha Force members, but the animosity between the two units remained almost palpable—and she had come here to help the general work with the unit reporting to him.

"Hey, Lieutenant," Jason said as he held the building's door open for her to exit. "What're you up to now?"

Had he read her mind? Or was her dejection obvious?

She pasted a smile on her face as she looked at him. Then it turned more genuine. It was hard to stay depressed in the presence of a guy so great-looking, so cock-sure of himself, who teased sexily with every gaze of his golden eyes.

"Just thought I'd head back to the BOQ and do some reading. I'm tired of excitement for now."

"Well, if you'd like just a little more excitement first—fun stuff, nothing heavy—you could join me. I'm heading over to the kennel to pick up my best friend."

She tilted her head at him, slightly puzzled. "I assume, if you're going to the kennel, that it's—"

"Yep, my cover dog, Shadow. I've been letting him hang out with his buddies much too long lately. It's time he spent some quality time with me. And with you, too, if you're interested."

"Cover dog?" She had thought Shadow resembled Jason in wolf form but still… What did that mean?

"You've been at the kennel, seen some of the dogs," Jason said. "They're mostly trained for K-9 uses, security and bomb sniffing and all that. But in addition—well, all of us shifters have a pet who looks like us in our animal forms. That helps confuse people who don't really know, or understand, what Alpha Force is about. If they happen to see a wolflike dog, they're much more likely to assume it's a wolflike dog than a shapeshifter. Same goes for Colleen Hodell's cougar-resembling cat. Smaller, of course. She keeps Puka in her BOQ unit."

Fascinating, Sara thought.

"With all that was going on," Jason continued, "I figured Shadow would be better off there, with company, than hanging out with me, but I miss the guy, want to spend some time with him."

"Sure," Sara said. "I'd love to play with Shadow."

And you, too, she thought, but didn't say it. Yet suddenly she felt much more lighthearted because she wouldn't be alone, at least not for now.

Knowing she'd be in Jason's company a little longer had nothing to do with it.

She loved it!

While Sara was growing up in Cleveland, Ohio, she'd had a dog—a small one, a Shih Tzu mix named Sissy, who had loved to play fetch with nylon bones. She'd been a sweetheart. Sara had missed her as much as she'd missed the rest of the family when she'd left home to attend Kent

State to study political science—and to join ROTC, since she'd known she wanted a career in the military.

Sissy was gone now, and Sara hadn't gotten to know the dog her parents had subsequently gotten from a rescue organization very well, mostly because she visited so infrequently.

She'd forgotten how much she enjoyed dogs—until that afternoon.

Jason and she each had a dog leashed beside them as they left the building housing the kennel on its main floor. Jason's was, of course, Shadow.

He had also gotten her a dog for companionship that afternoon. "This is Duke," he'd told her as he handed her the leash of a large shepherd-wolfhound mix. "He's the cover dog for the second in command stationed here at Alpha Force, Lieutenant Patrick Worley. Patrick's been on vacation with his wife, Mariah. She's a nature writer and they went back to Alaska, where they met, for a couple of weeks. They're due back tomorrow, but we've all been exercising Duke in the meantime."

And now, Sara was running with dogs and Jason on the neatly trimmed lawn beneath canopies of trees, and between some of the cookie-cutter low buildings that filled Ft. Lukman, including the one that housed the general's, and Drew's, offices. The one holding the kennel—and the lab areas below—was on the periphery of the rest.

Sara knew she was a bit out of shape despite all the calisthenics she performed as a matter of course nearly every morning at home, as part of her military regimen. But she hadn't run like this for—well, forever.

"Please, wait!" she finally cried to Jason, who was ahead of her with Shadow. Duke tugged on his leash to catch up. "I need to rest."

"Is that an order, Lieutenant?" Jason called. He'd turned and was running backward. At least his pace was slower now.

"That's an order," Sara gasped, stopping altogether. "Duke, come here."

"Here, let me give you a lesson in training these guys." Jason was suddenly right beside her, and the dogs, too, had stopped. Both large canines were panting heavily. So was Sara. Jason barely seemed out of breath, although Sara did see patches of perspiration near his armpits, and his forehead, too, was damp.

She must look awful, she thought—definitely sweaty and breathless and generally a mess.

So why, when Jason looked at her, did he smile so sexily?

Hell, she knew why. That was his usual look. But if he was totally turned off by her, he was kind enough not to show it.

Which in a way was too bad. Maybe it would make her stop lusting for this highly inappropriate soldier.

"Okay, Shadow." Jason stood straight as he looked down at his dog. He raised one hand and pointed to Shadow's rear. "Sit." The canine obeyed immediately. "Now you try it with Duke. That's elementary, and they've all been taught the same commands."

Sara did so and found herself surprisingly pleased when Duke sat, stood and gave her his paw, all on command. "Is he trained for any of the K-9 things you mentioned, like sniffing out drugs or whatever?"

"Sure. They've all been taught some of that, too. A few are real experts, and they're used when that kind of help is needed. But most of these guys are just excellent camouflage pets." He paused. "Are you ready to take Duke back to his quarters? I'm keeping Shadow with me tonight."

So he would have company, even though it was just a dog.

Sara would be on her own—which never used to bother her. She'd find male companionship now and then when she wanted some, but not here, of course.

"Tell you what," she said. "I saw an outdoor eating area at the base cafeteria. Why don't we grab dinner together with both dogs—part of their training, of course." And definitely not fraternizing. Or at least arguably not, if anyone called her on it.

"Fine with me." Jason gave her one of those hot grins again, as if he knew exactly what she was thinking. "You hungry now?"

"Hungry enough." Under other circumstances, she'd go shower and change clothes before having dinner with a great-looking guy.

But now, it was better if she stayed grungy and unalluring. Much better.

Because even if she hadn't yet been able to get her attraction to Jason completely under control, at least he couldn't possibly find her appealing.

Jason kept the dogs company while Sara went inside to grab her dinner.

He'd have liked to have accompanied her, even paid for her meal, but it was better this way.

No way could it look like a date.

Especially since the cafeteria was filled with both Alpha Force members and those from that damned Ultra Special Forces Team.

Jason sat at a table for two, bending over and petting the dogs. Talking to them.

It kept him from having to speak with anyone nearby— who mostly seemed to be USFT guys. Too bad he didn't know what their special skills really were. What the hell made them more ultra than regular Special Forces?

He wasn't about to ask. Probably no Alpha Force member would. Better that both units keep pretty much to themselves for now, till given orders otherwise to start whatever joint training was planned for them—although he had no doubt that these guys had at least some idea what made Alpha Force so special.

"They've got Salisbury steak as their special tonight." Sara had returned, carrying a tray, and Jason inhaled the aroma of the dish she had mentioned. Smelled good. He figured he'd get some, too, instead of his usual T-bone here.

This cafeteria was used to serving Alpha Force members red-meat entrées.

"Did you get enough to treat these fellows?" Jason gestured toward the dogs, whom he'd given commands to lie down and stay. Their noses were in the air, though—both of them.

"I didn't think people food was good for them."

"Not as a general diet, but treats don't hurt. I'll get a little extra."

He went inside. When he came out again with his tray a few minutes later, the dogs hadn't moved.

A couple of those damned USFT guys had, though. They were close to Sara, apparently hitting on her. Both were in camo uniforms, and they also wore the insignias of a lieutenant and a captain.

Her rank and above.

She seemed friendly enough to them, too, chatting. He focused his excellent hearing on the conversation before joining them.

Sounded innocent enough—maybe. They were asking about her work for General Yarrow, what had happened to his Jeep, how he was doing.

Did these guys already know? Were they trying to learn how much Sara knew?

Oh, but she was cagy in the responses Jason heard, though. All she said was that so far she'd heard of no indication that the fire in the vehicle had been anything but some kind of weird accident. And since the general was okay, that was all she needed to know.

Jason took that opportunity to sit back down across from her.

Shadow and Duke stirred. He looked at them both and said, "Stay," and they did.

"So how's the Salisbury?" he asked Sara, ignoring the others.

"Pretty good." She hesitated only a moment before saying to Jason, obviously for the benefit of the other officers, "So after dinner you'll teach me the commands you use for getting these guys to fetch?"

"Sure will," he said, and smiled at her.

And loved the way she smiled back.

Sara hadn't imagined that having dinner with Jason would turn into a land mine of possible dangers, but it had, at least in a way.

She didn't, couldn't, trust those USFT guys until what had happened to the general's car was explained, but she'd been trying to both answer their questions and interject some of her own to find out if they were just stringing her along while knowing the answers themselves.

But there'd been no indication of that.

And she had of course wanted to make it clear that she wasn't simply fraternizing with Jason.

So why did the idea feel so good?

The USFT group returned to their prior table. Jason and she took their time finishing their meal. Jason even gave her some of the meat he'd saved to give to Duke, while he did the same with Shadow.

And then they left.

Sara would have loved to take Duke back to the BOQ as her companion that night, but Jason had already said that his master, Patrick Worley, would probably be back soon. No sense for her to get any more involved with the dog— either for her own sake or for his.

She enjoyed the way they sauntered, though—Jason and her and both dogs—back to the edge of the base and the kennel.

She felt almost mournful putting Duke back in his enclosure, even though he went leaping inside to be greeted by other base canines.

Then she walked back out again with Jason and Shadow.

It was starting to get dark. "We'll accompany you to the BOQ," Jason told her. "Not that I anticipate anything bad happening on the base, but in case you need backup we'll be there."

She didn't need backup. But she appreciated their company—for more reasons than gentlemanliness on the part of Jason, which she figured wasn't his normal demeanor.

Was he, after all, as attracted to her as she was to him?

On one level, she hoped not. It would only make it harder for them to stay apart, as they had to do.

On another level…well, why shouldn't it be as difficult for him as it was for her?

"Lovely night tonight," she said to make conversation as they strolled toward her quarters.

"Yeah." By the location of his voice, she could tell he was looking at her, and she felt herself begin to blush.

"Glad the general might be here tomorrow." She hoped that her change of subject would be a turnoff to him. It was to her.

Kind of.

She knew what would be a real turnoff to her. "So when

will you be shapeshifting again? I've heard that you Alpha Forcers don't always have to wait until a full moon."

"That's true. And I don't know."

When they reached the front door of the BOQ she looked around, hoping someone else would be there so the parting would be brief and simple.

They were alone.

She bent and patted Shadow. "Good night, guy." She stood again. "And good night, Jason."

She didn't expect it…did she? But he leaned down toward her and planted just the hint of a kiss on her mouth—leaving her wanting more. Much more.

"Good night, Lieutenant." He backed off, grinned and sauntered away, whistling an unidentifiable tune.

Chapter 7

Turning away from the BOQ, Jason yawned. He didn't bother covering his mouth. No one was around except Shadow, and the dog wouldn't be offended.

And besides, yawning in the face of an officer might only make him feel better.

Not if it was Sara McLinder, though. He'd much rather leave a favorable impression with her. Like that kiss.

Too bad he hadn't dared more with her...yet. But his body was still reacting to that little peck.

It had been a long day. A lot had happened—starting from when the general's car had caught fire.

Jason knew he was dog-tired. Loved that expression. It certainly fit.

But feeling that way wouldn't stop him from what he still had to do.

He stepped up the pace as he and Shadow headed back toward the building housing the kennels...and the labs. While hurrying, he called Noel Chuma.

"Is Simon Parran doing anything tonight?" he immediately asked when the guy, not a shifter but one really good aide to some of those who were, answered the phone. At the moment, Noel was assigned both to Lieutenant Simon Parran and to Sergeant Jason Connell.

Jason never had to guess who had priority in the case of a conflict.

"Nope," was Noel's response. "Are you?"

"Yeah. You near the lab?"

"I can be there in five minutes."

"Me, too. See ya there." Jason ended the connection.

He had lied to Sara. She'd asked if he planned to shape-shift anytime soon. He'd claimed he hadn't decided on a time.

But he had already intended to shift tonight. He still needed answers about the damage to General Yarrow's Jeep. They all needed answers. And his plain, ordinary human senses weren't nearly as much help as his enhanced wolfen senses might be.

"Hey, boy," he said to Shadow as they finally reached the door to the building they'd been heading toward. The dog's tail wagged. "I'll leave you with your buddies again. If all goes well, I'll be back for you in a little while and you'll go home with me."

Not that his quarters, in the building housing the base's NCOs, were especially lush. But he liked having Shadow around for company and believed that his dog, too, preferred being out and about, at least some of the time, rather than hanging out with his canine pack.

Jason swiped his key card and they entered the building on the main floor where the kennels were located. By the time he had let Shadow into the large enclosure with his closest canine friends—including Duke, who greeted him nose to nose once more—Noel Chuma had caught up with him.

Noel had dark-toned skin. Though he was on the short side, he had the build of a guy who worked out a lot. Maybe that was how he made up for not having all the abilities of the Alpha Forcers he helped. He hadn't bothered putting on his uniform that night, but instead wore a black T-shirt over equally dark jeans. The better not to be seen when Jason left him in the woods later.

He'd also thrown a backpack over his shoulders. "Hi, bro," he said. "Let's go downstairs. I need both a light and some elixir."

"Sounds good."

At the door to the stairway, as Jason prepared to swipe his other key card, he noticed some scratches in the paint. "You seen this?" he asked Noel.

"No." The other man bent down to scrutinize the area. "You think someone tried to break in? One of those USFT guys?"

Alpha Force had beefed up security in this building when they'd anticipated the arrival of another unit to be stationed at Ft. Lukman. There were two types of key cards— one to enter the kennel area upstairs, which were given out to nearly anyone who might need to help out with the dogs, and a second kind to get down to the highly classified lab area. Not many of those were available.

And it now appeared that someone who didn't have the second kind of key card had gotten frustrated about that.

Too bad they'd decided against using security cameras— but there was too much of a chance that pictures taken of shapeshifters could get into the wrong hands. Or even on the internet.

"Could be one of them—although as far as I know they're not aware of the importance of the lab facilities down there. Tell you what. You tell my cuz about this while I'm shifted, okay?"

"Yeah."

They headed downstairs and emerged about five minutes later with all Noel needed in his backpack, closing and locking the door carefully behind them. Without discussing it, they both walked straight into the depths of the woods nearest the building, which was in a remote site on the base.

There, Jason drank the elixir and stripped while Noel aimed the light at him. Immediately, Jason felt the initial throes of his shift.

"Have fun," Noel called. "And be careful. I'll call Major Connell and hang mostly near here, but I'll be around if you need me."

Jason answered with an acknowledging growl.

Jason bounded even farther into the cover of the thick trees then followed the inside of the base's fence around its perimeter. He didn't have time to revel in his wolfen state. Not at this moment. But he loved the feeling. Always.

Right now, he needed to get to the area around the main entrance where the fire in the general's car had first been noticed.

It was dark, late enough that not many people were out walking the grounds either on official security patrols or otherwise. Good. He barely had to hide. And some of those he saw were part of Alpha Force so there would be no repercussions, even if they noticed him.

He reached the area closest to the BOQ, though there was another building paralleling it that was nearer to him. He spared a quick glance and sniff in that direction.

Too far and too late to smell the appealing scent of Sara McLinder. She had to be inside, in bed.

Alone? Probably. Even so, he uttered a low growl at the thought she might not be, then made himself hurry forward. He had much to accomplish.

There were more bushes for camouflage near the entry drive and its security kiosk. He waited for a minute, his long, smooth muzzle in the air, inhaling the smells. He doubted that any useful scent would remain, though it had

*appeared that the general's car had first started to burn in
this area, or just beyond.*

*Vehicle odors here. Some human scents. The nearest
trees and other vegetation. The merest hint of the residue
of the smell of fire.*

Nothing helpful.

*As always, 24/7, there was a guard inside the kiosk. Of
course the guards had high security clearances. Although
none were Alpha Force members, they knew that some delicate and highly covert training exercises were held inside
this fence. They also knew to ignore anything...unusual.
And absolutely to keep it to themselves.*

*Even so, Jason was cautious as he slunk under the fence
and outside the base. He knew the most likely way the
general would have approached the entrance. He stayed
hidden in the surrounding trees as he trotted along that
route, once more using all his special senses to identify
anything unusual.*

*Unlikely, of course. He'd found nothing in the car that
explained what had happened. It was improbable that
someone had hidden an incendiary device inside the Jeep
before the general left D.C. The idea that a person just
outside here could have somehow done something to set
the fire...*

*He had driven past this area before, seen and sensed
nothing unusual, but he'd been in other vehicles and not
particularly close.*

Now though—

*Wait! Jason found himself coughing, his head nearly
touching the ground as he inhaled...what?*

*He had just reached the corner almost a half mile from
the base's entrance where the general would have turned
off another road. There was a stop sign. Stones on the street
and at the roadside that Sara and he had noticed before.*

Had they been thrown onto the road to slow the general's car?

There were lots of trees around. Places where someone could have hidden, then somehow lobbed something into the back of the slowed vehicle?

Jason couldn't focus on his speculation, since he had not stopped gagging. Fortunately, whatever it was did not negate the effects of the Alpha Force elixir that allowed him human consciousness, but there was something on and in the ground that reeked. Made him feel ill.

Was the area rigged for this purpose: to prevent an Alpha Force shifter from scenting someone, something, that would give a clue to what had happened to the Jeep?

Jason was sure of it—as sure as he could be about anything while feeling so miserable. Too bad he couldn't hold his breath. Would that help?

It was dark here, no streetlights, so he couldn't even attempt to use his most vital human sense and look around for anything causing the problem.

He would come back, in daylight, in human form.

Then maybe he would find answers.

For now, he coughed some more, and headed slowly back toward the base's entrance.

Sara felt exhausted after such a stressful day—a day that had ended with that kiss, admittedly fairly tame, by Jason Connell.

She'd tried lying down on her sofa in the BOQ, reading to put herself to sleep by the light of a table lamp. She had even chosen another complicated book on military strategy.

It didn't help—not any more than her attempts to sleep on the night of the full moon after seeing the pack of wolves she now knew to be Alpha Force shifters.

Was that why she couldn't sleep now? Was she thinking too much about Alpha Force? Shapeshifting?

Jason?

Of course not. She was worried about General Yarrow and what had happened to him earlier that day.

Not that she could do anything about that now...could she?

Hell. She wasn't sleeping, anyway. She hadn't even changed out of her camos.

Why not just go outside and take a short walk to exercise and wear herself out?

She slammed the book down on the low coffee table, stood and headed for the door.

She didn't want interaction with other people, so she took the same set of stairs she'd used before to avoid the main doors.

There was a light outside the door where she exited. Off to her right was the building's primary entry, so she decided to go left.

Especially since a couple of officers she recognized stood just outside the main door, talking. One was Lieutenant Manning Breman and the other was Captain Samantha Everly, both members of the Ultra Special Forces Team.

But before Sara started off, she heard something in the distance. Someone coughing? It sounded more like a sick animal.

Not only that, but she saw a movement in the gap between the two low buildings between the BOQ and the trees that lined the base's outer boundaries. Something low.

The size, perhaps, of a wolf. A wolf that resembled Shadow, Jason's cover dog.

Which meant it resembled Jason, too, at times. Not that her brief glance could tell her that for certain....

Making an immediate decision, Sara changed her mind

and approached the two from USFT. No sense taking chances about their noticing the creature sneaking around in the not-too-far distance.

Just in case.

"Hi," she called, loudly enough for the wolf—or whatever—to hear. "I couldn't sleep. You, too?"

In the artificial light, Manning Breman looked moderate in height and chubby-cheeked, and he immediately smiled when she approached. "Yeah, I just came out here to—"

"To meet with me," Samantha broke in. She, on the other hand, wasn't smiling. She was about Sara's height but a lot curvier in her uniform, and her light brown hair was gathered with a clip on the top of her head. "We had some planning to do for our next USFT exercises." She looked tellingly at Sara, as if ordering her to leave. She was a captain, so she could actually give that order if she chose to.

For the moment, though, she didn't—and Sara wanted to waste more time. "Really? What kind of exercises do you do? I know you're special forces, but I have to admit my ignorance. I don't really know anything about your unit, and—"

"Well, it's nothing like your damned Alpha Force," Samantha said. "No claims, or actuality, of any woo-woo stuff. We're just damned good soldiers with strategic and fighting skills that are highly classified. All I'll say is that we're the best, in fact, chosen from other special-ops teams. But we're not about to tell you anything else, Lieutenant."

Sara felt affronted. On the other hand, it was in the best interests of General Yarrow, Alpha Force and even herself not to antagonize any members of this unit—for now.

"I understand," Sara said. "Sorry. I'll leave you alone now." She noticed Manning's frown at his superior officer until Samantha looked his way. He gave a brief shrug of his narrow shoulders in Sara's direction then aimed a concerned expression toward the woman beside him.

Apparently, the guy didn't necessarily agree with his boss, but he obeyed military protocol and didn't voice an opinion.

Sara turned and strode off. Instead of the walk she had planned around the building, though, she decided to head in a different direction.

Down the center road of the base.

The one that would take her to its farthest building, the main quarters of the cover dogs, and hidden laboratories, of Alpha Force.

In case she was right about the nature of the animal she had glimpsed and heard, she believed it—he?—would be heading there.

Jason was in a downstairs lab. He had just changed back to human form and lay on the cold, hard floor. He hadn't even wanted to go into the small office to sit on a more comfortable chair.

Noel had ushered him down there after seeing the wolf's condition, helped him into his clothes, made a call or two.

"So," Noel said. "You okay? That looked like a pretty rough shift, and you weren't looking so great before, either."

"Something was definitely wrong," Jason said then coughed again. "Suspicious," he managed to hack out.

"What was it?" He looked up at the sound of the female voice to see that Sara had joined them.

Sara. She must still have the general's key card to get down here. What had she been doing outside her quarters?

Talking to those USFT people? Was she conniving in some manner with them?

Even if she was, she had managed to help him that night.

And she surely was much too smart to collude with them in public.

"Don't know." He coughed again.

"Don't try to talk," Sara said. She looked toward Noel as if to get his concurrence.

"That's right. Tell us later what happened. Right now, just relax."

He continued just to lie there and listened as Sara, bless her, explained to Noel what had occurred from her perspective.

"I didn't know for sure it was Jason, or even a shifted Alpha Force member," she said, "but I heard a strange noise like coughing then saw the form of a canine in the distance. I'd noticed a couple of the USFT people standing outside the BOQ and figured I'd better distract them, just in case."

Jason couldn't stay quiet at that. "I saw you. Wondered. Thanks."

At her bright, pleased smile, he wanted to kiss her again. Only better.

Instead, he just coughed.

"Are you going to be okay?" She sounded worried.

He nodded. "Just wish I knew what it was." Each word came out softly and slowly as he kept trying not to cough.

"We'll figure it out." This time, the speaker was Major Drew Connell, who'd just arrived. "Let me examine you, maybe run some tests." His cuz was obviously wearing his medical hat at the moment, which pleased Jason.

"Fine," he said. "Noel, would you walk Sara back to her quarters?"

"Sure," his aide said, though he sounded worried. "Unless you think I can help here, sir." He was obviously talking to Drew.

"I think you can help best by doing as Jason suggested. Then return here and we'll talk about what we find."

"And you'll let me know, too?" Sara asked.

"Absolutely."

Chapter 8

The walk back to her quarters with Staff Sergeant Noel Chuma felt tense to Sara—and not because of her companion. Noel seemed like a nice enough guy who stayed friendly while constantly surveying their surroundings, doing his job of protecting her.

Maybe his efficiency was part of what disturbed her. It was as if he assumed there were people—or whatever—watching them, ready to attack.

She wished she could refute that possibility.

Instead, she decided to talk to him, without, hopefully, distracting him too much.

"How did you get recruited into Alpha Force?" she asked.

"I like challenges." He glanced down at her beneath the dim light with a huge grin. "And what could be more challenging than helping out a whole group of shapeshifters?"

That gave Sara pause. "Then you knew about them before you joined?"

"I was already in the military, spent a year deployed to Afghanistan, and figured I'd had enough combat experience to ramp my military career up a notch. I started asking around, learned that there was this highly covert unit that needed some extra guys, so I threw my name onto their list of possibles. I heard from Major Connell a couple of days later. He came to see me at my base in Texas, which seemed unusual. I assumed I'd be the one who'd have to travel. I guess I answered his questions okay since he put me at the top of his list. That was when he started asking really weird questions about what I believed about people and the universe and things, or creatures, that were unusual. Guess I did okay there, too, since he offered me the position—after swearing me to absolute secrecy. Now, here I am!"

And so was she, Sara thought. She had also been vetted—by General Yarrow before he took her on as an aide. But he hadn't been as upfront as Noel described about the units that were under his particular aegis.

She might never have known about Alpha Force and what it really was if he hadn't come to trust her implicitly.

Was she happy now? Well, she liked that he did trust her. She liked working with the general.

But did she like being here, in this situation, being surrounded by people whose characteristics still seemed unreal, no matter what she'd seen?

Amazingly, the answer was yes. Or it would be if they figured out what had happened to Greg Yarrow and his vehicle, and resolved that satisfactorily.

Including finding out what had sickened Jason, in wolf form, that evening.

They reached the BOQ, and Noel offered to accompany her to her unit to make sure everything was okay. Sara still felt somewhat spooked, so she agreed.

All seemed fine. It was empty. At this late hour, they didn't even see any other building occupants up and about.

Noel left after a pleasant goodbye, leaving Sara wishing things had turned out way differently that day, on many fronts. But at least the general would be okay. And it was still much better that Jason hadn't been the one to walk her home.

Jason. How was he doing? Well, she could always call, as an interested superior officer, to find out.

As she pulled her cell phone from her pocket, it rang.

It didn't show a name—but the number had a local area code.

"Hello?" she said.

"Sara? It's Jason." There was still a raspiness to his voice, although it could just have been the connection. "You back at your place?"

"Yes. Our walk here was uneventful, and Noel just left." She paused for only a second. "How are you feeling?"

"Mad."

"I mean—"

"I know what you mean. Nice of you to ask. I'm fine. And I also want to find out what caused that reaction. Fast."

"Then you'll be—"

"Checking it out tomorrow, after a good night's sleep."

"I'll help," Sara said, not sure what she could do that would be useful. But whatever it was that had affected Jason so badly had to be related in some way to the cause of the burning of General Yarrow's car.

She wanted answers—and, she realized, not only because the general had been harmed. She sought retribution for Jason's sake now, too.

Just because he was a member of Alpha Force, on the general's team, she told herself—recognizing it was at least a partial lie. She cared about what happened to Jason— more than she should, and for reasons she didn't want to think about.

But she did think about them when Jason prepared to hang up. "By the way," he said, his tone soft and somehow amazingly sexy over the phone. "I called to make sure you got there okay, but I also wanted to thank you."

"For what?"

"For having my back. If you hadn't distracted those USFT guys, they might have noticed a coughing wolf sneaking around the base. Not good."

She considered sloughing off what he said, but realized he not only was right, but that she appreciated his acknowledgment, too. "You're welcome," she said, equally softly. "I know you'd do the same if the situation warranted it."

"Count on it," he said with no hesitation. Then he paused. "So...see you tomorrow."

"Absolutely," she said. "We'll try to figure out what you breathed in while you were shifted."

"*I'll* try to find out," he contradicted sharply. "There's no need for you—"

"I'll be helping out, Sergeant." She used a no-nonsense military tone.

Another pause. Then, "Thanks, Lieutenant." And he hung up.

Leaving Sara wondering if she had made a mistake.

She wondered that far into the night.

Jason slept on and off that night in his small, private quarters. He told himself that his intermittent coughing, which hadn't completely gone away, was what kept waking him.

Or maybe it was Shadow's restlessness. He had brought his cover dog back when he'd left the building housing the lab and kennels. He was glad for the company. Shadow was his real bud. Gave him affection without asking anything from him but pats on the head and treats.

But Jason knew that it was partly irritation that kept him from sleeping soundly.

He recognized that he had to talk to Drew about the strange scratches on the door to the lab.

But even more, there was the stark reminder that Sara

McLinder wasn't just a woman who happened to be hot and attractive to him.

No, she was definitely hands-off. A superior officer. The kind of woman who thrived on giving orders.

Well, he may have had to buckle under and join the military to redeem himself. Stuck himself into a position where he had to take orders, since that was preferable to prison. Maybe even stay for the rest of his life, since he wanted continued access to the Alpha Force elixir.

But that didn't mean he had to like all aspects of it. Or to feel attraction to a woman who could force his submission by just tossing words at him.

No matter how much she turned him on.

He eventually gave up and got out of bed around six-thirty. He showered, put on his uniform and took Shadow for a walk.

Lots of people were up and about already at Ft. Lukman. Some were Alpha Force members, wolf shifters who were also walking their cover dogs, including Seth Ambers and his dog Spike, Marshall Vincenzo and his dog Zarlon, and Jock Larabey with his dog Click.

"Morning," Jason said as Shadow and he caught up with them just outside the base's primary office building. The dogs all traded greetings by sniffs.

"Heard about what happened last night," Marshall said in a low voice. He was a generally quiet guy, about Jason's height and built even more muscularly—had spent his childhood, while not shifted, doing martial arts, Jason had heard. Zarlon looked more like a German shepherd than most of the cover dogs, and Jason had seen that Marshall, too, resembled a shepherd when shifted.

"Yeah," Seth said. "You okay?" He, on the other hand, looked more like a football player while in human form.

Spike resembled a wolf and had a hint of wildness about him, but he obeyed Seth just fine.

Jock gave a nod toward Jason, lifting his massive shoulders as if he was ready to hear the worst. His dog Click had a touch of German shepherd in his wolf appearance—but that was okay, since so did Jock while shifted. "What we heard sounded bad, but you look all right. Are you?"

Jason figured he might be asked how he felt a lot today. "I'm fine. I just want to figure out what happened."

"We all do," Seth said. He might even more than other Alpha Force members. From what Jason had heard, Seth had been injured months ago during a training exercise with another military unit—while in wolf form, too. "In fact, there's already a contingent of people who met at the labs early this morning for orders and information. They're already preparing to collect samples of dirt and vegetation in the area where you were walking. They're also looking into whether someone tried to break into the lab and said you reported scratches on the stairway door. Didn't they contact you?"

"No. Where are they now?"

"Still at the lab," Jock answered. "Drew was there—said you'd described where you'd been checking things out while shifted last night, so I guess that was why no one got in touch with you. They probably figured you ought to rest."

"Like I said, I'm fine," Jason responded, holding back his irritation. He didn't like people making assumptions about him any more than he enjoyed taking orders—but the latter was a necessary evil as long as he stayed in the military. The former? Total garbage. "Think I'll go see if I can give them any more info before they go off on some wild-goose chase."

He gave his usual halfhearted salute to the three lieutenants, aiming it even more toward their dogs, who probably deserved it more than the humans. Then Shadow and he stepped into high gear to hurry to the lab building.

When they got downstairs to the small office near the spacious lab facilities, Sara was there with Drew, Jonas Truro and Colleen Hodell.

"Good morning, cuz." Drew appeared surprised to see him. The others, too, sounded as if they hadn't expected him.

"What're you up to?" Jason asked.

"We were just going to try to retrace your steps yesterday," Sara said. "While you were shifted. When you inhaled—whatever. That's what we intend to find out. Just in case—well, we've been speculating that it was intentional. That someone who knew about Alpha Force's nature, and its wolf shifters, planted something to hide evidence of what they did to set the general's car on fire. We decided to collect a lot of samples this morning from the route you took." How could she look so calm and concerned in the face of the perfidious act she was engaged in? That they all were doing—solving his issue without even asking his advice.

But Sara's involvement was the most biting of all. Which didn't make sense. Jason should have been more upset about Drew's cutting him out.

"And how, exactly," he said, "do you intend to retrace the steps of someone without asking that someone exactly where he walked?"

"You told me most of it last night," Drew said. "I did look at those scratches on the door, too, by the way. We'll be doing more investigation of that, too."

"And I saw you on at least part of your walk while ill," Sara reminded him. "Plus, we spoke with the general to confirm the last part of his route before he turned into Ft. Lukman."

"I've just been handing out some sanitary and sealable

containers from the lab for collecting samples," Drew said. "I figured this was a good group of people to conduct the examination. Jonas has a medical background, Colleen— as a shifting feline—won't necessarily react the same way to a contaminant as a werewolf, and Sara—" He seemed to hesitate.

"I just insisted on being included," she said, "as a key representative of General Yarrow." She stared with her flashing blue-green eyes, as if challenging him to tell her to bug off.

Which he wouldn't. In fact, he found her dedication admirable, although he'd never admit that to her.

"Fine," he said. "I insist on being included, too, as a party with a whole lot of interest in what happened. Besides, it won't hurt to have a shifter in human form along to check out the odors without having the even more acute senses of a wolf."

The entire group soon walked up the stairway from the underground lab, all of them carrying paraphernalia for collecting dirt samples.

As they started along the walkway toward the base's entrance, Jason found himself beside Sara.

Not that he'd planned it that way…or had he?

"Guess you got your way," he said to start a conversation—or argument, whichever worked out.

"What do you mean?" Her tone sounded innocuous, as if she didn't recall pulling rank on him over the phone last night.

"I mean, here you are, helping out."

She glanced at him with her sparkling eyes, which again contained a challenge. "Yes, I am. Any problem with that?"

"No, ma'am." He gave her a salute that arguably looked real, then glanced around. The others were ahead. It might look as if he gave a damn if he stepped up his pace to catch up.

Sara stopped altogether, reaching to grasp his arm. "Look, Jason, I didn't intend to start a war between us, but my assignment as an aide makes me want to know everything, solve all problems and..." She looked away. "I was worried about you yesterday." She glanced back, raising her chin almost belligerently. "If I'm going to be hooked up with Alpha Force for a day, or a week or month or longer, I intend to do all I can to help it and all its members. That includes helping to discover sources of anything that can harm any of you, to the extent I can. So if you don't like that, tough."

To his chagrin, he did like it. He liked her.

In fact, at this moment, he had a much-too-strong urge to kiss those defiantly pursed lips once again.

Instead, he just grinned. "Oh, I do like it, Lieutenant, ma'am. If anyone can solve this mystery, I'll put my money on you."

But it didn't appear that this mystery would be solved any more quickly than determining who might have tried to get into the lab area, Sara thought a while later as she stood with Jason, Jonas and Colleen near the stop sign about half a mile from the entrance to Ft. Lukman. She had hooked the straps of her backpack over her arm so she could access its contents and stick whatever she collected into it most easily.

The general would have made a right turn here onto the final road to his destination. Since he'd have stopped, this was a logical place for someone to do...well, whatever was done.

Especially since Jason had noted that this was the vicinity where he had first inhaled whatever had made him ill last night.

Jonas Truro, despite being trained as a medical doctor, dug in like a regular enlisted guy to pick up some of the stones they'd noticed before and examine them minutely, hanging on to only one or two that he said were just samples. He threw the rest back along the roadside with a shake of his head and a shrug. "They seem like regular stones to me."

And Jason, even with his enhanced senses while in human form said he didn't perceive anything about the rocks other than usual natural odors.

Sara had been watching Jason carefully, trying to guess, from his expression and demeanor, not only if he sensed anything off, but also if he was feeling okay.

He glanced back often, sending her looks that seemed both exasperated and challenging, as if still not thrilled that she had insisted on coming along. She kept her expression neutral, but she would have loved to challenge him right back.

Trees grew close to the roadside, with decaying vegetation between the trunks. Jason again gagged despite his senses being so much less acute than when he was in wolf form, so it was up to nonshifters Sara and Jonas, and cougar shifter Colleen, to collect samples of stones and dirt and plants—mostly dead leaves and grass—and even a few pebbles.

If there were traces of something placed there to veil evidence of who had been there and what they had done, something shifted werewolves might otherwise have noticed and possibly even figured out, it would need to be ID'd in tests that would analyze those samples. And that could take time.

In the meantime, whoever was guilty of placing it there,

and doing whatever was done to the general's car, would be free. Maybe escaping, or maybe hiding in plain sight at Ft. Lukman. A member of the Ultra Special Forces Team? If so, why?

Or perhaps there was another culprit or motive that Sara hadn't yet considered. The guilty person could even be an Alpha Force member, but what motive could they possibly have?

"I think we're through here," Jason finally said, but Sara was glad when he added, "Agreed?" at her sideways glance. Maybe he needed reminding, but at least he had acknowledged, in some manner, that he was in the presence of superior officers.

And then he coughed again.

He may have tried to hold her back, but the reality was that she should have pulled rank and not let him come along. He had no business being here, where he'd come across something harmful yesterday.

On the other hand, his presence was helpful, since he'd been able to point out precisely where he had prowled in wolf form, and where he had first sensed whatever he had inhaled.

"Yes," she said, "but let's walk exactly the path you took to get back on the base, from here till we get to where I first spotted you opposite the BOQ."

"I'm fine with getting away from here, too," said Colleen Hodell. She was a friendly, pretty woman with pale feline eyes that seemed almost translucent. Her tawny hair, though layered, was longer than Sara's and had become mussed in the slight breeze wafting around them. She had stayed with the group yet wandered toward the fringes of the areas they explored as if believing the answers were even less obvious than the others might have considered. "My other senses are different from those guys', but I feel a bit like gagging, too. Damn, it's frustrating to be here and know this is a vital location for what happened to General Yarrow and only be able to pick up dirt, not find anything helpful."

"I'll second that." Jonas Truro had started out wearing a camo cap over his dark hair but he'd taken it off and shoved it into a back pocket. His frown appeared as exasperated as Sara felt. They were supposed to find something here. And maybe he, as a doctor, figured he'd have better insight into the chemical reaction Jason had suffered.

But apparently he didn't—although he had collected the bulk of the samples they were returning with. Like Sara and Colleen, he was carrying the pack that contained all he had gathered.

They all walked back together to the base's gate where they checked in with the sentry guarding the entrance.

"I want to get all the samples right to the lab for handling," Jonas said.

"Good idea," said Colleen.

"I'd still like to retrace my steps of last night," said Jason, "in case something useful comes to mind."

She knew better, but Sara had seen Jason's difficult trek through the base yesterday. What if he suffered a relapse, despite being in human form?

Or was she just looking for an excuse to stay with him?

Either way, she said, "I'd like to continue this recon as we discussed before and follow everything Jason did last evening to look for additional evidence. Can you take my samples with you?" At Colleen's nod, she handed the other woman the backpack containing the sealed packages and tubes filled with all she had collected.

The other two hurried along the road toward the far side of the base—and the building containing the underground lab. Did they have enough technical personnel and expertise to conduct all the analyses here? Maybe, Sara thought, since apparently they did all their own blending of shape-shifting formula there. But analysis and creation could be quite different.

Well, that definitely wasn't her expertise.

Organizing was. So was following through.

"Okay, let's trace your exact footsteps from last night," she told Jason.

He grinned down at her, but his expression appeared wan. "My pawprints, you mean?"

"Yeah," she said, finding herself smiling at the reminder rather than recoiling at it. Interesting.

Instead of strolling down the road, they went behind the low buildings on the base's far side. Part of the area was paved, but a lot of it abutted the narrow groves of trees that formed the perimeter of Ft. Lukman inside its fence.

Jason's gait was slower than Sara had seen it before in human form, and she kept her pace equal to his.

They had almost reached the area between buildings where Sara had spotted Jason last night when he said, "You know, I thought I smelled something else when I got here, but I was feeling too awful to check it out."

"Let's look now," she said.

Together they entered the forested area. Although it was daylight, once they walked into this place of heavy growth they were surrounded by shadows. Sara heard the singing of several species of birds, overlying other soft sounds like small animals scurrying around dead leaves at the base of the trees. No one could say this place was anything but fully alive.

"Do you smell anything unusual now?" she asked. All she sensed was the green, healthy scent of growing trees, interspersed with some heavier, darker odors of decaying undergrowth. But she realized that her sense of smell was nowhere near as acute as his.

"Nothing unusual," he said. Even so, he walked farther into the forest and Sara followed. "I just wish…well, whatever happened must have been centered on the road outside, like we thought. I'm just mad at myself now for not having protected myself from whatever was left there. I already suspected some kind of terrorist act or sabotage or—"

"It's not your fault," she interrupted sharply, then paused at the way his golden eyes widened. They'd both stopped beneath some fairly low branches, in shadows.

He might have been surprised at her outburst, but she, too, had been surprised that this jaunty, devil-may-care guy actually did care. Blamed himself for the harm that someone else had caused him. At least he wasn't blaming himself for what had happened to General Yarrow…was he?

"I know it's not my fault," he said softly, his gaze grabbing hers and latching on with a hot intensity that seemed to come out of nowhere. Or had she anticipated—hoped for—it all along? "But thanks for the vote of confidence."

She opened her mouth to say something casual, but nothing came out. Not while she continued to look into his eyes, see the heat blazing between them, feel a sensuality rising within her from far below that didn't belong in this cool, neutral surrounding. That didn't belong inside her at all.

Sara wasn't sure who moved first, but she was suddenly engulfed in Jason's strong embrace. His mouth came down on hers, softly at first, then picking up heat and fierceness and intensity that she felt helpless to do anything about but respond in kind.

No. She never felt helpless. This was exactly what she wanted, precisely where she wanted to be: in Jason's strong, sexy embrace. Kissing him as if there were nothing, no one, in the world but them. As if their attraction was fiery and wonderful and inevitable. And not forbidden by who, and what, they were.

Their lips parted, their tongues met and teased and tested one another as if in anticipation of a mind-blowing sexual encounter.

Sara felt the hardness of Jason's erection press against her and pushed harder toward him. If only…

But as her hands raced under his clothes and up his back to clutch his heated flesh, she heard, in the distance, the sound of conversation. Someone must be on the sidewalk on the other side of the nearby building.

Or so she hoped. Surely they weren't any closer.

But the sound brought her back to reality. Instead of pulling him closer, she pushed him away.

"I—I'm sorry," she gasped. "This wasn't right."

"Oh, I'd say it was very right," Jason muttered.

"I mean—"

"I know exactly what you mean." He looked down with both heat and sorrow in his gaze. "Nowhere to go from here but back to the lab, right, Lieutenant?"

Sara closed her eyes at the jab, the reminder that she didn't really need—that even ignoring that the hot, enticing, utterly sexy man who'd kissed her was also a shapeshifter, their lives, their careers, their military ranks made it impossible for them to do even what they had done, let alone follow through and engage in the hot sex suggested by their heated embrace.

"Right, Sergeant," she finally said, putting as much strength and distance as she could into her voice despite her continued breathlessness.

Without looking at him again, she hurried from beneath the trees and onto the path behind the nearest building.

She thought she heard Jason following but didn't turn to confirm it. She walked between two buildings, ironically in about the same location as she had spotted Jason yesterday. She reached the sidewalk nearest the road through the base where a few other people strolled on the sidewalk ahead of her.

And as she looked toward that road, she saw a car carrying General Yarrow drive by.

Chapter 9

Sara had peeked into General Yarrow's Ft. Lukman office before but hadn't gone inside.

Not without the general there.

But now he had arrived. Safely, this time. He still looked pale in his camo uniform as he sat behind his attractive antique mahogany desk. Maybe even frail, although she would never dare to tell him that.

At the moment he was chatting with Major Drew Connell, who sat on one of the couple of chairs facing the desk.

A short while ago, as Sara had neared the base's main office building, she had seen the general being helped from the car being driven by an enlisted man—who'd presumably picked him up and brought him here from the hospital. Drew had obviously been expecting him and accompanied the general into the building.

From what Sara had seen, still at a distance, the general had refused further assistance, even an arm to hang on to.

Sara hadn't asked for an invitation. She was still the general's aide. She had turned quickly to see that Jason had followed her here. She gave him a quick nod that she hoped appeared dismissive, even though her glance settled, for just an instant, on those lips that had created so much emotion—and desire—within her.

Wrong. How wrong that had been. And the general's presence only reinforced how foolish she was.

Despite how good that kiss had felt…

She had quickly reached the building, then hurried up the stairway to the general's second-floor office.

She'd wanted to interrupt his conversation with Drew. Maybe even to hug him in relief that he was okay.

But that was almost as inappropriate as her sharing a kiss with an enlisted man.

Instead of doing anything else, she had simply come in and saluted General Yarrow. He had saluted back as if all was in order and nothing bad had happened.

"Have a seat, Lieutenant," he had told her.

"Yes, sir." She had quickly obeyed.

Now she remained there quietly as he continued to talk with Drew.

She liked the general's office. It suited him, with its decor that spoke of his love of both the United States and history. The U.S. flag that hung on the brass pole behind his desk was similar to the one he had in his much more formal office at the Pentagon. Nothing else resembled his usual digs. Oh, sure, she recognized a lot of old books on the sumptuous wooden shelves behind him—the ones with military history and regulations.

But then there were the antique-looking volumes of old classics, from Bram Stoker's *Dracula* to Jules Verne's *20,000 Leagues Under the Sea*.

And was that what she thought it was? Before coming here, she would only have laughed had she heard he had an original script from the classic movie *The Wolf Man*. Now she recognized how fitting that was.

"Our investigation is still inconclusive, Greg." Drew brought Sara's attention back when he looked at her for confirmation. His golden eyes, so like his cousin's, flashed as if he was furious that such an event could have occurred under his watch.

"That's right, General," Sara said. "But we're still working on it." She related how Sergeant Jason Connell and she had brought a vehicle back to the base to move the remains of the car, and how automobile expert Jason and others had studied those remains. She caught Drew's expression as she described all his cousin had done so far.

Then she looked at the general. Her CO looked older now than his actual age: sixty-four. He took good care of himself, and most of the time he appeared younger, possibly because his hair was really black—and from what she gathered, he didn't do anything to keep it that way. It had receded quite a bit, though, around his temples.

He frowned a lot even before—although right now the expression seemed etched into his long, lined face.

But he needed to know everything, at least all that was related to what had happened to him. As far as Sara knew, Drew hadn't mentioned to the general the scratches on the door to the lab. Maybe he'd already had someone examine it and determined it was nothing.

Taking a deep breath, Sara told the general about seeing Jason in shifted form last night after he'd gone to the area near the base where the car might have been ambushed.

"That's why we think this was an intentional act of sabotage," Drew said.

"Especially since Sergeant Connell was taken ill after visiting that site," Sara added, then described Jason's coughing and how she had accompanied him, and other Alpha Force members, to that area to collect samples that were being analyzed.

"I see," the general said slowly when she was done. He leaned forward, folding his arms on the top of his desk as he looked at Sara. She expected more questions about the investigation.

Instead, his expression lightened. He even smiled. "So Sara, what's your opinion of shapeshifters now?"

She stared at him. What did he expect her to say?

When she remained silent, he continued, "Just wondering. Every time I hinted at the real nature of Alpha Force after you started reporting to me, you laughed it off."

"I'm not laughing now," she said, keeping her tone bright. "It's really amazing."

She wasn't about to give an opinion of shapeshifting, let alone the existence of a military unit like Alpha Force. In fact, at this moment she wasn't really sure what her opinion was.

Except that, as she considered it, the face of Jason Connell—and the feel and taste of his lips on hers—insinuated itself into her mind.

She felt herself start to flush and looked down at her hands, hoping that neither of the others in the room noticed.

"Amazing, huh?" The general sounded amused. But then his tone hardened enough to make her look up. "I'd just like to know whether the *amazing* nature of Alpha Force is what caused someone to mess with my Jeep. I loved that old thing."

"They messed with you, too, General." Sara knew her anger and indignation were clear from her tone. "I'm sorry about your car, but…well, you could have been killed."

"And whoever it was apparently went to some lengths to conceal his identity and method—especially from anyone, human or otherwise, with keen senses," Drew said.

"Yeah, looks that way," agreed General Yarrow. "In fact, I'd like you to contact your cousin and tell him to come here now, Drew. I want to talk to him more about what he sensed when he went in shifted form to check it out."

Meaning that Major Connell would be bringing Sergeant Connell to this office. While Sara was here.

Only a short while after they had embraced in the woods. And kissed.

Lord, how they had kissed....

"Well, it sounds as if you have a lot to discuss," Sara said. "You won't need me—"

"Yes, we do, Lieutenant," the general replied sharply. But the expression he leveled on her looked curious. And shrewd. "You were helping in the investigation. I want you to join in our discussion. Unless you have something better to do?"

"I'll do whatever you'd like, sir," Sara said. Within reason, of course, although she wasn't about to tell him that.

But she did have something better to do. Almost anything would be better than being in Jason's presence at this moment.

The general's gaze had not moved from her face as he said, "Then stay here, Sara. It'll be good for all of us to get both your take on things and Sergeant Connell's." His smile broadened, then faded.

She now believed in shapeshifters. What about mind readers?

Or was she just being much too obvious in her demeanor and desire to get away before Jason arrived?

"Drew, give Jason a call. Sara, you hang out here for a short while, at least, and see if you can contribute to what the sergeant says. Then you can leave, if you'd like."

"Yes, sir," she said formally.

And then she sat and waited as Drew called his cousin.

When Jason's cell phone rang, he wasn't surprised to see that the caller ID said it was his cuz.

He had seen General Yarrow being chauffeured onto

the base in a black military-looking car that looked nothing at all like his Jeep.

He wondered whether the general would do something about the loss of the car he'd seemed to care about so much. Get another Jeep?

Jason would be happy to discuss possibilities with him.

But following the general when he'd spotted him hadn't been an option—first because he was a general and probably had little interest in talking to a lowly sergeant who fixed cars.

Second because Sara had seen him, too, and clearly was following the general to wherever he ended up on the base.

At the moment Jason was in the underground lab where Colleen Hodell and Jonas Truro had taken the samples of dirt and leaves and all they'd collected from near the road to analyze what had made him cough and feel sick.

But he'd half expected the call from Drew.

He said hi, listened, then said, "Be there in a little while." Then he turned to Jonas.

They were in one of the large, sterile labs. Jonas, who worked on the shifting elixir, had started an initial analysis of what they'd found.

"Anything helpful?" Jason asked. He'd let both of them down here using his own key. Neither had mentioned the scratches on the door.

"Not yet. And our facilities are more for trying new formulas out, not figuring out what other stuff contains." He was dressed all in white in a clean-room kind of outfit that contrasted with his moderately dark-toned skin, including a hat holding back his wavy, black hair.

Jason wore something similar, as did Colleen. Wearing all that white clothing made the feline in human form seem almost ethereal. Interesting, Jason thought. With her pale skin showing but not her tawny hair, she looked more like what she was than she normally did: a shifting cougar.

She'd been in the lab before. All Alpha Force members spent a lot of time here. She'd seemed fascinated by the experiments that Jonas had launched into right away. Jonas had been part of Alpha Force for a while and knew his way around this facility. Though he wasn't a shifter, he sometimes acted as a shifter's aide—and also helped Drew modify and even test his newest formulations of the elixir.

"I've got to go now, at least for a little while," Jason told Jonas. "The general's back and Drew wants me to join them to talk about what's been going on."

He didn't mention that Sara was there. If he did, he'd undoubtedly think about the kiss they'd shared.

That kiss he should have restrained himself from.

Too many complications now—including the fact that, given the opportunity, he'd do it again.

"Good." Jonas shook his head. "So far I'm not finding anything helpful, but even with my medical background I don't really feel competent to figure out how whatever may be contained in these samples led to your reaction. We'll need to send everything to another lab."

"What kind of lab?" Colleen asked.

"I don't know yet, but someplace with professionals who are a lot more sophisticated in analysis of possible toxins than anyone here is."

That was definitely out of Jason's realm of knowledge, too. He could analyze pretty much anything having to do with cars and most other vehicles. But though he didn't know what had caused his problem, he damn well wanted to find out.

In fact, he had already scheduled an examination with both Drew and his wife, Melanie, a veterinarian. He would have both the human physician and the animal doctor do what they needed to ensure there wasn't anything nasty lurking inside him.

But that was later tonight, when he could shift in their presence.

Right now, he had a meeting to attend—one that might be a hell of a lot more difficult.

Sara would be there.

Oh, yeah. She was there.

Was she ever.

When Jason arrived, saluted the general then asked after his health, Sara remained seated. As always, she looked beautiful.

But remote. She barely glanced at him despite that damned kiss he'd stolen from her.

Well, hell, she'd participated, too. And now she acted like she'd never even seen this lowly sergeant before.

He'd do something about that…sometime. When he could. But not now, with his cousin Drew greeting him effusively and dragging a chair for him from a neighboring office.

Which his cuz ironically placed between his seat and the one still occupied by Sara.

What else could Jason do but sit down there? Toss her a half smile. Then turn all his attention back to the general.

"Thanks for asking about how I'm doing," General Yarrow said from behind his awfully nice-looking, old desk. In fact, Jason considered him an awfully nice-looking, aging military geezer. Even though, at the moment, he looked nearly as pale as the white stripes in the flag hanging behind him. "Now I want to hear how you're doing. I heard you may have inhaled something harmful while trying to figure out what happened to my poor Jeep."

"Yeah, maybe." Jason gave a brief description of his shift

last night to check things out, his finding nothing useful but smelling something intense and awful while in wolf form that led to his coughing spree.

"Several of us accompanied Sergeant Connell back to the area where he first smelled whatever affected him," Sara added before Jason got into that part.

"Nothing conclusive there, either, General," Jason said. "I figure, though, that the fire was somehow set by whoever disguised his scent that way. That only makes me even more determined to figure out what was done to your Jeep. I liked the damn thing—and I'm sure that's nothing compared with your feelings for it."

"Thank you, Jason," the general said. "I think we're all as determined as you to figure out what was done to cover up how my car was sabotaged. You could have been harmed, too." He looked at Drew. "I assume your cousin's health has been checked to make sure no ongoing problem was triggered."

"I'm feeling fine," Jason broke in, then sagged a little. "But I'm letting them do a complete analysis of everything inside me tonight—in both forms." Not that he looked forward to it. But it was necessary, though the coughing had stopped and he felt no further effects.

As a car expert, he knew that people who had car problems were better off having the vehicle checked out for residual issues. Same went for living beings—especially shifters. It wasn't like he could just drop into any medical clinic anywhere if he started to show symptoms again later.

Besides, he might as well take advantage of his cousin's being a doctor.

Sara had turned to stare at him. Her amazing blue-green eyes looked as if they might be trying to disassemble his brain to learn what was inside.

"But it's just a precaution, right, Ja—er, Sergeant?" she

asked. "You said you're feeling okay." As if she realized that she sounded as if she might actually give a damn about how he was feeling, she added, "I'd really hoped to find out what gave you that coughing problem. I felt…involved with it, you see, sir." She related how she had noticed the slinking wolf in the distance when she was outside the night before.

Before she added in how she had assisted him at the time, Jason inserted, "Lieutenant McLinder helped me a lot then. She distracted a couple of members of that Ultra Special Forces Team who happened to be outside at the same time."

"Oh, yes. That's one of the reasons I'm here," General Yarrow said. "Why I headed to Ft. Lukman in the first place. I've set up a meeting with the commander of the USFT at this facility—General Myars. I know that relations between the two units are rather strained and I want to see what we can do about it so we can start our planned exercises."

"I respectfully suggest that the solution is to have those…er, difficult troops deployed elsewhere, Greg, and plans dropped for our working together." Drew leaned forward in his chair. Jason knew that look on his cousin's face. It meant sincerity, determination—and definitely intention to be heard. "I know they've all been vetted, so their suspecting that the other unit they're interacting with here has shapeshifters should be fine, since they supposedly understand how covert things are, but, well, someone may have attempted to break into the lab." He described the scratches on the door. "Maybe they know more than we think—or are taking steps to find out."

"I gather they're also doing things that must be kept completely under wraps." General Yarrow shot a glance toward Drew. "Scratches, huh? But no indication they got inside?" When Drew shook his head, the general continued,

"Well, it's mutually beneficial, not to mention useful to the U.S. military, to have them stationed here right now. We'll just need to direct our security forces to be more on alert."

"I understand, sir," Drew said. "But to have two units functioning so closely together with apparent animosity from one toward the other—"

"And from that other right back at 'em," the general said. "Look, that's one reason I'll be meeting with General Myars. I want to find out if we can find common ground between Alpha Force and the USFT. Encourage military camaraderie and get all of you to work together—the usual."

"But what if USFT members were involved in sabotaging your car, sir?" Sara's voice was quiet, but it lacerated the peacefulness of the conversation.

Jason admired her for bringing up the obvious, especially when it clearly wasn't what the general wanted to hear.

"It's possible," he admitted.

"Even probable, Greg," Drew said. "Who else around here would have wanted to harm you?"

"You, of all people, can figure that out, Drew," the general shot back. "It's been a while, but you were right there in the middle of the animosity between the visitors and residents of Mary Glen due to their legends about shapeshifters."

"You're right, of course—at least back then," Drew agreed. "There were both werewolf fans and haters around at the time who thought shifters could be real and hanging out around town. But we resolved that. Some were killed—and we caught who was committing the murders for motives of their own."

"But some remaining townsfolk may not yet be appeased," Greg said, "and even then there was some speculation in Mary Glen about whether there were shifters at Ft. Lukman."

"Could be," responded Drew. "We won't eliminate any possibilities for now."

"Good," said the general. "Right now, I want you to walk me through everything that happened and what you've learned about it. Let's start with a visit to my poor car. Then we'll walk the path. Agreed?" He looked at Drew.

"Fine, General. I'll come along. But Sara and Jason know a whole lot more about it than I do, so we'll follow them."

Sara felt even more uncomfortable now. She was essentially under orders to be in Jason's presence, so that helped. No one would officially question their being near one another.

But she definitely questioned the wisdom of that.

She hung back, following General Yarrow and Jason, who took the lead as they walked from the office building toward the garage where the Jeep's hulk was stored.

"Everything okay, Sara?" Drew's voice from beside her startled her, even though she was aware of his presence.

"Yes…more or less," she said, wishing she could be candid with Drew. Ask a few questions.

His wife, also a nonshifter from what Sara had heard, had been in a similar position to her. Well, not exactly. She had apparently fallen in love with a werewolf, then married him and they had a child, a little girl.

Sara was merely attracted to Jason. But Melanie Connell hadn't been in the military so there'd been no policy against fraternizing to keep them apart.

And…well, hell. Drew was a good guy. A doctor who had the best interests of the troops below him as well as all shifters at heart. He was even the person who'd mostly developed the elixir all the shifters in Alpha Force now relied on to help them control what they did and their consciousness while shifted. He was nice. Intelligent. By the book.

And then there was his cousin Jason, who had joined the military under duress—to keep from going to prison for car theft, of all things.

Sara should focus on that, and not all the man's intelligent analyses of what had happened to the general and his car.

Nor how hot Jason was.

She'd heard of another couple, Lieutenant Quinn Parran and Staff Sergeant Kristine Norwood, whose fraternizing was simply being ignored here at Ft. Lukman, thanks to the unofficial camaraderie of Alpha Force. But Sara wasn't really an Alpha Force member. She wasn't actually stationed here, and her presence was temporary.

No, fraternizing wasn't her destiny.

They'd reached the parking-lot building. Jason had directed them all to the entrance nearest where the car's remains now lay and used a key to open it.

He held the door open for the general then for Drew... and Sara. She met his glance—and was dismayed to see how icily he looked at her.

Obviously he, too, had decided to back off.

Which made it a little easier for her to talk to him... through the unwanted sorrow she felt at his attitude.

"Thank you, Sergeant," she said softly as she walked by him.

And felt a tiny stab of pain in her butt, as if he had pinched her.

She gasped and turned back to face him, but he had already let the door shut and was passing by her to catch up with the general.

He led them all into the secluded area where the Jeep's

hulk still rested. A uniformed guard still stood there, a private whom Sara had seen and talked to before named Kerry Browning. He had been the sentry at the gate when General Yarrow's car was set on fire. He saluted them, and Jason told him it was okay to take a break while he showed the general what was left of the car.

Without looking at either Drew or her, Jason started walking around the remains with the general, pointing out the charred elements of the front first, the wheels with burned tires, the engine compartment then the driver's seat where the general had been sitting when the Jeep caught fire.

After that, they walked to the back of the chassis and Jason showed the metal framework that had supported the canvas cover, which no longer existed. He went to a storage trunk with a lock on it where all the ashes, and the residue of the items found in them like the general's fishing pole, overnight bag and other stuff, had been stored.

Then Jason went through the scenario as he said he believed it had happened, where the canvas had caught fire first then the flames had moved through the vehicle, causing the general's smoke inhalation and more.

"Very interesting," Greg said as Jason finished up. "And thorough. But we still need answers."

"We're still working on that, Greg," Drew said. He explained the investigators who were due to arrive the next day from D.C.

While they talked, Sara found herself beside Jason. She shot him a look that she hoped appeared withering, as if she were responding only now to what she thought she had felt.

A pinch on the butt?

She must have imagined it. Jason appeared so interested in the others' conversation. So serious. And innocent.

She took a step toward Greg and Drew so she could

hear them better, only to have Jason take the same step beside her.

She turned to look quizzically at him.

That was when he gave her a wink.

Chapter 10

General Yarrow seemed tired after their visit to what was left of his car. Maybe his fatigue was partly depression, but Sara knew better than to ask something like that. Instead, she did what any good aide would do: she told him to go rest while she set up the meeting that was the reason he had originally come to Ft. Lukman.

Walking with the general to discuss plans also gave her a good excuse to avoid Jason, who remained, for now, with what was left of the vehicle. He couldn't get away with that pinch, but she hadn't yet figured out how to deal with it.

"How would 0900 tomorrow morning be, sir?" she asked as she accompanied the general to the BOQ. His quarters were in the same building as hers, but it held a wing for VIPs. "Or is that too early?"

He'd already said that General Myars was planning to arrive at Ft. Lukman this evening. She wanted to arrange things for the convenience of her CO.

"That should be fine—on the late side for Hugo, if anything. Liking to start working early in the day is about the only thing we see eye to eye about." The general's smile appeared wry, and Sara wondered how the conclave between the two senior officers would work out.

"And let me confirm this," she continued. "You want it to be a one-on-one session between General Myars and you."

"At first, yes," the general said. "I want a brief meeting with Hugo and then get everyone in both units together to talk, clear the air and exchange information."

"If all goes well," Sara couldn't help saying.

"It will go well," the general responded grimly.

They continued to discuss plans for the meetings as they approached then entered the building and climbed the stairs to the second floor. They stopped outside the general's apartment. Even the hallway in this wing appeared more sumptuous than the one outside Sara's regular officers' digs on the same floor at the far side of the building. It might as well have been a world away.

He didn't invite Sara inside, which was fine with her. He unlocked the door then said, "First get the place confirmed with Drew. We'll meet in my office for the initial meeting then go to the large assembly room when we get everyone together."

"Yes, sir," Sara said, making a mental note.

"Then call Hugo. Make sure you make it clear you're contacting him on my orders. Otherwise, he probably won't even talk to you. Feel free, by the way, to tell him to call me to confirm that. Either way, give me a call after you've spoken with Hugo and let me know if we're on. Once we're square with a time, contact Drew and have him get our Alpha Force members there, too. Oh, and here. These are for you." He handed her a set of card keys that he said were duplicates of his that would let her into the kennel building and the labs below, which she had already returned to him. "I know I don't have to remind you to keep these to yourself, but you may need to set something up in the lab areas sometime."

Sara was glad but a little surprised. Only the general, and those members of Alpha Force with a need to work in the labs, had key cards to get there. All, though, had access to the kennel floor above.

That was that. Sara had already programmed Major Drew Connell's number into her smartphone, so as she headed down the hall to her own quarters she called him. No problem there, setting up the time and place. She was also able to get the number for General Myars's aide, Captain Rynton Tierney. She needed to use appropriate protocol to get through to General Myars despite being under orders to speak to him.

She entered her apartment and sat on the well-worn couch in her main room before calling Captain Tierney. She wished she'd brought a cup of coffee from the cafeteria. She didn't have any to brew in her kitchenette, which was fine since it wasn't equipped with a coffeemaker, anyway.

She heard background noise in Tierney's phone. "We're on our way to Ft. Lukman now," he said. "In the car. I'll hand the phone to General Myars."

Just like that, Sara was able to schedule the meetings the next day that General Yarrow had requested. "We'll be at Ft. Lukman within the hour," General Myars said. "We've already arranged for quarters while we're there." His tone suggested he wasn't pleased about it. "It's not the night of a full moon, but I understand that isn't necessarily a prerequisite. You can tell General Yarrow that I do not wish myself, or anyone in the Ultra Special Forces Team, to be subject tonight to little green men—oh, I mean attacking werewolves or whatever."

And then he was no longer on the line. Probably a good thing, Sara thought. The animosity had been almost palpable.

She called Drew back to confirm everything so he could get the Alpha Force members primed to attend the all-hands meeting the next day.

"Something wrong?" Drew asked.

"Just…well, I'm not holding out a lot of hope for the meetings to go well." She related her conversation with General Myars to him.

"Sounds like, even though he was polite enough to visit General Yarrow in the hospital, Myars isn't overly fond of werewolves." Drew sounded half-amused—and half-angry, if Sara was any judge of it over the phone.

"My take on it, too," she agreed. Apparently, even if not all USFT members knew about the Alpha Force shifters, their CO was aware of the nature of the unit.

"Is General Yarrow available to meet me again tonight?"

Sara told Drew that she had accompanied him to his quarters.

"I'll give him a call. I'd like to strategize with him. You, too. But you'll need to come to our labs. My wife, Melanie, and I will be conducting some tests on Jason—we want to make sure that whatever my cousin inhaled is out of his system with no lasting effects, in either of his forms. It's not something we want to delay anymore, so we've got him joining us tonight."

Sara paused. Did she want to see Jason at all? Even if she did—well, he would be transforming into his wolfen form then back, if she understood what Drew had said.

In a way, that might be perfect. She felt much too attracted to him as a human, and watching him shift once more might be enough to permanently end that attraction.

And that was exactly what she needed.

"I need to call General Yarrow to confirm that we have things set up," she told Drew. "I'll ask him to join us tonight at the lab. What time?"

"Nineteen hundred hours."

Which was only a couple of hours away.

"Fine," Sara said. But she would not look forward to it.

* * *

Jason didn't really want to do this. "I'm fine now," he told Drew, who'd made him take a seat in a downstairs laboratory on one of the most uncomfortable chairs he'd ever sat in. It was plastic and canvas, faced a small desk in the large lab with its complicated layout and it sucked.

Or maybe it was the anticipation of what was to come that made Jason feel so uncomfortable.

It was early evening. Jason knew he had to take some of the elixir in a short while so he would shift here. That was the only way that his cuz and cuz's wife could do a thorough inspection of him to make sure that whatever he'd breathed in last night was all the way out of his system.

"We'll make sure of it." Drew looked like the damned soldier he was, in his camo uniform—and yet, he had put all the garb over it to prove he was a doctor, a white lab suit.

His wife, Melanie, was a pretty lady, with bright blue eyes and long brown hair she had fastened back behind her neck. Nice, too—full of sympathetic smiles. She'd left their daughter, Emily, at home with a trusted neighbor who babysat so she could come here and help out.

No camo uniform on her, but she wore a similar lab outfit—because she was a veterinarian.

"Okay," Jason said resignedly. "Get it done."

Drew's turn first. Using standard medical stuff Jason had seen before, he checked Jason's heart rate and blood pressure. "All seems fine there." He sent him to the adjoining bathroom with a small container so he could provide a urine sample. But then Drew took out what Jason hated: needles. He looked away when Drew pulled his arm straight, used some kind of cleaning stuff in the crook of his arm and drew blood. "I'll analyze this tonight," he said.

Which Drew could do on his own. Jason's cuz was more than a medical doctor for humans. He was the one who'd taken the old, standard family elixir that helped a bit while they were shapeshifted to allow shifting outside the full moon—when it was effective—and turned it into something that not only worked all the time but did a damned good job, plus it let every shifter who used it keep their human awareness while in their alternate form.

In addition, thanks to sometimes incorporating another formula developed by a different Alpha Force member, Dr. Simon Parran, they were working on being able to avoid shifting during full moons, as well as other improvements.

Jason wasn't the only one who was happy about that.

When Drew was finished drawing blood, he patted Jason's back. "You can breathe again, cuz. For now. But we'll want you to shift in five minutes so we can check you that way, too."

"Fine." Jason continued to sit for a short while longer, staring out over the lab. It was full of shiny metal cabinets with glass doors that Drew said were always kept locked, even though the bulk of the already prepared elixir was now kept in a secured refrigeration unit down the hall. Some cabinets had equipment on top—really sophisticated-looking microscopes and stuff Jason couldn't identify but figured it was state-of-the-art. Computers, too, on shelves here and there. The place was inevitably kept clean and sterile, the better for ensuring that the amazing elixir could be brewed without any contamination.

As Jason sat there, he thought he really was still unwell. He was hallucinating—wasn't he?

For two people had just entered through the lab door. General Greg Yarrow...and Lieutenant Sara McLinder.

What were they doing here, especially now?

This was his time here to ensure he was okay.

And he was just about to shift into wolfen form. Surely no one thought he'd do that in front of these nonshifters—

even though he'd already shifted before in Sara's presence. But it had been his choice then. He'd wanted to have some fun with her.

It wouldn't be fun to tease her here, in the presence of all these other people, particularly when his shift would be for medical purposes.

Some other time, though...well, sure, it would be enjoyable to do that again.

Especially after that kiss.

"Hi, General, Lieutenant," he began, drawing himself to a stand.

But before he could get closer, Drew and Melanie had positioned themselves between him and the newcomers. "Welcome," Drew said. He turned briefly, glanced at Jason, then back toward the others. "You know, General, this is not the most auspicious time for you to observe another shift here."

Which implied the general had seen shifting here at Ft. Lukman before. But it hadn't been Jason who had changed then.

"No," the general said, "but with our meeting coming up tomorrow, I want to observe a shift generated by the most current version of the Alpha Force elixir in case I have to describe anything about it."

"Or defend it." Drew didn't sound happy about that.

"That's right."

Melanie got closer to her husband and put her arm around his waist. "If those special forces guys don't like the idea of shifters, they don't belong here," she said to the general.

Jason could see Sara at General Yarrow's side. Her eyes widened as if she couldn't believe that someone would confront her commanding officer that way.

But of course Melanie wasn't a member of the military despite her close affiliation.

"Maybe not," the general said with a shrug. "But they are here, and we need to do the training for the planned joint mission as soon as possible."

"Even if they're willing to harm you and Alpha Force members to make some kind of point—one we don't even get?"

That surprised Jason. It was Sara this time who confronted her commanding officer. Not only that, her gaze had slipped from the general to Jason, as if she might actually give a damn that he'd possibly been harmed.

An unwelcome yet enjoyable warm and fuzzy feeling swept through Jason. He shot her a quick smile. For an instant, she returned it then seemed to catch herself and resumed the grim, remote expression she'd had before.

"Hey," Jason said. "Bring on that super elixir, cuz. I'm ready to give the general and lieutenant a demo of exactly how wonderful the stuff is right now. And I can't wait till Melanie gets the chance to give me her best veterinary checkup and extract some of my most vital bodily fluids." He winked at Sara, who stared at him in apparent shock.

Then he strutted across the lab to the refrigeration unit where small amounts of elixir were stored.

He was in wolfen form.

Unlike how he usually behaved during a shift, when he almost always was outdoors and able to prowl, he was confined in a room with others.

Mostly nonshifter humans.

No specially designated aide had assisted him. Drew had handed him the elixir. He had drunk it, then walked beyond the rows of sterile cabinets to take off his clothes.

Drew had also followed with the light needed to effect

*the shift and aimed it at him. General Yarrow had been
with him, watching the whole thing.*

*The shift had commenced nearly at once. That was when
both Melanie and Sara had joined the general and Drew.*

Jason's shift had occurred in front of all of them.

*He had tried to observe Sara's reaction—especially at
first, when his still human organs would be visible to her—
but his discomfort shifting, and the presence of other people, distracted him.*

*When it was finished, she hadn't run screaming out of
the room. Neither did she regard him with contempt.*

*But she did regard him with... He wasn't certain what
she was thinking.*

*Immediately, Melanie Connell had started her poking
and prodding of his wolfen body. Even drew blood and
saliva and urine, although peeing into a cup while shifted
was far different from doing it in human form.*

And then she was finished.

*He sat on the cold floor of the lab, relatively motionless
despite wanting to run.*

*But his dosage of elixir had been small, so he knew he
could change back fairly quickly.*

*That was when he would learn what Sara McLinder
was thinking.*

It was all a scientific experiment. Neutral observation of
an interesting phenomenon. Yet another act in her capacity
as General Greg Yarrow's most trusted aide.

Sara had nearly been able to convince herself of that
when they had all watched most of Jason's initial shifting
into wolf form. That was something the general had really
wanted to do, so what could she do but stay by his side?

And then, after all the veterinary tests Melanie conducted on Jason, it had been time for him to change back.

Right there, in the lab, since General Yarrow had also wanted to see that.

As a result, Sara had gotten to see a lot. More than she wanted? Well…yes and no.

Close up this way, it was fascinating.

In this very controlled, very human, very clean environment on a pristine white floor: a body changing, from a man, standing then crouching while arms and hands changed to legs and paws in a more compact form. A muzzle, hair erupting everywhere. Low moans and growls of discomfort and pain.

And then a wolf.

Afterward, back again. Similar, in the opposite direction. That was where Sara could have lost control if she hadn't considered in advance how to handle this.

For when it was over, there was Jason in all his naked glory. Again.

Only for a moment, of course. Well, several moments in which Sara pretended to look elsewhere while Drew brought a blanket over to cover strategic areas as he handed Jason his clothes once more.

Jason seemed a little out of breath even after he'd donned his clothes. As if they'd planned it in advance, they all headed for the small lab office area and took seats around the desk. Four of them were clad similarly in their camo uniforms, but Melanie, who, like Drew, had removed her lab jacket, wore a button-down shirt over navy slacks.

"Good," General Yarrow said at once. "Not that I'm any kind of expert, but the shift looked quicker, more controlled, than I've seen it before." He looked toward Jason. "How are you feeling? I take it that nothing you inhaled before inhibited the process, but are you inclined to cough any more than usual, or is there any other difference that you sense?"

"No, sir," Jason said. "I'm really feeling pretty well now—subject, of course, to how Drew and Melanie tell me I should be reacting."

They all laughed. Even Sara, who had once again wound up sitting beside Jason. She hadn't planned it. Had he? Drew was the one behind the desk, since the lab was his venue.

She tossed a glance at Jason to find that he was leveling a look at her, too. Was he challenging her to say something?

It wasn't as if she hadn't seen him shift before.

General Yarrow was the one, though, who got her to talk. "So, Sara," he said, "I've no doubt that you believe in shapeshifting now." His tone was teasing and ironic, like a father who'd told his skeptical kids there was a Santa Claus and had introduced them to a store version at Christmas.

Bad analogy, Sara thought. First of all, most kids continued to believe in Santa for a while, even after they're told Jolly Old Saint Nick is just a myth.

Shapeshifting was definitely real, even though she hadn't believed in it at all when her paternalistic commanding officer had hinted about it before.

She'd now seen it herself. Several times.

"Yes, sir. In fact, as I'm sure you know, I've believed in it for a couple of days. But you have to admit that, in the regular world before I met Alpha Force, it wasn't odd of me to have my doubts."

"Not odd at all," Jason said. "But isn't it more fun to believe?" His lowered brows and grin made it clear he was teasing. Maybe even trying to remind her of his hotness during the process when he was unclothed and his masculine organ was so erect—and so obvious.

"Definitely. You know, I really like dogs. Haven't been able to own one since joining the military, but it's fun to be around them here—or at least canines of varying types."

The look she tossed back at him was all innocence, as if she hadn't gotten what he'd been trying to do.

He laughed. "Any time you want to work with Shadow and me, or any of the other dogs, you're welcome. And you know we shifters are generally assigned assistants who help by bringing our elixir doses and lights along to wherever we need them. Why don't you give that a try one of these days, too?"

"I just might do that," Sara shot back, then hoped her small flinch wasn't too obvious. She was acting as if the two of them were alone, not in the company of others, including her commanding officer.

"Really? Interesting thought." General Yarrow's lined face grew pensive. "I could possibly assign you to stay here on a longer-term, temporary-duty status once we reach whatever agreement we work out with the USFT, to make sure it is honored. You'd have a dual function of working directly and deeply with Alpha Force to be able to assist even better with my reports—as shaded as they are—to the highest-ranking officials who supervise these special units."

Uh-oh. That wasn't what Sara had intended. Staying here? Being assigned to work closely with Alpha Force, with Jason on indefinite TDY? Bad idea.

And yet she found the idea intriguing.

"Well, everyone, I need to go take Jason's samples to my clinic for analysis first thing tomorrow, and then I have to go home and get Emily," Melanie said. "Would any of you like to join us for dinner?"

She had stood and was regarding all of them, Jason included. But Drew nixed that invitation—as well as the implied one to Sara. "Sorry, but I'd really like the general to come to our place so we can talk. Maybe we can invite all of you some other time."

"That's fine," Sara said, not wanting Melanie to feel uncomfortable. Although, as the wife of a military officer, she probably felt outranked now and then, anyway. And since that officer was not only a member of Alpha Force but also a shifter himself—well, Sara felt sure that Melanie knew how to cope with situations that Sara couldn't even imagine. "I was planning on just grabbing something light at the cafeteria and taking it back to my quarters. I want to go to bed early so I'll be rested to assist with anything I'm needed for tomorrow."

"You can go ahead, Mel," Drew said. "I'll also do my analysis first thing tomorrow, since Jason seems to be okay. The general and I will join you at home soon—right, sir?"

That was fine with General Yarrow. Sara decided to take the opportunity to leave then.

So did Jason. She felt a little uncomfortable as they walked out together.

"Want to grab dinner in the cafeteria?" Jason asked, staying much too close beside her as they walked up the stairs to the main floor.

No, is what she thought. *Bad idea.* But what she said was, "Sure." And in fact, it wasn't really a bad idea, if she might be staying at Ft. Lukman for a while. Getting to know some of the other Alpha Force members better in a group setting couldn't hurt. And in preparation for the meetings tomorrow, it also wouldn't hurt for her to watch the reactions tonight from any USFT people who were there and potentially further brainwashed by their general.

Surely Hugo Myars wouldn't be at dinner there—would he?

He wasn't. In fact, not many members of the other primary unit at Ft. Lukman were in the small facility that night. Probably a good thing.

But Staff Sergeants Noel Chuma and Rainey Jessop were

there, as were shifter members of Alpha Force Lieutenants Seth Ambers, Colleen Hodell, Jock Larabey and Marshall Vincenzo. They'd taken a table in a corner, and Jason pulled a couple of additional chairs up to it before Sara and he got their dinners from the cafeteria line.

Sara chose a large chopped salad with steak chunks in it. The steak theme remained major here—undoubtedly because of at least some of the troops stationed on this base. In fact, almost all of the others had brought beef dishes of one kind or another to the table.

She mostly listened to the dinner conversation—which primarily centered on grumbling about Alpha Force's relationship with USFT and how no one was looking forward to tomorrow's meeting. They also talked a bit about their respective backgrounds, what the shifters' lives had been like before joining Alpha Force. They'd all had practice being secretive, but some had had easier existences than others.

Sara couldn't help looking at the shifter members with a different focus now. Not only had she seen Jason shift up close and personal today, but she might also be taking on, at least now and then, the function that Noel Chuma and Rainey Jessop had in assisting shifters.

She still wasn't sure how she felt about that.

But everyone treated her as a comrade, not with the remoteness she had concerns about since she unabashedly represented their commanding officer, General Yarrow.

She liked these people.

She wondered how their unit was trained to assist the rest of the U.S. military, but the general had indicated, before she believed in shifters, that the group was working undercover in some very interesting situations—and had already helped to thwart biological warfare and other major threats.

And now she could be, indirectly, part of that very useful function.

Eventually, they all finished. Time to leave.

With Jason? Yes, it seemed that he intended to walk her back to the BOQ, notwithstanding the fact that she had other officers here who could keep her company.

Although…as they started to walk past the enclosed parking structure that housed the remains of the general's car, Jason looked at her. "There are a couple of things I thought of that I'd like to check out on the car," he said. "Care to join me?"

There was something in his look that she couldn't quite read. A challenge?

Well, if she was going to remain part of Alpha Force, even for a short while, she had to stand up to Jason's challenges and then some.

Even more, she had to master the deep sexual attraction that stirred her insides with just the slightest heat of his gaze.

"Sure," she said. "Let's go."

Chapter 11

"Here we are." Jason turned to Sara as they reached the main entrance to the post's parking garage. "I'll call ahead and warn the guard that we're coming."

She looked at him quizzically. "Okay, but I'm still not sure what we're looking for tonight."

"I have a couple of ideas I want to test." Jason pulled his phone out of his pocket before she could ask anything else.

Only one guard was stationed outside the room where what was left of the general's car was stored, since that room was secluded and locked. Jason had access with a key, but the couple of times he'd visited here, he'd called the guard first on his cell phone, warning that he was about to get company.

Jason had made sure he was on a first-name basis with each of the guards he'd met who were charged now with the duty of ensuring that no one disturbed what little evidence there was on what had been done to General Yarrow's prized Jeep.

It was only a little more than a day since the incident, and the military crime-scene team Drew had finally zeroed in on wouldn't be there until tomorrow, or maybe even the next day.

Jason doubted they'd find anything he hadn't already seen, but hey, that was their expertise. Maybe, if they got their butts in gear and arrived, they'd actually figure out what had happened.

And who'd done it.

Meanwhile, his mind had been working double-time on things he may have missed when he'd looked before. Though he couldn't come up with anything he should have done differently. Maybe he needed to look again at the small stuff, in case he'd missed something while preoccupied with his coughing spree. Surely there'd been something important he hadn't focused on.

Sara and he hurried up the stairs to the third floor, then exited the stairwell. The room was at the far side of the garage, not far from the ramp they'd taken when they used the rented truck to bring the remains inside. Jason didn't wait for Sara to keep up. He just hurried toward his destination.

As anticipated, a sentry stood there with arms crossed, a weapon on his hip. When he spotted the two people approach, he snapped to attention, his hand over his gun. Then he relaxed and saluted. "Sergeant Connell," he said then looked toward Sara.

"This is Lieutenant McLinder, Kerry. Like I told you on the phone, we need to go see the general's car again."

"Yes, sir. Hi, Lieutenant McLinder." Sounded to Jason as if they'd already met. For now, the private stood out of the way, allowing Jason to hold the door open for Sara.

Inside he flicked on the lights. In the center of the room, where they'd left it, was the mess of charred metal and more.

"What are we looking for this time?" Sara had moved around him to approach the hulk.

"Wish I knew," Jason said. "But I've got to have missed something before. And it sure would be handy to have whatever that is with us at the meeting tomorrow. Whoever did this has to be a USFT member, and I'd love to wave evidence in their faces to see whose reaction gives them away."

Sara turned toward him again. She was smiling, the expression lighting up every inch of her gorgeous face beneath that sexy cap of blond hair. "Love the idea, but I don't think it'll happen. Even if we find something, whoever did it has to be craftier than that. He—or she—will look at that piece of evidence with an expression as bewildered and innocent as everyone else's."

"Ah, Lieutenant, you forget. A quarter or more of the people in that room'll be shifters. We don't rely on looking at someone's face or even body language to tell us what they're thinking or feeling."

"You mean that—"

"Fear has a scent, and we're all familiar with it." He grinned.

Dumb, but he felt a swirl of pride inside as she flashed him an even broader smile that he read as admiring. "Know what?" she said. "We're going to find something here today that you can wave tomorrow to see the reaction—even if we actually come up with diddly squat."

His turn to look at her with admiration. They were definitely on the same wavelength.

He found that idea to be hot. In fact, he found everything about Sara to be hot.

They spent about half an hour going over the car again. Once more, they wore latex gloves and held flashlights. Lots of seared and melted metal, ashes, pieces and puddles and ruined rubber and the kinds of things Jason expected and had noticed before. He didn't see any more paraphernalia that the general might have been transporting in the back of the car.

Jason had already interfaced with the soldiers charged with initial checking out and photographing the scene be-

fore the car was moved, who'd looked into the general's
overnight bag that had been in the front seat with him.
They'd found nothing with the remains of the general's
clothing and personal items beyond what Jason had already
noted there—and none of it had provided any clue as to
what had gone wrong in the Jeep.

No indication that anyone had set the general's miscellaneous stuff to smoldering before he'd gotten on his way
here.

Then Sara and he got into the box at the side of the room
where ashes and debris were stored, stuff like the remains
of the general's fishing pole and hooks and other uniden-
tified metal items.

Sara knelt on the hard floor beside him, also scanning
the detritus with her lovely blue-green eyes as if this additional viewing would somehow yield results.

Her sigh told him that she felt as ineffectual as he did.
Why did that feel so appealing? He wished he could reassure her that she was a big help here—but knew that
wouldn't go over well. Not when they weren't finding answers.

Jason wished, for a moment, that he was in wolfen form.
Might he smell something that would be helpful?

Just in case, he closed his eyes and let the smells filter
into his nose as he inhaled, carefully and slowly. There
was no indication that whatever had triggered his bad reaction was present, but he didn't want to take any chances.

Scents were merged here, but he could tell the difference
between the ashes of the canvas and the odors of charred
metal, burned rubber and the rest.

And yes, there was more. The fishing line? Maybe.
There were several smells he believed to be melted plastic.

But that proved nothing.

"Anything interesting?" Sara said from beside him.

When he opened his eyes, she was watching him intently, as if trying to vicariously participate in what he was doing.

He enjoyed that look, her seriousness. The way the intensity of her expression made him feel as if she were studying him, getting inside him, wanting more of him.

That was only wishful thinking…wasn't it?

"Maybe," he said. "But nothing I can really follow up on, at least not yet."

"So we'll just wing it tomorrow," she said decisively.

He liked the way she said *we.* And the way she tilted her head, as if soliciting his agreement.

"But I can't help agreeing that we're missing something," she added. She turned back toward the box of debris. "Maybe the experts will figure it out when they sift through these things, but I wonder if there's something in here that the general couldn't possibly have had in the back with his stuff."

"Let's make a list of what we find. Take a few more pictures. We'll run the details by the general tomorrow. All he saw, when he was here checking over what was left, was the big picture. Maybe seeing and hearing about the small stuff will trigger him to suggest more clues."

"Good idea."

They spent another fifteen minutes there. Sara moved from angle to angle and shot photos, and Jason made the list of items they surveyed. That seemed backward to him. He was the kind of person who took action, not the kind who kept track of things. But Sara seemed happy this way, so he didn't object.

Task completed, she stuffed her camera back into her pocket. She looked so woeful that he wanted to kiss her, to distract her from all that was bothering her.

Hell, why give himself an excuse? He just wanted to kiss her.

"Guess we're done here," he said unnecessarily.

"Guess so," she agreed.

As they both headed toward the door, Jason said, "Sounds like I still won't have an opportunity to return the truck to that service station tomorrow and retrieve my own car. I've been in touch with them but I'll have to make sure it's still okay with them. Uncle Sam's paying for the rental, but I can't help worrying about my Mustang."

Her smile was broad and amused. "I'd worry about it, too, if I had a great car like that."

"You really like it?" He felt himself lighten inside. Well, anyone with a brain and a heart would like that red, classic delight of his.

"Of course," she said. "I told you so before." As their eyes met, he felt some really top-grade tingling way down in his body. Tingling that told him her attitude—everything about her—was making him hot.

"I still need to go get it," he said. "Right now, though, I'll check on the truck. I've got it parked on another floor."

They left the room, locking it behind them and making sure that the sentry was back on guard. Then Jason led Sara down the stairs to the second floor.

The garage contained a lot of cars parked in parallel rows but was devoid of other people at this late hour. The truck was right where Jason had parked it, at the end of a row near a concrete wall where it wouldn't get in anyone's way. All looked fine with it.

Jason glanced around. "Is your car here?"

"No. I've left it in one of the outdoor lots near the BOQ."

"Well, we can still check on one of my other cars."

She blinked at him. "How many do you have?"

"Two here. A few more with family back home in Wisconsin, where I grew up."

"Legitimately acquired?"

He stared, offended, till he saw the twinkle in her eyes. "Some are. Some I stole."

"Really?"

"No," he said, grinning. "Like I told you before, the ones I stole have been returned to their rightful owners, damn it."

Her look suggested that she was trying to feel shocked but not succeeding. He liked that teasing look. In fact, there wasn't much about her that he didn't like.

"Let me introduce you to the other vehicle I brought here," he said. "I even bought it in Maryland a short while after I arrived."

He motioned for her to follow. He led her to a silver Toyota hybrid SUV that he'd bought used but in pristine condition. It was useful—and it was a gorgeous hunk of car.

"Nice," she said, and her sincere and impressed tone got to him.

"Yeah, nice," he said and took a step toward her.

What was it about this guy that turned Sara into a totally different person every time they were together?

She wasn't a car groupie. She just considered them handy transportation. But she knew that Jason had gasoline in his veins, a love for cars that at one time, at least, had gone way beyond sensibility.

And now…now he was up close and personal with her. Right beside this nice, utilitarian but attractive vehicle that he apparently owned.

Not only that, but he was *really* up close and personal with her. If he took just one more step—

He did take it. And suddenly, she was in his arms.

His kiss was astoundingly hot and sexy as he thrust his tongue into her mouth. She felt like melting and exploding, all at the same time. She responded with gusto, expecting—wanting—more. Lots more.

But just as suddenly, he stepped back.

"Don't see anyone around, but you never know," he said huskily. "Care to see my accessories?" He winked one of those golden eyes of his and she was lost.

Her own return laugh was soft and full of…what? Challenge? Sex?

Hell if she knew. But in only moments she found herself entering the back of his car. The seats were already down, forming an upholstered bed that looked much too enticing.

Especially with Jason's hands guiding her inside.

She didn't resist. Didn't want to resist—although she did take one furtive look around to ensure that they were still alone.

And then there they were, with the door closed behind them, both kneeling on the SUV's bed. Jason wasted no time in taking Sara into his arms. Kissing her again—so hard and so sexily that she nearly toppled over.

Which wasn't a bad idea. The surface was softened by the light upholstery, but it wasn't particularly comfortable for kneeling, even in her camo uniform's slacks.

But instead of lying down, Sara just snuggled herself closer to Jason's muscular body. Awkward? Yes. But even so, against him this way, she could feel how hard he was below. Without thinking, she urged her own body even closer and heard him moan softly.

That did it. She wanted him. Wise or not. Forbidden or not. Or maybe that was a factor in wanting him. Rebelling against who and what she was? She'd never done that before, but maybe, just maybe, she was starting now.

She pulled back enough to start unbuttoning the top of his uniform without breaking their kiss. Turned out he had the same idea, for suddenly her shirt was open and pulled back, baring her to him.

Only, when she got through unbuttoning him, she was

enthralled by the sight of his hard, wonderfully toned chest. Apparently servicing cars, or being in the military, or both, sculpted this sexy man's muscles into perfection.

She, on the other hand, wasn't completely naked above— not at first. But she felt one of his hands touch her breasts, rub against them so her nipples hardened, and then her bra was off, too.

"Sara," Jason gasped, laying her down gently onto the carpetlike surface. He sucked first one breast, then the other, into his mouth as his tongue teased her nipples.

She was far from passive, even as she moaned at his utterly sensual activities, his gentle attack on her vulnerable, eager body. She reached into his pants, grasping his hard erection and pumping it gently with her hand.

He moved so quickly that she was barely aware of it, but in moments he was naked against her. She imitated his motion, and the rest of her clothing was gone, too.

And then he touched her, right there in her most sensitive area. Grasped her, rubbing gently, moving one finger, then more than one, inside her in imitation of the sex act that she suddenly craved.

Only— She couldn't, could she? Not without protection, even with a being who was entirely human, and his differences from her, although not obvious now, suddenly leaped into her mind.

She stiffened.

"Wait," he said. He let go of her, leaving her bereft despite thinking it was for the best. But as she watched, he wriggled between the two rear seats and up into the front of the vehicle. Lord, what a view. His long, sinewy, hard legs ending in a tight butt she wanted to stroke and squeeze, but she couldn't reach it. Not now.

She heard the glove compartment open, and in seconds he had retaken the position he had just left—almost. She saw him struggle to open a small package but his hands were trembling and he was taking too long.

But he was prepared, bless him.

"Let me," she said, taking the condom from him. She got the wrappings off—and had the additional pleasure of sliding it gently, teasingly, onto him.

With a growl that was entirely human, he repositioned her onto her back and thrust inside her. He was still, as if savoring the moment, and she did the same.

And then he started pumping, gently at first and then with more and more intensity. She groaned in ecstasy, and when she finally reached the most amazingly powerful orgasm of her entire life, she had to stifle a scream.

Minutes later, or was it hours? Sara still lay on her side on the stiff, uncomfortable surface at the back of the SUV. She was breathing deeply and erratically, and the fact she was facing the similarly still—but really ripped—body of Jason's didn't help her calm her respiration.

She still felt damned attracted to him. If she weren't so exhausted, maybe she would attack him again and engage in more feral, uninhibited, mindless sex.

Only…well, she wasn't really mindless.

Even so, her gaze locked on to his for a long moment, and she knew that, if she let herself, she would be absolutely hypnotized by his smug grin.

As if the words were extracted from her by some kind of woo-woo sci-fi mind meld, she heard herself say in an irregular voice, "That was amazing."

But at the same time, reality was starting to reinsert itself into her mind.

Yes, he was one damned sexy guy. What she'd experienced was incredible.

But he was a subordinate in the military, which made

what they'd done forbidden—especially for someone like her, who toed the line implicitly. Or always had before.

And in addition to that little problem, another insurmountable barrier remained between them. Jason was also a shapeshifter.

"It was," Jason responded to her comment. "But there's always room to make it even more amazing…soon." As if his body responded to what he said, Sara saw his sex organ start hardening once more.

Despite her fascination, she made herself stare at his face again. But she didn't respond to his suggestion.

Once she regained her senses, she'd never want to have sex with him again.

If she ever regained her senses….

Now though, physically sated, she relaxed against him while catching her breath, and allowed her mind to glom on to the curiosity that had invaded her from the time she'd begun to believe Jason was truly a werewolf.

"You told me before that you'd let me know what it's really like to be a shapeshifter," she murmured against his chest.

He put his arms around her and held her close. "It's incredible," he said, and she felt his breath rippling the hair on top of her head as he spoke. "The change? It's uncomfortable, and yet it feels like being reborn every time. In both directions."

"Which do you like better?" she asked. "Human or wolf form?"

"Love 'em both, for different reasons." He paused. "At the moment, human's in the lead."

She heard herself chuckle. And then she said, "Did you have a hard time while growing up? Were there regular humans around, and did you have to hide who—what—you were?" *And did that, somehow, lead to your becoming a car thief?* she wondered, but she didn't ask.

"Our family was pretty much located in remote areas of Wisconsin," he said, drawing her even closer. "And yes, there were still a lot of 'normal' people we had to keep our secret from. But we weren't too far from Madison, so we were always able to shop there for stuff our neighbors wouldn't understand, even some kinds of chemicals. Over generations, our ancestors had started fooling around with an elixir to help us decide when to change and all—similar to the one Drew has been developing for Alpha Force, but his is a whole lot better, more sophisticated now, than what he and I grew up with. And its current formulation is proprietary to Alpha Force, which is one reason I'm here and will be staying, at least for now."

"How did you all… I mean, is there a whole community of shapeshifters where you're from, or only your family?" She was finding this description fascinating, which surprised her. She always had a streak of curiosity that controlled who she was…but who knew she'd find something she'd considered pure fiction—before—so interesting?

"There are a bunch of us," he responded. "Not all are in the same area, and not all are part of our family, but we do keep in touch."

"And what do you do there about—" A sound startled her, interrupting her question, but she stopped herself from gasping aloud. A car must be driving by. She heard the noise of tires on the concrete floor and froze.

Just moving her eyes, she glanced upward. There were no lights on in the SUV. The only illumination was dim and came from recessed lighting in the parking garage. Plus, the vehicle's windows were tinted.

And Jason and she both were lying chest-to-chest—

and how sexy that felt—on the folded-down backseat, way below those windows.

They had to be invisible to anyone driving by.

Thank heavens.

She looked at Jason, though, realizing that she was trembling a little. He was grinning, apparently at her horrified reaction about potentially getting caught here. She glared, but at least he wasn't moving. Although she wouldn't put it past this man to stand up, turn on the lights and flaunt all he had.

If the driver happened to be female, she'd get one hell of a show.

But fortunately, Jason was wiser than that. He stayed as still as Sara did.

In less than a minute, the noise receded and was not followed by the sound of any other vehicle.

"I think it's time to go." Sara drew herself up slightly, still hiding herself in the corner between the farthest-back side window and the rear one, and hurriedly donned her clothes.

With what appeared to be a sorrowful shrug, Jason also knelt and began to dress.

Sara tried not to look, but she nevertheless saw enough to feel regret that such a gorgeous, hard, utterly sexy body would soon be hidden from her view.

Until the next time that Jason had suggested...?

No.

There could be no next time.

Reading Sara McLinder's face was even easier than reading a car's maintenance manual.

Jason purposely made dressing himself into a show, as he'd done with his body when he had shifted in front of Sara so many times now.

Even though she'd been curious, had asked a lot of good questions about his background and all, she regretted what they'd done.

But damn, she'd enjoyed it, too.

Even admitted that—a few minutes ago. But he bet that if he asked her now, while she finished dressing as she hid as best she could inside the back of his SUV, she'd pretend she'd never meant anything of the sort. Had maybe enjoyed slumming just this once.

But that was the one and only time.

His presumption was unexpectedly painful. It challenged him, too. They would do it again. He'd make sure of it. Or at least he'd do his damnedest to seduce her sometime in the future.

The near future.

"So what do you think of my second car?" he finally asked, keeping his tone light.

"Nice," she said, although she didn't sound serious. And then, still buttoning up her camo blouse, she stopped and stared at him. "Did you plan this? Did you bring me to the hauling truck—and then this car—because you wanted us to get in the back here and…and make love?"

He could see by her rattled expression that she sought the right euphemism, one she could live with, for the various words and descriptions out there for having sex.

"I thought about it," he admitted easily. He'd thought about having sex with Sara since he'd met her. "Our respective quarters wouldn't be exactly the easiest places to get down and dirty like this, would they?"

"No. And that's a good thing." Sadly, every bit of her gorgeous body that had turned him on so much it hurt was now covered. Oh, her bustline was obvious even beneath her shirt, but her being in uniform was definitely not the most exciting view of her he had seen.

"Okay," he said. He didn't want to get into a fight with her. Not now. But he could see by her angry expression that his agreeing with her hadn't pacified her, either.

He wanted to grab her. Shake some sense into her.

Better yet, turn her on again.

Instead, he turned away and grabbed the inside handle of the vehicle's back door. He levered it and pushed it open.

"I'll get out first," he told her, which he did. He looked around to ensure they were still alone. "It's okay now. Let's go."

Chapter 12

Sara's bed in her BOQ apartment was a hell of a lot more comfortable than the bed of that SUV she'd left only about half an hour ago, alone, stalking out of the garage ahead of Jason—even though she knew he was behind her, keeping watch.

Which made her feel protected. But she didn't need protection. She could take care of herself.

So why wasn't she sleeping…again?

Last time she'd had insomnia, it was because she'd thought she was hallucinating after seeing all those wolves.

This time…no hallucination. She had just experienced the best sex of her life. With the wrong man. Or whatever he was.

He'd described his background—some of it. And he'd even suggested they'd partake in another heated encounter someday. Another bout of unforgettable, incredible lovemaking with a man—yes, he was at least partly a man—who seemed to anticipate every touch, every kiss, every thrust that would make her giddy and turn her into a heap of mindless sensation.

She didn't even want to think about it.

Which meant she thought about nothing else, except for her fascination—no, her fury with herself—far into the night.

She was relaxing, at least, when she suddenly jolted to attention in her bed with the ringing of her smartphone.

She glanced at the caller ID.

Jason.

She ignored the sudden moistening and twisting down below, where he'd made her feel so good. Why would he be calling at this hour?

Was something wrong again at Ft. Lukman? With General Yarrow? Something else?

"Hello?" Her voice was all professional. At least she hoped so.

"Hi, Sara." His deep voice made her insides react even more. He didn't sound frantic or upset. But why was he calling?

"Is anything wrong?"

"Yes," he said immediately, and her heart started thumping erratically.

"Tell me."

"I can't sleep. I'll bet you can't, either. I don't suppose you'd like to get together again so we could relax one another. I'd like at least some rest tonight. Lots going on tomorrow."

"You have a lot of nerve," she spat out. "What's going on tomorrow is just one of the many reasons we are not only staying apart tonight, but what happened...well, it was a mistake. It won't happen again. Do you understand?"

"I hear you." She heard him, too—including the laughter in his tone. "Good night, Sara."

Damn. He hung up, and she'd wanted to be the one to end the call.

She felt furious—with not only him, but herself, too.

But as she lay there, rehashing not only his phone call but their unforgettable lovemaking, she found herself smiling, too...even as she finally felt sleep coming on.

* * *

Sara hurried from her apartment first thing the next morning. With the upcoming meetings, she didn't have time to obsess about what had happened last night.

As she walked down the hall toward the stairway, a door opened. Colleen Hodell ran out, almost bumping into Sara.

"Sorry," the tawny-haired lieutenant said, her feline-like eyes wide. "I'm meeting Rainey for a quick breakfast and I'm late."

"She's your shifting aide, isn't she?" Sara felt curious about how a cougar-shifter handled her role here among all the wolves.

"That's right." Colleen seemed to hesitate then smiled. "You haven't met Puka yet, have you?"

"Puka?"

"My cover cat. I keep her in my apartment rather than having her stress out among all those dogs. Come on in. Rainey can wait a few more minutes."

"Thanks."

Colleen's apartment was as small as Sara's, with nonde-script but comfortable-looking furniture and a tiny kitch-enette, but she had been there long enough to add some personal touches such as photos on the wall of lots of cats.

Some were wilder kinds of felines, and Sara couldn't help wondering if they were real pumas and jaguars and tigers—or if they were shapeshifter felines, like Colleen.

"In here." Colleen gestured for Sara to join her near the kitchenette. "This is her favorite spot."

The cat that lay on a fluffy, orange pillow at the far side of the narrow tile floor was large for a kitty, maybe twenty pounds. She was as tawny as Colleen's hair, and her face looked like a miniature version of a mountain lion.

"She's lovely," Sara couldn't help exclaiming. She con-sidered herself more of a dog person, yet this cat was not only unusual but the stare of her brown eyes appeared highly intelligent. "Where did you find her?"

"I knew when I joined Alpha Force that I'd need a cover animal." Colleen crossed the floor, reached up and opened a cupboard door. She removed a box of feline treats and fed a couple to the cat, who rubbed against her leg. "My family always kept cats around that resembled us as much as possible while shifted, so I just brought Puka with me."

"Where are you originally from?" Sara said, wondering if it was any harder to keep a shifting cougar's identity secret than it was a wolf's. She now knew a bit more about where Jason had come from. Colleen had given some of her background the other night at dinner but Sara didn't recall what she'd said except that she wasn't among those shifters who now liked to complain about their prior lives.

"Oh, the Midwest."

"Is your family—"

"Yeah, they're still there."

Colleen's abruptness suggested she didn't want to answer a bunch of questions. Maybe she truly was concerned that she was late for her breakfast with Rainey. But after her conversation with Jason, Sara was curious.

"Are they all shapeshifters?" she asked. "Are there a lot of cougar shifters? I gather there are quite a few wolves. And did you have to hide from regular humans while you were growing up?"

Colleen's sigh was deep and she didn't meet Sara's eyes. "I don't generally talk much about my background." Her voice was hoarse. "You're right—there tend to be a lot more wolf shifters than feline, and there are more of us than there are other shifters, like birds. My family is small. We all shift under a full moon so, hiding—yes, that was a lot of what we did when I was a kid. I'd wanted…well, I thought my life would change a lot when I found Alpha Force and was able to join up. And it did. But…" Her voice trailed off, and Sara didn't prompt her. Maybe that was enough. "But my family," Colleen finally went on. "They're still there. It's hard for them, and I'd love to help them. I—" She turned toward Sara. "Okay, enough of that."

"Sorry for being pushy," Sara said. "But I didn't even believe there were shapeshifters before, and now that I know there are I'm really curious."

"No problem." Colleen bent down and picked up her cat. "Anyway," she continued, "Puka is mostly an indoor cat, and you can't really train cats the way they do with the dogs, so she's my furry apartment mate."

Despite her reluctance to talk about her past, she apparently had no issues about talking about her cat. "Have you ever had to use Puka to protect you as a shifter by proving there's a genuine cat around?"

"A couple of times, but not around here."

"I figured," Sara said. "Not with Alpha Force being the primary unit stationed here."

"Yeah, but even around those USFT guys…well, I know some have figured out what Alpha Force is all about."

"And they're about to learn more," Sara agreed. "Today."

"Which means we'd both better get going." She reached down and stroked Puka. "See you later, little girl."

That cat wasn't a *little* girl, in Sara's estimation. But she did enjoy watching Puka stare with interest as her best human friend said goodbye.

Jason wasn't invited to the initial preparatory meeting that morning.

He understood why. He wasn't the general or his aide, like Sara, nor a commanding officer of Alpha Force like his cousin Drew or Lieutenant Patrick Worley.

He definitely wasn't even aligned with other NCOs from that damned Ultra Special Forces Team.

Nah, he was just a peon. A mere sergeant who shape-shifted, fixed cars…oh, and occasionally helped to save a general's life.

Or spent a really great night with that general's aide.

So he just waited in the cafeteria, along with other Alpha Force members who were also eager for their part of the meeting to start—like shifters Seth Ambers, Jock Larabey, Colleen Hodell and Marshall Vincenzo, and nonshifting aides Noel Chuma and Rainey Jessop.

But they weren't alone playing with their breakfasts and speculating about what was to come. Oh, no, some of those damned USFT guys were there, too. Jason didn't know all their names, but they sat at their tables eating, drinking juice and coffee and, undoubtedly, gossiping, since they sent a lot of glares toward the Alpha Force folks, who only glared back.

And the meetings today were supposed to somehow promote accord and working together?

Good luck.

For fun, Jason decided to stick a baiting knife into the tense atmosphere. He stood with his cup of coffee and went to the row of dispensers to top it off with some hotter brew. Instead of returning to his original seat, he sat at the USFT table and gave a smile of utter innocence. "Hey, you guys going to the all-hands meeting later?"

"Yeah," said a woman whose ID tag said she was Lieutenant Swainey. "We'll be there." She said nothing more at first, but Jason continued to stare at her smoothly attractive African-American face with his goofy yet challenging smile. "Will you?" she asked, as if she had decided to follow his unspoken instructions.

"We sure will. I'm looking forward to hearing how we're

all going to work together like one big, happy family." He widened that faux smile.

"You're the guy who works on cars, aren't you?" asked Lieutenant Brown. He was a big guy who'd apparently either chosen to wear his camos tight or he'd been beefing up his body since acquiring his uniform.

Jason wouldn't want to get into a physical altercation with the muscular lieutenant. But a battle of wits? Anytime.

"That's right," he responded. "You have one that needs work?"

"No, but I heard you did a pissant job of fixing your General Yarrow's."

That brought a titter from everyone else at the damned USFT table and nearly made Jason stand up and tip it onto their fat little laps.

But some of those from his own table now stood behind him. This could get out of control really quick.

He thought then of straitlaced, by the book—almost— Sara. What would she think if he primed the atmosphere here so that nothing could be accomplished at the later meeting?

Hell, he figured the meeting would be worthless, anyway. No need for him to cause any additional ill feelings right now. So instead of accusing these guys, or someone in their unit, of sabotaging General Yarrow's car, he simply said, "Yeah. Unfortunately, it was too far gone to be saved. Fortunately, the general survived."

"Yeah, fortunately." Brown's tone made Jason want to slug him.

"I need more coffee," Jason said, standing. The Alpha Force members who'd joined him looked surprised.

Hey, he'd gotten a reputation not only for talking out of turn but acting that way, too. Sometimes. When it didn't threaten his ability to stay in Alpha Force and therefore out of prison.

But these folks didn't really know him. And if he'd surprised them this time? Well, hell. That felt good...and he knew he'd do it again.

The preliminary meeting of the topmost officers stationed at Ft. Lukman was nearing its end.

It had taken place at the front of the base's assembly room, even though they all could have fit into General Yarrow's sumptuous office.

Sara understood why that hadn't happened. Her CO hadn't wanted to make it appear to the other general, Myars, that he intended to take charge.

But it had become crystal clear nearly immediately who had not only the power here, but the knowledge and intelligence to get these people talking—and to prepare for the larger upcoming session, too.

She couldn't help wondering where Drew's "cuz" was but forced herself to cast all thoughts of him aside.

Two of General Yarrow's subordinates who were the local officers in charge of Alpha Force were inevitably present: Drew Connell and Patrick Worley, who was back on base temporarily but due to leave again that afternoon.

General Myars had a couple of his immediate reports present, as well: Captains Samantha Everly and Rynton Tierney.

Sara recalled her brief discussion with Samantha the night that Jason had been in such bad condition while shifted. The captain seemed less animated now, although she undoubtedly tried to take her cue from her commanding officer. Today, the clip holding her light brown hair was at the nape of her neck instead of on top of her head.

Sara was more interested in watching Rynton Tierney,

who held a similar position to hers with the other general. He appeared less engaged than Samantha listening to the conversation. In fact, he seemed more inclined to watch the Alpha Force members from across the narrow aisle between the seating areas. Did he know, or just suspect, that some of them were shifters?

The two generals' initial conversation was standard cordial B.S., with Hugo Myars commenting on how well Greg Yarrow looked despite his ordeal the other day.

Greg, similarly, asked Myars about his trip here and how things were going with him at the Pentagon and Ft. Lukman.

Useless stuff. At first.

Sara noticed with relief that General Yarrow looked a lot better than he had even on his arrival yesterday. Maybe it was because he was no longer pale, but his lined face was florid beneath his dark hair as he faced off with his counterpart about what they intended to do at the later meeting.

General Myars looked ten years younger than Greg, despite the fact his hair was sparser and its short style displayed strands of gray within its brown. Maybe it was because he was stockier. The flabbiness of his cheeks shoved out most wrinkles. He was taller, too, though part of that height was due to the exaggerated heels on his military boots.

But once the polite initial conversation was ended, he seemed ready to shout and storm and do anything he could to rattle General Yarrow.

Including insult his subordinates.

Both generals sat at the front of the room, beyond the tiers of chairs holding underlings like Sara. She couldn't hear all they said when they lowered their voices for more serious conversation—and wished, for once, she had a few of the enhanced senses of Alpha Force members who sat with her in the first row of seats. They must have heard it all.

With the little she did hear—and the animosity emanating from Myars—Sara had a hard time staying silent and not jumping in with her own opinions and accusations. One or more of these people may have been the ones who'd ruined Greg Yarrow's prized car—and tried to injure, possibly kill, him.

Damn them.

She wouldn't ask Drew or Patrick what they heard when the two men's voices were lowered. But if Jason had been here? Well, even though she had to stay away from him personally, the bond they'd started to forge would have allowed her to ask him.

After five minutes of the heated, low-voiced exchange, Greg stood and looked at the members of the small audience.

"Here's what we decided, ladies and gentlemen." He glanced at Myars, who stood quickly beside him. "General Myars and I will each introduce our units briefly to the entire group when everyone is here and seated."

"We'll describe again what sets our units apart from each other, and from all others in the military," Myars added.

"Then we'll describe the joint maneuvers we intend to hold here," Greg continued, "demonstrating those special skills to one another and seeing how we can work together—because we've been primed about a very special, critical mission that the government intends to send us both on. That's why USFT was sent here, to where Alpha Force is stationed, to see if we could join forces and get the kind of result our government needs."

"I'm sure we can work together, sir," Samantha Everly said immediately, undoubtedly kissing up to her CO. "USFT

can do anything—even if it involves danger…and weird-
ness."

She pointedly shot a glance toward the other side of the
aisle, where Sara sat with the Alpha Forcers. Apparently,
Samantha had a pretty good idea of what special abilities
the other unit had.

Sara wished she knew what skills above and beyond
standard the USFT members had. If they behaved this way
with shapeshifters, Sara suspected their abilities were more
similar to what was considered normal, even if they were
somehow enhanced.

The all-hands meeting definitely promised to be interesting.

Especially because…everyone in both units was expected to be there.

Including Jason.

And his offbeat sense of humor.

Sara had a feeling that whatever the USFT's special abilities, if Myars, Samantha or anyone else in that group decided to diss Alpha Force and its highly unique capabilities,
some members of Alpha Force would reciprocate in kind.

Jason, in particular, would get a kick out of making fun
of them.

That was neither professional nor military, Sara knew.
But even tamping down all memories of the night they'd
shared, she couldn't wait to see Jason…and hear his reactions.

Chapter 13

Jason entered the administration building near the assembly room at least fifteen minutes before the session was to begin.

He wasn't alone. The other Alpha Force members he'd been with were there, too, talking and joking in the concrete-and-tile foyer till it was time to enter the room.

Jason often hung back when forced to attend meetings. Alpha Force might be an exceptionally good job for him, but, hell, it was still the military.

Only today was different. He was interested in what this session was about.

What were the special skills of those damned USFT members that made their higher-ups consider them appropriate to train, then deploy on a major assignment, with Alpha Force?

What was the point of basing them here, at Ft. Lukman, then waiting weeks before holding this kind of assembly to inform the groups what their respective future roles would be?

How had the earlier meeting gone—with the two generals?

With Sara's presence.

While waiting, his group linked up almost as if under orders to do so, ignoring the similar gathering of their rivals. Nemeses?

Jason wasn't the only Alpha Force member who mistrusted them.

"You ready?" Colleen broke into a conversation among Noel, Jonas and Rainey, who were trading humorous suggestions on how best to act like a shapeshifter's aide. They'd kept their voices low. Even if a lot of the other Alpha Forcers here could hear them, the damn USFT guys would stay oblivious.

Jason looked around and saw that the door to the assembly room had been opened. Sara glanced out before turning and walking back in.

"Showtime," Jason acknowledged. He kept his pace slow enough not to look eager to get inside. His habits were known here, including his lack of enthusiasm for meetings. No use changing that now and triggering any speculation.

There'd be plenty of speculation about the truthfulness, and completeness, of whatever they were told in the meeting.

The USFT group had noticed the open door, too, and headed in that direction. Jason turned enough to inhale their scents—standard shower soap and deodorants and the usual, but also more, caused by emotions. Sweat from fear? Heated by anger?

What the hell did they have to be angry about?

But their filing through the door was accomplished politely as they allowed others through first.

In the crowd, it was harder to scan the place to locate Sara. Yet it was almost as if he had a direct link with her— her light citrus scent, her connection with General Yarrow. All Jason had to do was check the front of the room for the two generals, and there was Sara standing, unsurprisingly, at Yarrow's right arm.

The two COs stood by chairs facing the crowd. Each gestured toward where they wanted everyone to sit.

There were a few seats left in the first row. Jason despised being up front—but it was the only way he'd get to be near Sara. He took one of those seats and waited.

Not long after his entrance, the room was apparently filled with all who were expected. Sara returned to the door and closed it. She turned before heading back to her seat, looking into the crowd.

She met Jason's eyes. She blinked then chilled her expression.

He nodded coolly, as he would toward any acquaintance, even a superior officer. Even so, she sat down in the last remaining seat in the row, which happened to be directly at his left.

Yes! But he didn't look at her.

The meeting began. General Yarrow took a step forward, placing himself a little closer to the crowd than General Myars. Myars tried to join the other man until General Yarrow's glance made him stop.

Interesting. Jason had been curious about their dynamics. Would Myars continue to take a more minor role?

"Thanks for coming, everyone." Yarrow raised his voice so it projected over the crowd. Conversations in the ten or so sparsely occupied rows of seats all stopped. He waited a moment then continued. "I know there've been a lot of questions you've all had over the past weeks, especially since the Ultra Special Forces Team arrived at Ft. Lukman. I am fully aware, and proud, that both the members of Alpha Force and USFT have been highly vetted and know not to talk about anything they know is confidential, and that has led to some…let's just say suspicions and lack of camaraderie around here. That was part of the plan. We wanted to see the reaction."

Murmurs circulated through the audience. Jason knew the other Alpha Forcers could pick up what was being said as well as he did. In fact, they were among those commenting, or swearing, or both, about the so-called plan.

Most had found seats near the front of the crowd, which meant that the USFT folks hung out mostly farther back.

Seth Ambers, in the second row, stood and saluted. "Permission to speak, sir?" The guy who looked like a moose, or at least a football player, would have dwarfed the general if they'd been closer. But Seth, a medical doctor as well as a shifter, was completely gentle…with those to whom gentleness made sense.

"All right, Seth," Yarrow said.

"I'm sure I'm speaking for everyone here when I say that we all really hope that the purpose of this meeting is not only to formally introduce the two groups, but also to explain the plan, and why we were allowed to get together with our counterparts before but not do much more than say hi."

Myars took another step toward the seats and scowled. His mouth was open as if he intended to berate Seth for daring to even suggest that the plan was anything but perfect.

But General Yarrow turned, blocking Myars as smoothly as if it had been choreographed.

Jason grinned. He used his peripheral vision to look sideways at Sara and saw her brief smile, too—although it quickly disappeared.

But General Yarrow was a peacemaker as well as a fighter. He said to Seth, "That's exactly what this meeting is about. In fact, I request that General Myars tell us all about USFT, why it is so ultra special. I'll then explain a bit about Alpha Force, and then together we'll outline the training exercises we plan here—and the mission on which most of you will be deployed if all goes well."

Jason leaned forward in his seat. So did most of the

others in Alpha Force. This was what they'd all wanted
to know.

"Okay," Myars said. "The Ultra Special Forces Team—
you're all exactly what that name describes. You've proven
it before. And whether or not you work directly with…
Alpha Force—" his tone sneered, though his face remained
visibly blank. Jason glanced at General Yarrow, whose eyes
had narrowed, but he, now seated, said nothing "—you will
prove it again."

Sara wanted to yell at that general for not acting wholly
professional. For insulting Alpha Force with his tone and
attitude.

Instead, she just clamped both hands into fists.

And glanced sideways at Jason. His hands were fisted,
too.

Almost involuntarily, she looked at his face. Didn't
smile, but nodded her head in acknowledgment that he,
too, was riled—but also acted professionally within military protocol.

He, on the other hand, shot her a very quick grin then
looked at the two generals once more.

At least General Myars finally got into what he was supposed to talk about: what USFT was all about.

"All members of the unit had to pass some very tough
tests. For example, their eyesight is far better than most
people's."

Sara had noticed that none wore glasses except sun-
glasses, but she'd just assumed some wore contact lenses.
Apparently not.

"Plus, they're highly trained in all special forces skills.
Most important, they are the most elite of all snipers."

Myars went on to explain the extent of their vetting,
their initial training, their ongoing perfection of their skills.

In other words, they'd been selected as the best of the special forces best. Some had been Navy SEALS. Some had been Army or Marines Special Forces. Some had been Air Force Special Ops.

Now they were all members of the Ultra Special Forces Team.

When he was done, the members of that highly skilled unit stood and cheered themselves. To be polite, Sara rose and found that the Alpha Forces joined her to applaud the others.

Then it was General Yarrow's turn. "I don't think it's a huge secret here, but all of you USFT folks were also chosen because of your security clearances, and understanding of clandestine operations and how to stay quiet about them."

Sara heard quiet muttering behind him. She couldn't make out what was being said, but knew that the shape-shifters in the room would hear it.

She was glad when Jason bent toward her and whispered, "Here's what was said: 'Oh, yeah. They're going to feed us that line again. Shapeshifters. Yeah, right.'"

"You know," General Yarrow said, "I heard someone comment but my ears aren't good enough to hear what was said. Drew, did you hear it?"

Major Drew Connell was also in the front row, a few people down from Sara. He stood—and repeated what had been said, verbatim. "The shifting members of Alpha Force also have enhanced senses while in human form," he said coldly, looking at the back row where Lieutenant Cal Brown sat.

The large soldier squirmed a bit, and Sara knew he was the one who'd spoken—especially when Jason confirmed it.

"And yes, the special talents of many Alpha Force members include shapeshifting," General Yarrow continued, as if he were describing the features of an outstanding new car. "What some of you USFT personnel thought was just a ruse on the recent night of the full moon was real."

No one spoke, but Sara sensed a lot of discomfort in the room. As she turned to look, she saw a number of personnel from the other unit moving uneasily in their seats.

Greg Yarrow didn't offer details about the shifting elixir, but he said that the next few days at Ft. Lukman would be critical. Obviously, those within the two groups had not yet bonded simply because they were fellow members of the military. That had been the hope when the USFT unit was first sent here. Neither group had passed that test. They had stayed separate and even seemed somewhat antagonistic.

But that had to change. Now they needed to show they could get along under many different kinds of conditions—conditions that each group would be permitted to manufacture.

If all went well, they'd then be put through joint exercises…and only then would they be told what their real assignment would be.

"Only if you've convinced us you can work well together," General Yarrow finished. "Right, General?" He looked at Myars.

"That's right," the other man said. "Otherwise, we'll call an end to the experiment, and both units will show a failure on their records."

"Permission to speak, General Yarrow?" That was Colleen Hodell, who'd sat in the second row. She was on her feet, saluting.

"All right, Lieutenant," Yarrow said.

"I know this isn't a question that'll lead to better relations between the two units, sir," she said, "and none of us wants any failures on our records. But everyone in Alpha Force will want the answer." She pivoted, first toward the people at the front who were in her unit, and those more toward the back rows who were not. "Has anyone found an answer about what happened to your car, General Yarrow? I mean—are we sure it wasn't damaged, and your life endangered, because of the lack of...well, camaraderie here?"

Jason felt the tension in the room rise. He didn't need his enhanced senses as a shifter for that. Even so, he inhaled the heated scents of anger enough that he felt his whole body tense.

Beside him, Sara also stiffened in her seat. He glanced at her and saw that her eyes were wide and worried, her full lips pursed in concern.

She looked as if she'd have shut the Alpha Force member up if she'd been able. And she clearly wasn't going to do what they'd discussed previously: hinting that they'd found a clue on the Jeep implicating USFT.

She didn't need to. Not now. Colleen had come pretty close to doing so, and the tension in the room could be sliced with a combat knife.

He didn't turn around to look at the USFT troops, but their scents suggested anger.

Of course they were all real military sorts. Unless ordered to fight—or otherwise given official approval—they'd hold it inside. And stew. And say "yes, sir" and "no, sir" and bite their tongues.

And potentially find underhanded ways of avenging their unit's honor.

Jason expected General Yarrow to respond, possibly even to scold his own Alpha Force member, to keep the peace.

General Myars beat him to it, stomping forward at the front of the meeting room. "Is that intended to be an accusation against anyone within USFT, Lieutenant? If so, you'd better be more specific—and have proof, not just insinuations."

"Sorry if I was out of line, sir." Colleen hung her head so that her light brown hair spilled forward over her face for a moment. But then she looked around again, a smile that looked rueful momentarily lighting her felinelike features. "I just meant that I would much prefer it if we weren't so—isolated here. Wouldn't it make more sense for our two units to mingle more?"

And was the fact that they hadn't before a factor in what had happened to General Yarrow—and to him, for that matter? Jason thought that was too simplified.

But sometimes the simplest answers were the right ones.

General Yarrow stepped forward, taking his place again beside the other general. "I think Lieutenant Hodell is right in what she just said." Yarrow was much too polite to hint that she might have been right before, too. "In fact, it's also my opinion that we all need to commingle more, and that has been my opinion for a while. That's one reason I came here, to Ft. Lukman, to set things right before we attempt to meld the two forces for an exercise—and then, if all goes well, in the field. So here's my order for tonight. I want each of you to pair up into groups of two members from your own unit, then hook yourselves up with one of the pairs from the other unit. You'll eat dinner together. Then later tonight, we'll conduct a preliminary exercise here at Ft. Lukman to see how your respective strengths can complement each other." He looked at General Myars. "Are you in agreement, General?"

The flabby officer said nothing for a moment, appearing as if he were trying not to throw up.

But then he answered, "Yes, General, let's give it a try."

And it would just be a try, Jason thought. He glanced

toward the woman beside him. Sara looked as skeptical as he felt.

"Then…everyone, dismissed," called General Yarrow.

Interesting, Jason thought as Yarrow immediately stomped into the crowd and confronted Lieutenant Hodell. The conversations around him were immediately too loud for him to focus in on that particular one, even with his superior hearing, but he'd have loved to catch what the general was saying to the lady shapeshifter.

Congratulating her for bringing the issue to a head—or reaming her for not staying in her place?

The conversation he did hear loudest, since the participants stood beside him, were among other officers in Alpha Force, including Sara. They stood near the front of the room, keeping their voices low.

"How should we pair up?" Sara directed the question to Drew.

His cuz's golden eyes narrowed. "I don't know whether General Yarrow intends that any of us do some shifting tonight to show these…fellow soldiers…who we really are and what we can do, but just in case I think we should have a shifter and nonshifter in each group. Not necessarily our usual group of shifters plus aides, although that would be all right, too."

In what seemed like moments, they'd chosen their groups: Drew with Jonas Truro, Simon Parran with Noel Chuma and so forth.

Was Sara intending to work with Colleen when the general was through with her?

Jason decided not to wait to find out. "Would you join up with me, ma'am?" he asked, trying to act as subservient a soldier as he could. "Unless, of course, your preference is to work with Lieutenant Hodell."

He caught the horror in her glance as she looked around

and saw that most of the other Alpha Forcers had decided on their partners. "I may just sit this out, Sergeant," she said.

"Whatever you say. Only…" He let his voice trail off.

"Only what?" Her lovely brow puckered.

"Well, for one thing, if we…" He leaned closer and whispered, "If we do shift tonight, all the usual aides already have paired up for this, so I'll need some help. And even if we don't—well, I'm really interested in how this works. How we get along with members of the USFT, see them strut their stuff, try to work out the camaraderie that General Yarrow's so eager to promote."

That got Sara's attention. Her blue-green eyes glanced upward, then glommed on to his as if she had been struck by what he said.

"Wouldn't you like to be part of that, too?" he pushed. "So you can report to the general how it all seems to work out. I'll bet he'd love to have an insider like you tell him about it."

Her smile was wry as she looked up into his face and shook her head slowly, as if in amusement. "You really know how to pull my chain, don't you, Sergeant?" He didn't like that she wasn't using his name, but in this location he definitely got why.

And her chain wasn't all he'd enjoyed pulling before.

Although, judging by the heat in her look, she didn't need a reminder.

"Okay," she said. "We're a team for this evening. An official Alpha Force team." She paused. "It might be good this way to have an officer in charge as well as a subordinate, to show whoever we get from the USFT how Alpha Force is an excellent, smoothly functioning military unit."

Jason read into what she said. In other words, he was to follow her lead. Her orders. Be a good member of the damned military and follow all the rules.

Not to mention showing the other guys what a great soldier he was.

Could he do it?

Hell, yes.

Especially if it got him extra brownie points with his cousin and the commanding general...

And Lieutenant Sara McLinder.

Chapter 14

This was becoming unnerving to Sara. But she could, and would, handle it. Even though it seemed contrary to most protocol she had learned since joining the military.

The protocol she had been comfortable with.

Right now she stood on the periphery of the improved areas of Ft. Lukman, beyond the buildings and at the edge of an outdoor parking lot—near where the forest within the base's boundaries began to grow.

Not far from where she'd gone her first night—and been confronted by that apparent pack of wolves.

The early-evening air was crisp, but her discomfort wasn't the result of her camo uniform not being warm enough. No, it was more internal.

Especially because she stood beside Jason, who was acting all soldier, all professional. Seeming even to enjoy it.

To enjoy being her partner in what was to come.

That only made her even more uneasy. And not just because being with him stoked her heated recollection of the time they had spent together. And how sexy he was. And how she lusted after him no matter how much she doused those thoughts with the iciness of reality checks.

That was much easier to ignore when she wasn't with him. But she'd been, and would continue to be, in his company a lot of the time she was here at Ft. Lukman.

She wasn't alone with him, of course. She was among all these teams of soldiers who had been ordered to work hard to get along together. Ranks didn't matter.

Their units did.

And as to members of Alpha Force, the preference was that one of the pair be a shapeshifter, and the other not.

She could have said no when Jason asked to team up with her. It was probably a bad idea.

Especially since she might have to not only watch him shift, but help him, too.

"All right, everyone." That was Major Drew Connell shouting to be heard above all conversations. From what Sara could tell, everyone was at least making an effort to achieve the camaraderie that they'd been ordered to do. "Here's what we'll do."

"My cousin likes to give orders," said Jason to the two members of the Ultra Special Forces Team who were now part of their team: Samantha Everly and Manning Breman. How odd—or contrived—was it that they'd been the ones Sara had talked to in the middle of the night to keep them from seeing Jason in wolf form?

But Sara liked that Jason was acting as he should—trying to make friends with these two.

Samantha looked offended, though, at the friendliness of a mere sergeant. She kept her chin raised, which made the brown hair clipped at the back of her neck seem to dig into her. Her arms were crossed over her full chest encased in her camo uniform, and her expression seemed… well, haughty.

To Jason's credit, he didn't appear to notice.

Manning, on the other hand, seemed all graciousness. The tall, pudgy guy laughed at what Jason said. "Isn't it a downer to have to report to your own relative?"

"Sssh." Samantha scowled at them both. "We need to hear this."

Sara said nothing. Samantha was right, but she didn't want to acknowledge that to the bitchy woman.

"First thing, we'll have our Ultra Special Forces Team members demonstrate their sniper proficiency," Drew continued. "For those of you who don't know, we have an outdoor shooting range near the fence at the back of this forest area."

Sara hadn't seen the area but figured that all shifting members of Alpha Force knew every inch of the base.

They'd have seen it while on the prowl.

"Let's head there, and we'll get a demo of the abilities of the USFT members. I've heard about them but really look forward to seeing it with my own eyes."

Drew motioned for everyone to follow. The closest to him, his own temporary team, consisted of his aide, Jonas Truro, as well as USFT members Rynton Tierney and Vera Swainey.

Sara noticed some of the other teams, too—around six in all. One consisted of Simon Parran and his aide while shifting, Noel Chuma, plus two USFT members Sara hadn't met yet. Simon's wife, Grace, wasn't included in this exercise.

Another team included Colleen Hodell and Rainey Jessop along with USFT member Cal Brown and another one Sara didn't know.

They all trudged through the woods. It was still light enough to see their way around the trees, though the area was blanketed in shadows.

The shifting Alpha Force members would have no problem. The sounds of everyone's footfalls on fallen leaves, and the twittering and shrieks of birds above, along with the smells enhanced by the sudden occupation of this area, would be child's play to their keen senses.

Sara made sure to keep up with teammate Jason. For safety's sake. Not because she was happy to be in his company.

When she tripped once over a fallen branch, she ignored her impulse to grab his hand and hold on. But he seized her arm and helped to keep her upright—before quickly letting go.

"Sorry, ma'am," he said, the perfect soldier—for the moment. "You okay?"

"Yes. Thank you." She managed a glance in the near darkness and caught his amused expression. He enjoyed the show that he and the others were putting on.

Sara couldn't make out much of the conversations of the groups heading through the forest. For a moment she wished, as she sometimes had before, that she had the senses of a shifter—utterly absurd. She hadn't even wanted to believe in them, and now that she did it wasn't logical to want to share any of their characteristics.

In a short while, they reached the far side of the forest. There, Sara saw a long fence that marked the perimeter of this part of Ft. Lukman. It wasn't standard chain link but was composed of some high, substantial-looking metal material.

Which made sense if this was a shooting range. She believed the other side of the fence was public parkland. No one would want any hiking civilians injured by unrestrained gunfire.

"Okay," Drew said loudly then turned to his new team member Rynton Tierney. "Please tell us again what your unit's special abilities are and explain what they'll demonstrate here."

Every team now stood in the clearing. Were they each getting along? Well, the members were all still alive and not shouting at each other, so Sara figured they were at least pretending to be buddies.

"This area is a good one, even at twilight," Rynton began. He explained again that most of the special nature of the USFT members involved their perfect—no, better than perfect—vision and accuracy in aiming weapons. "We've all been vetted to make sure we can do even more than an ordinary sniper—and you all know that the military's regular snipers are far from ordinary."

He went on to talk briefly about how the USFT members' accuracy in aiming and more had been recognized and lauded at the topmost echelons of the military—including its commander in chief, the president of the United States.

Then it was time for a demonstration.

The special M25 sniper rifles and ammo had already been brought to the area and secured there. Rynton opened the case that had been hidden at the edge of the woods. He also introduced a couple of privates who were members of USFT, and who had acted as sentries over the equipment.

For the next half hour, while the area grew darker as night fell, each USFT member provided a demonstration of his or her prowess, firing into wooden targets in the shape of people—and never missing the area of the heart or head, or wherever else they said they were aiming, even as each stepped back to be farther away in the blackening night. Then the targets were set to moving on their platforms. Fast. The perfection of the hits didn't waver.

It definitely was impressive.

But soon—maybe too soon—it was over.

Time for Alpha Force to conduct its own demonstration.

Sara wondered how Drew intended to carry this off. She knew he'd discussed it with General Yarrow, but she hadn't been included in the process.

She hoped that, for the sake of the modesty of Alpha

Force shifters, they weren't just supposed to drop their drawers and change in plain view.

Fortunately, that wasn't the plan.

"All members of the USFT, please stay here. For security's sake—and mostly because I don't think any of you really want too much information here—we'll head into the nearest building, then return in shifted form."

"What if we want to see it all?" demanded Rynton Tierney. "That's what General Myars expects."

"The shifting process is highly classified," Drew shot back. "We saw the results of your abilities and training. That's all we'll show you of ours."

He gestured for the members of Alpha Force to follow.

Sara was glad she was among them. But was she about to see a lot more nudity than Jason's?

If so, she'd handle it as she'd handled everything else in the military.

The nearest building, a storage depot, had already been organized for the night's activities. Drew's wife, Melanie, was there, and she had taken charge of the shifting elixir. There were plenty of vials as well as boxes of the lights used to trigger the shifters' changes.

Each Alpha Force team was directed into a different storage area. In each case, the Alpha Force members consisted of a shifter and an aide.

Which meant Sara would become Jason's aide.

Drew approached her before he went off with Jonas. "Are you okay with this? You've never acted as one of our aides before."

"But she did see our pack that first night," Jason reminded him. He looked oh so smug when he glanced toward her, but was the picture of military propriety when he faced his cousin.

"Yeah, and I gather she's also seen you shifting since then."

"Yes, sir." Sara nodded, not looking toward Jason. "It's fine. I can handle it, sir."

Poor choice of words, she realized immediately, and felt herself flush. What she could and would handle right now was the light, and Jason's clothing.

But she would be seeing a lot more than that which she might desire to handle...again.

Drew didn't need to know that. Fortunately, he either didn't catch her slip or didn't interpret it as she did. "Fine. If you're all right with it, that'll help a lot, since our members have already paired up. You understand that it's fairly simple. Jason drinks the elixir and removes his clothing, you shine the light that resembles the light of a full moon on him and he changes. You take charge of his clothes and return them to him when he changes back again. Because this is a limited exercise, he won't drink a lot of elixir and will shift back in a short period of time. Okay?"

"Yes, sir," Sara said. And it *was* okay.

She would make sure of it.

And keep her damned, easily ignitable lust under control.

Jason had to hand it to Sara. She did everything just right.

Which was too bad. He saw her staring only momentarily at his private parts when he stripped after taking the elixir in the small room to which they'd been directed.

"Are you ready, Sergeant?" she demanded while he stood there in all his naked glory.

Just knowing she was there, this woman with whom he had so recently made memorable and magnificent love, made his cock stand up even larger and harder than usual.

Damn, he wished he wasn't about to shift so he could take Sara into his arms once more.

But that wasn't to be.

"I'm ready, Lieutenant." He drew out the last word as if he made fun of it. He watched as she pulled out the light and turned it on.

Before she aimed it at him, he couldn't resist. He flexed himself down below, and had the pleasure of seeing her eyes widen, her lips part, her body tense—but only for a moment....

That was when his shifting started and all things within him began to change.

Jason accompanied his pack members as they all stalked into the lobby of the storage building—all shifters within Alpha Force who were on duty on base. That included the sole feline member, Colleen, now a cougar.

The rest, including Jason, were all in wolf form. The other feline members of Alpha Force and its sole avian member were not present.

Together the pack walked, one by one, out the door, their human assistants following.

Outside, in darkness illuminated only by dim lights attached to the building, waited the members of the other unit now at the base, the ones who had perfect aim with sophisticated weaponry.

Did any wish they had their guns on them now to aim at the wild animals who faced them, waiting for their reactions?

Some came forward, including their current officer in charge since their general was observing from a distance with General Yarrow while this exercise took place.

Captain Rynton Tierney drew closest, even put his hand

out to touch the canine at the lead, the most alpha wolf present, Drew Connell.

Jason tensed, ready to spring to his cousin's defense if needed.

But Tierney just shook his head as he stroked the wolf like a dog. "This is amazing." Then he looked beyond the pack and the cougar toward the human aides who had followed them out. "If it's real. I've seen the dogs here at Ft. Lukman who look a lot like these animals."

"They're cover dogs. And have you seen the cover cat? I have."

That was Sara's voice from behind him. She was speaking up for Alpha Force, this woman who hadn't wanted to accept the reality of its existence.

Jason's human consciousness was highly enhanced by the special elixir Drew had developed. He knew what he was hearing.

And if he could have, he would have turned to thank, and congratulate, Sara McLinder. Maybe even kiss her in appreciation.

But he would have to wait for that.

For now, he waited to follow Drew's lead.

Sara wasn't surprised that Rynton Tierney didn't simply accept her answer: that these shifted Alpha Force members were exactly what they seemed and that cover dogs that resembled the wolves remained in the kennel area. Colleen's domestic cat that looked like a small cougar remained in her quarters.

As a result of his skepticism, Rynton sent a couple of USFT members to the building housing the kennels. The shifted Alpha Force members could start their planned demonstration, anyway, while that part of the cover story was confirmed.

Sara knew what else was in that building, downstairs and hidden away. The USFT troops didn't need to visit there. As a result, she requested that Noel Chuma, Simon Parran's aide today, accompany them. He'd be able to ensure they saw what they were after without heading below ground level to the highly classified and critical lab area.

With Noel gone, Sara would keep careful watch over the shifted wolf that was Simon as well as her own current charge, Jason.

Jason. In wolf form, he was sleek and gorgeous and alert, staying by her side, at least for now. Sexy? No, not this way…but somehow the idea of his having two such different personas didn't turn her libido off, not even now.

All Alpha Force and USFT members went outside together and stood in the pale glow cast from lights at the top of the building. USFT Lieutenant Cal Brown, on the four-member joint team that included Colleen, seemed particularly interested in the sleek feline, talking a lot to the cougar as if she were human—which she was. He goaded her, urging her to find prey within the darkened woods and go in for the kill as her real feline counterparts would do in the wild.

Unsurprisingly, the cougar growled and roared. But to her credit, she didn't attack the man who taunted her.

Sara marveled at the situation. She'd have heard something from General Yarrow if there'd even been any similar kinds of exercises between Alpha Force and other military units. She had heard of only one—and although she'd not been informed of all the details, she'd gathered that the humans had interacted with canines they hadn't been informed were shapeshifters.

Previously, she hadn't believed they were, either.

Soon it was time for the demonstration that had been planned in advance by the Alpha Force members. First the nonshifters gave a couple of easy commands—things that perhaps even real wolves could be taught, but only with time and patience. The idea was to prove that these creatures understood language and could react to it appropriately—better than a true wolf would do, even after training.

"Use your left paw and scratch at the bark of the nearest oak tree," Jonas Truro instructed his charge, Drew Connell in wolf form. The rest of the shifted creatures were to sit and wait, which they did.

Of course Drew did as commanded. Sara had been told that all shifting members of Alpha Force had the consciousness of their human form while changed, thanks to the elixir that Drew had blended and continued to upgrade.

Next she told Simon Parran to find the tote bag she had brought along and take the bag of rawhide dog chews out of it. She'd left it behind a bush near the storage building, and he found it with no trouble.

She offered one to each of the wolf shifters. Most, but not all, accepted the treats. Each looked at her as if in thanks. This wasn't, of course, anthropomorphism. These animals truly were human some of the time.

But they were wild creatures in more than looks, too. After all the other, easier exercises had been performed, Rynton said, "I want to give an order, too." He didn't ask if it was okay. Instead, he approached Jason.

Which made Sara stiffen. Would he perform well? She didn't want her primary charge for this night to be the one who somehow ruined the fragile détente between the two units.

On the other hand, with his contrary, sometimes antimilitary attitude and offbeat sense of humor, he might decide to act like…well, a real wolf.

"Go catch some prey. I don't care what it is. A rodent, a bird—but act like what you look like. Got it?"

Sara watched the face of the wolf that was Jason. She tried to read the expression but couldn't.

Then he raced off into the forest.

The entire crowd stood watching. At least a few of them stood. Some Alpha Force shifters sat on their haunches as they followed Jason with their eyes.

Would he come back?

Their attention was interrupted by the return of the guys who'd been sent to check on the cover animals. Noel Chuma was with them.

They approached Rynton Tierney, who stood with Vera Swainey and Manning Breman.

"Yep, there were a bunch of dogs in those kennels, Captain," said one of the USFT privates. "Want to see the pictures we took?"

He did, looking at the illuminated photos on the digital camera proffered by the soldier. He passed them around, too.

He then looked at Sara. "So those cover dogs do exist, along with the…shifters we've got here."

"You still don't believe?" she challenged him.

Maybe they'd have to allow at least this man, or perhaps General Myars, to watch a shift no matter how much violation of privacy that caused.

As long as they didn't take pictures….

That was when a wolf leaped out of the forest, into the sparse light near where they all remained, waiting.

He approached Captain Tierney. There was something in his mouth—and Sara shuddered. It looked like a rat.

She expected him to place the dead creature on the ground in front of the captain's feet.

Instead, the wolf that was Jason got up close and personal with Rynton Tierney, his filled muzzle just over the guy's shoe. He stuck his nose between Rynton's shoe and his pants leg.

And let go of the still-living rat.

It scampered up Rynton's leg inside his camo trousers. That was obvious by the bulge that moved upward.

Rynton shouted, "Get it off me! Get it off!"

As some of his underlings raced to get to him to help, Sara watched the wolf sit down. Raise his muzzle in the air. A howl that sounded full of pleasure soon filled the air. And when it stopped, Sara would have sworn that the wolf was smiling.

Chapter 15

It wasn't long after Jason's return with the rat that everyone—the humans, at least—agreed it was time for the Alpha Force shifters to change back.

"You're still not going to let us watch, even after that nasty joke?" Rynton's voice was harsh. He hadn't stopped scowling since his minions captured and dealt with the rodent he'd demanded be brought back as proof of cognition by a shifted wolf.

After all that, he still didn't believe?

"Alpha Force's position is that no one outside the unit can be permitted to watch a shift, Captain," reminded Jonas Truro.

Sara had an idea, though, that should satisfy even the most skeptical USFT member. "We each assisted our charges in separate rooms before. I don't believe they have alternate entrances or exits, so you could stand in the hallway and watch them enter in animal form and come out as humans."

"That's better than nothing," Rynton grumped.

As a result, they all trooped back into the storage building. Sara noted that the cougar that was Colleen Hodell was followed by Cal Brown, who appeared much too interested in her. Fortunately, her aide Rainey stuck with them.

In a short while, they were all in separate, closed rooms

once more. The walls appeared to be thick, and were fairly soundproof.

The shifters often made noises during the process that the USFT personnel didn't need to hear.

The empty elixir vials and lights had already been gathered up by some Alpha Force nonshifters and taken back to the underground lab. The storage rooms, therefore, contained only the usual shelves and boxes, plus backpacks holding the shifters' clothing.

Sara entered the room where they'd been before with only the slightest trepidation. She steeled herself to see the shift. And Jason. Naked.

She would act totally professional.

She shut the door behind Jason the wolf. "Are you ready?"

She still wasn't exactly certain what precipitated the shift back to human form. It had to do with the amount of elixir that was drunk, but apparently, the shifter also had some choice.

Jason's response was first to look at her. Then he started turning in a circle, like a dog outside tamping down imaginary grass to prepare the perfect place for its eliminations. But in moments he stopped and lay down.

That was when the shift began. His limbs began to elongate. His fur receded into his body, which grew. His muzzle lifted into the air as he moaned softly, then started to disappear and morph into his facial features.

The rest of his body began to change, too. His external canine organs became human. Sexual organs. Sexy as Sara remembered.

She closed her eyes. He should have privacy.

And she needed to regain control over her libido.

"Sara." It had only been a minute or two that she'd

looked away, with her eyes closed. The word wasn't enunciated quite right, but the voice was arguably human.

She turned and looked.

There was Jason. In all his naked glory.

She quickly moved her gaze from his genital area to his face, then hurried across the room to her backpack. Damn! She should have had his clothes ready.

Or had she subconsciously awaited this moment, prolonging her ability to look at his firm, toned—hot—nude body once more?

"I'll have your things to you in just a minute," she called.

She extracted his camo uniform and underwear, then turned toward him.

He was standing there, all human. His broad shoulders were hunched a bit and he slumped, his head forward, as he seemed to catch his breath.

But oh, what a view.

She didn't even try to stop herself from looking. At least he wasn't meeting her gaze.

But if—when—he did? They couldn't take the time to make love again. Not now. No matter how much she suddenly ached to do so.

People were outside, perhaps counting the minutes until they emerged. Other Alpha Force members might already have completed their shifts and left their rooms.

Frustration or not, she strode forward, holding out his clothes. For a moment, his golden eyes met hers. He smiled…but it disappeared into a serious, formal gaze.

Still undressed, he took his proffered clothing and stepped back. "Permission to get dressed, ma'am?" he asked, not sounding at all teasing. He even saluted.

"Of course, soldier." She saluted back. Then she added softly, "Jason, I liked the way you acted out there with

Captain Tierney. And I like even better…well, the way you look now."

He merely blinked, said, "Thank you, ma'am," and turned around.

Hurt, Sara watched from behind as Jason started donning his clothes.

It was one of the hardest things Jason had ever done: turning his back on an obviously sexually aroused Sara McLinder. Pretending he didn't care. That, this time, he was the one who observed military protocol.

But he'd had to do it. No way could they satisfy their lust right now. And yes, he felt lust just by looking into Sara's interested and provoking expression.

Just that look had caused his erection to harden even more, but he tucked it into his pants.

He wanted Sara. Again. More. Often.

But that was foolish. She had apparently accepted, at least on some level, that he was a shifter. Yet the reality was that they had no future together. Getting up close and really personal more than they already had today could only lead to further frustration, and maybe even heartache.

He needed to try to find another noncommissioned officer who might accept who and what he was. Maybe even a private. Someone who was already a shifter? Unlikely in the military unless she was already in Alpha Force, but who knew?

So far, the only women he'd had relationships with had been near home. Nonmilitary, of course. Nothing serious, just companionship and sex. None had been shifters, so some of the fun had been in keeping his true status from them.

He hadn't regretted leaving any of them behind when he'd had to join Alpha Force.

He'd finished donning his clothes. Now he turned around.

Sara must have been watching him. She suddenly swung away and seemed to examine some of the shelves along the wall of this storeroom.

"Thanks, Sara," he said softly. His body moving almost involuntarily, he approached her. Touched her arm.

She pivoted, and suddenly she was in his embrace. He moved so his mouth was hard upon hers. Her arms went around his neck, pulling him down, closer, as her lips opened for him, her tongue speared out to play with his, and her soft, supple, altogether sexy body pressed close against him. Really close...down below.

He groaned, rubbing harder against her. Aching to remove those clothes again.

He was suddenly startled by a knocking on the door. "Hey, cuz, you shifted back yet?" yelled Drew.

Sara pulled away, her expression horrified. "We have to get out of here," she said. "I didn't... I mean, we shouldn't..."

"You're absolutely right, Lieutenant," Jason made himself say as coolly as possible. "Time to put all of this behind us."

They all were to return to the assembly room after the exercise was complete.

Sara stopped in General Yarrow's office on the way to report how things had gone from her perspective before walking to the meeting with him.

She planned to tell him all he needed to know including, with regard to Jason, only that he had successfully shifted in a timely way, had shown himself in wolf form to the USFT members and had then shifted back again. Oh, and yes, the general was sure to hear about that little prank Jason had pulled with the rat on Rynton Tierney—but the captain had asked for it.

Sara smiled briefly at the recollection as she seated herself in a chair facing the general's desk.

But no sense revealing any of her thoughts and emotions—and definitely not her lust—relating to Jason.

"I think it was successful, sir," she told Greg Yarrow. "At least the USFT members appeared to accept the idea of shifting, although Captain Tierney made it clear he'd like to watch a shift for verification."

"What do you think about that?" His wide brow furrowed as he regarded her from behind his desk. He looked tired, and Sara wondered what had gone on during his interaction with General Myars while the joint mission between Alpha Force and USFT members played out.

"I'm aware that's against the protocol established by Alpha Force—that only unit members are supposed to have access while someone is shifting. I also know there have been some exceptions now and then, like me. And—"

"You're not an exception."

"Well, I'm not really a member of Alpha Force." Yet she felt now as if she had become one. She believed in, had seen, shifting. Wanted to learn more about how Alpha Force would be used in actual military deployments.

Especially the one being considered in conjunction with USFT.

The general smiled. "Sure you are, just as much as I am. You're my right arm, and though I'm not a shifter or aide, I'm close enough. That gives you standing with the unit, too."

She couldn't help grinning back. "Guess so, sir." She hesitated, then added, "Thanks, Greg."

"Oh, you'll pay for it, Sara. In fact, I'd like you to set up a lunch tomorrow for both units together—thirty people or so. In Mary Glen. Everyone'll be sleeping in tomorrow since it's so late now, so lunch will be better than breakfast.

There's a restaurant there—I don't remember the name—but it should be able to accommodate us, even on short notice. Ask one of the local Alpha Force members. They'll know. In fact, your shifting charge Jason Connell should be a good resource for that."

"I'll check with him first, sir." Sara hoped that the blush she felt creeping up her cheeks wasn't visible in the daylight of the general's office. "But just to clarify. We still have no intention of allowing any USFT members to actually watch a shift occur, right?"

"Did any of them doubt the reality of it after your exercise?"

"No one seemed to, especially after the human cognition of the shifted animals was verified." She described how Jason had stuck the rat up Tierney's leg.

The general laughed. "I might get chided about that from Myars, so it's a good thing you told me. But was that the only thing that gave them an indication shifting was real?"

"No, sir. Even though we didn't let them watch any shifting, they checked to make sure that the cover animals remained in the kennel areas when the shifted wolves appeared."

That caused the general to frown again. "And someone went with them? No one got down into the lab area?"

"That's right, sir. And afterward, they watched animals go into closed rooms with their aides, and only people exit from them after shifting." Sara hesitated. "You don't really trust those USFT personnel, do you, sir?" She didn't—not after what had happened to the general and his car. And the scratches on the door down to the lab. A break-in attempt? Not that anyone in USFT had been proven involved. Not yet.

"I trust them to do an excellent job doing what they do best—perfect vision and marksmanship to assist in the joint assignment we'll have with them if all goes well." The general was standing now. "But I really don't understand their attitude toward Alpha Force. Skepticism about shifting? That might have made sense before, but now they've seen enough to buy into its reality. And there appears to be on-going antagonism that I've not been able to nail down any answers about. Maybe this latest exercise will help dispel it. I certainly hope so." He turned and looked down at the computer on his desk, shifting the mouse. "It's time. We'd better get off to our meeting."

Sara couldn't help it. She scanned the crowd in the assembly room as she entered with the general, looking for Jason.

She had an important question to ask him, she reminded herself. She glanced at her wristwatch. She needed to find out what restaurant the general had been talking about to ensure she could line up a place for the units to have a joint lunch the next day.

Once again, Alpha Force seemed to have taken over the first few rows, with the USFT members planted in the rear. One good thing Sara noted, though, was that there were at least a few conversations in which members of both units participated. Those folks banded together along the side of the assembly room.

In fact, she was able to join one of the groups, since Jason was standing with Vera Swainey, Cal Brown, Colleen Hodell and others. They all appeared to be chatting amicably. Some held bottles of water from a case that had been left near the door.

Maybe the night's exercises really did turn the page on their attitudes.

Sara wended her way along the crowded aisle, overhearing brief snatches of conversations including jokes from

USFT members about renting an old version of *The Wolf Man* movie, and promises to teach Alpha Force members some tricks of the USFT shooting abilities if they'd teach them how to shapeshift.

Sara had heard that request before occasionally coming from some nonshifting aides of Alpha Force, but she'd also heard it wasn't possible.

She finally reached Jason's group but stood on its periphery, listening. Jason was describing some of the most unusual and fun things he claimed to have done while shifted. He looked amazingly good, his dark, silver-flecked hair slightly longer than when she'd first met him, his strong hands waving in punctuation while he talked...and his amazingly sexy body moving in emphasis, too. Sara listened to what he said, interested in his description of howling at an outdoor sign not far from Ft. Lukman that depicted a full moon to advertise some kind of beer, and playing tug-of-war while shifted, with Shadow, using as a toy a car rug he'd taken out of a military vehicle he was fixing.

"You mean sticking a rat up our CO's leg wasn't the most fun and unusual thing you've done?" Cal asked. The muscular guy stood straight and looked serious, as if he was attempting not to scowl at Jason. But then he broke into a large grin. "Never seen anything like that before."

"Well, I admit it was creative." Jason nodded. "But now I'll have to think of something to top that. Anyone want to volunteer for me to experiment on?"

"Hey, how about us?" demanded Samantha, a smile on her face. "I've heard rumors that the secret formula you shifters drink could turn us into shifters, too."

"Where did you hear that?" Jason demanded.

But Samantha just continued to grin, raising her brows. She had a bottle of water in her hand and she raised it, as if in a toast. "Here's to giving it a try someday."

"No," said Jason with as cold a voice as Sara had ever heard from him. "You won't. That's against orders, and whatever you've heard is wrong."

It was time for Sara to break in. "Hey, sorry to interrupt, but I have a question for you, Jason." As the others looked at her, she said, "Not sure yet if I'm supposed to let everyone know, but we're all getting together for a group lunch tomorrow. Assuming I get the info I need."

At the edge of the crowd, Sara explained. "General Yarrow said you could tell me the name of a restaurant in Mary Glen that can accommodate a group this size on short notice." She looked into Jason's golden eyes as she spoke and felt drawn in. She would get lost in them if she allowed herself to.

She looked down, drawing her smartphone from her pocket as both a diversion and a way to find contact information and location of whatever eatery Jason mentioned.

"I've only eaten there once, since everyone's favorite place is the Mary Glen Diner, but try Danny's Delicious Café," he said. "They're open twenty-four hours so you should be able to make the reservation now."

"Isn't that a new chain out of Baltimore?"

"Yeah, I think so. They're expanding."

The conversation was so mundane that Sara longed to say something to Jason to remind him she'd been there for him earlier, watched him shift, watched his mesmerizing, naked body...

What was she doing? He was acting completely professional while her mind exploded with everything she didn't dare think, didn't dare feel, ever again.

"Thank you," she said formally, moving her finger on her phone screen to locate the restaurant's listing. "I'll call them now." But she couldn't help asking, as Jason turned to walk toward the front of the room, "I don't suppose those rumors about the elixir are true, are they?" Not that she wanted to try to become a shifter.

"Of course not. And those rumors have to stop. I'll make sure Drew's aware of this nonsense."

She hesitated. "Will you be joining the group for lunch?"

She'd asked for it. Even so, a shiver went through her as he turned, said, "Oh, you can count on it," then winked. Again. The usual, carefree Jason back in charge.

Her insides turned momentarily to hot, flowing lava.

She made herself stare back at her phone and quickly exit the room to make the reservation.

Praying that no one else had noticed that damnably sexy wink.

Chapter 16

The meeting was fairly uneventful, but Jason understood why General Yarrow wanted to hold it, even this late at night. It allowed members of both units to suck up to their commanding generals and show how well they'd followed orders earlier and were now the best of friends.

Jason wondered if anyone was dumb enough to believe that. On the other hand, there seemed to be a bit more camaraderie between them now.

He himself was getting along well with some of the USFT members, now that he had managed, in an excusable way, to humiliate their captain.

He remained in the crowded room listening to the generals congratulate themselves and their subordinates, as if all ill will had now evaporated like steam from a hot spring. But he knew the heat between the two groups could rise again at any moment.

He still wasn't sure why.

He'd glanced often toward the door where Sara had gone to make her phone call. Was she using the lunch reservation for tomorrow as an excuse to stay away indefinitely tonight?

No. There she was. She slipped inside and stood near the door. The meeting was wrapping up, anyway. Both generals had gotten in their thanks and made it clear to their troops that what had been started tonight would be continued. That was an order.

As they were all dismissed, everyone stood and streamed toward the door. Sara moved out of the way.

He only wanted to say good-night. That was what he told himself. She'd have plenty of takers wanting to walk her to the BOQ, and it wouldn't be right to join them.

But she was apparently waiting for General Yarrow. The two top guys were among the last to leave, and Sara was still standing there when they, and Jason, approached.

"Did that place work out?" Jason asked before the generals reached her.

"Yes, it did. Thanks." As Yarrow and Myars joined her, Sara told them about the reservations she'd made for lunch tomorrow. Both gave her formal military kudos, and the three left the auditorium.

Jason followed. The generals were wrapped up in conversation as they walked through the building's lobby and out the door.

Good. That gave Jason the opportunity he wanted to say a friendly good-night to Sara.

"Same to you." She smiled, then looked beyond the generals where some of the USFT members stood in a group, talking.

"I'd like your help tomorrow morning, before lunch," Jason heard himself blurt, his voice low.

She turned back, surprise on her lovely face. "Are you shifting in daylight?"

"Oh, no, not that kind of help. Not about cars, either."

She smiled, and he suspected that would have been her next question.

"No," he continued, "I'm planning on a training session with Shadow and a couple other cover dogs. You worked well with us before, and I'd like to have you join us. Okay?"

"Sure," she said. "What time?"

* * *

It probably was a bad idea, Sara thought as she turned her back on Jason and joined the nearby USFT members to walk to the BOQ with them. Had they been waiting for her? Unlikely.

Drat, she thought a minute later. Cal Brown had probably gotten them to hang around for her. At least the way the large guy joined her immediately, as if claiming her company, suggested he'd wanted to talk to her.

Flirt with her?

Fortunately, Colleen joined them when they reached the main sidewalk. She started talking animatedly to Cal and Manning Breman, asking what they now thought of shapeshifting, and didn't they prefer cougars to wolves?

They all just laughed. Sara hung back a little, letting Colleen handle the requisite camaraderie.

She wondered how far behind them Jason was.

She knew better than to look.

She did, however, hesitate for a moment, pulling her phone from her pocket as if checking something. She surreptitiously glanced behind them—only to see one person not far behind.

Walking alone.

When he stepped beneath one of the lights along the walkway she confirmed what she already knew. It was Jason.

She felt a surge of warmth. Of knowing she was protected without needing protection.

She looked forward to that dog training session tomorrow.

When Sara finally got to bed that night, she figured she would sleep well. And probably would have if her phone hadn't rung.

"Sara? Sorry to call so late, but it's Colleen. Can I ask a favor?"

"Sure," Sara replied hesitantly. What could she possibly want at this hour?

But five minutes later, Sara had put her uniform back on and hurried down the dimly lit hall. Colleen opened the door to her apartment almost before Sara knocked.

"I really appreciate this," she said. "But Rainey has an upset stomach—maybe too much excitement today. And even though I just shifted back a short while ago after our exercise—well, I'm just so restless I need to do it again. Since my usual aide can't help, I hope you don't mind my bothering you."

The cat Puka came out to greet Sara but didn't stay in Colleen's small living room very long. She disappeared back into the bedroom.

Near the door, Colleen had set one of the backpacks that had become so familiar to Sara since she had begun working with Alpha Force. It probably contained a vial of the all-important elixir, plus a special light.

"I just need for you to come outside with me while I shift. I won't stay in cougar form long and I can shift back by myself, but I've never shifted with the elixir on my own."

"No problem." Sara figured it would be similar to watching Jason shift. Interesting, too, but in a very different way.

Sure enough, she found Colleen's shift fascinating.

Colleen stripped first and hid her clothes behind a rock in the part of the forest within Ft. Lukman where they'd gone. "I'll be able to find these here myself when I shift back," Colleen told Sara.

She'd already drunk some elixir. Now Sara shone the special moonlike light on her and watched as the woman began to writhe and grow tawny hair all over as she shifted into cougar form.

She soon gave a nod of her wild feline head toward Sara, then ran off into the woods.

As they'd discussed, Sara also left the backpack with Colleen's clothes. Had she really been needed here to help Colleen?

Maybe not, but the feline Alpha Force member apparently felt better having someone assisting with the shift.

And it gave Sara yet another perspective on shapeshifting.

Tired that night, Jason had fallen asleep in his tiny quarters nearly immediately. It had been late, so he hadn't even gone to the kennel to bring Shadow back. Of course, he'd be with the dog in the morning.

When he woke, he nearly sprang from bed in anticipation of the day. And it wasn't only because he'd have Shadow with him.

Hell, yesterday had had some pretty fine moments. Like shifting again in front of Sara.

And sticking a rat up a superior officer's leg with impunity. What a kick!

Now he would spend more time with Sara in a place that lent itself to having fun.

Maybe even get her sexuality stoked again.

He showered then dressed in yet another camo uniform. He was getting damned tired of looking like everyone else.

Welcome to the military.

On the other hand, Sara didn't seem to mind what he wore.

Although if he wasn't mistaken, she much preferred when he didn't wear anything.

Well, someday he'd go back to fixing cars for civilians and wear what he wanted. But how could he give up the Alpha Force shifting elixir with all its benefits?

Could he do it if it meant more time with Sara?

Yeah, like she'd pay any attention to him if he left the military.

Now it was still early. He met no one else on his quick walk to the cafeteria. There, he grabbed a steak and egg sandwich and coffee to go—after sharing a quick, meaningless, but enjoyable session of sexual innuendo with the female cashier.

He had something to do before going to meet Sara.

He headed first to the base's main garage. There, he checked the computer to make sure he wasn't falling behind on work on the rest of the base's vehicles. He had some oil changes to accomplish within the next couple of days, but the car washes and other trivial matters could wait.

Next he went to check on the remains of General Yarrow's Jeep—again. Some feds were finally scheduled to come to conduct an official investigation, so he wanted to make sure he'd done all he wanted to first.

The hulk was still locked in a secure area, although guards were no longer assigned 24/7. In fact, no one was here now.

And when Jason tried the door before inserting his copy of the key, it was already unlocked.

He froze momentarily, listening, in case someone had just preceded him inside. Even with his acute hearing, he heard nothing, so he slammed open the door and flicked on the lights.

No movement inside, no scent of an intruder. The remains of the general's car were still there, perched on the same spot on the floor, a sorry-looking sight to someone who revered automobiles as much as Jason did.

But there was more: a hint of an odor similar to whatever had started Jason coughing during his attempt to search for clues. It wasn't strong, but it still repelled him. Even so, he wouldn't let it control him.

He strode into the room. Approached the metallic remains still decorated with black ashes.

And was surprised to see that someone had set up an AK-47 aimed challengingly at the car, as if adding a new threat—or taunting and ridiculing the sorry attempt at an investigation that had already been conducted.

He checked. The weapon was even loaded.

Where had it come from? Was this a statement that one of the people Alpha Force already suspected actually had been the perpetrator—a member of USFT?

That was absurd. Then was it an attempt to frame the USFT?

If so, by whom?

Or was this actually a ploy by members of that unit to make it appear they were being framed…an attempt to further hide the fact that they truly had done something to set the general's car on fire?

Jason didn't know.

But what Jason did know was that it made no sense.

And that he had to notify his cuz. Immediately.

Though tired, Sara got up on time and reached the Ft. Lukman kennels at exactly 0900, the time Jason had said to meet him.

Jason, however, wasn't there.

Noel Chuma was, though. The sergeant who acted as aide to a couple of Alpha Force shifters seemed right at home with the dogs. He was already working with Zarlon, Marshall Vincenzo's cover dog, in a paved inside courtyard area, not far from the lush kennel areas where the dogs lived inside the building.

"Good morning," Sara called to Noel, who was using

treats to encourage Zarlon to walk on his hind legs as a human would. Probably a good skill for a cover dog to know, Sara thought.

"Hi, Sara." Noel gave a signal with his right hand to Zarlon, and the shepherdlike dog lay down and rolled over. "Are you just visiting, or is there something I can do for you?"

"Neither—but I'd like to join you with Shadow." Jason had told her he hadn't come for his dog last night.

Sara went to the kennel run, said hi to all the cover dogs present and patted a few heads. She then snapped a leash onto Shadow's collar. He seemed happy to see her, nuzzling her in greeting then ready to run.

"I don't know what all Shadow can do," Sara said after rejoining Noel. "And though I've seen one training session, I don't want to get the signals wrong."

"Here, let's trade." Noel handed Sara Zarlon's leash and said, "Sit," giving a hand signal that looked familiar to Sara. Then he started putting Shadow through his paces—including getting him to walk on his hind legs the way Zarlon had done.

"Hey, that's me over there," said a voice near Sara. She had her back toward the wall of the courtyard and had been watching the training so intently that she hadn't noticed it when Jason edged his way in.

She suspected, by the way he showed up practically behind her, that he'd planned it that way.

"You mean that dog who happens to resemble what you sometimes look like?" she said without looking toward him. "Nope, I don't buy it. He's much better behaved than you are in either form."

Jason laughed briefly, then paused. "Sorry I'm late," he said. "Something came up."

The sudden hardness in his tone startled her and she

turned to look at him. There was an expression on his handsome face that she couldn't read.

"What's wrong?" she asked.

"I'll tell you when we're finished here. In fact, maybe you can help me figure out how to play it when we're all together with our USFT buddies at lunch. One of them, at least, may owe me an explanation—not to mention Drew and General Yarrow. I just had a brief, unplanned meeting with both of them."

"Really?" But Sara couldn't ask more questions then. Noel approached with Shadow and challenged Jason to a doggy duel—Zarlon against Jason's cover dog. Which, in the hands of the right trainer, performed best?

Jason accepted the challenge, leaving Sara damned curious about what he'd been talking about.

But she had to admit—only to herself—that she liked his moves while working with the dogs. The two men looked as if they were training the canines for agility in the high-ceilinged internal courtyard, weaving their own forms between the obedient, nimble dogs.

Surprisingly, a few other people joined Sara's observation, including Colleen—who didn't look at all tired after her busy night—and Jock of Alpha Force, and Rynton, Vera and Cal of the USFT. They clapped and cheered along with her as Jason and Noel put the dogs through their paces.

Presumably the USFT members were welcome here, even when joint exercises weren't being conducted, as long as they were in the presence of Alpha Force members—upstairs, at least. But not in the highly classified Alpha Force laboratories below.

Cal stood close to Sara. Too close.

"Do you like dogs?" she asked brightly, taking a step away. "Aren't they wonderful?"

"I'd like to see those shifters do the same kinds of tricks."

Cal sounded condescending, strange coming from a man who always resembled a simian. Apparently, he hadn't decided to obey the orders requiring camaraderie. Or maybe he'd be friendly without sincerity.

In either event, Sara moved toward Colleen. "How are you this morning?" she asked to make conversation.

For an instant, Colleen looked startled, her feline eyes narrow in her pale face. Then glancing toward Sara, she smiled. "Just fine, despite not having a good night's sleep. I got some rest, though, and it was enough."

Soon the exercise ended. "Okay," Jason said, approaching Sara. "Shadow's telling me in canine-ese that it's time for a walk. Care to join us? Oh, in case you're wondering, I can communicate with other canines while shifted but not in any language. I teach them to follow commands in English. Gestures, too, just like everyone else does."

Feeling glad to get away from the others for a while, Sara agreed to go along. Aloud she said, though, to make it clear that the walk fit within the parameters of her job, "We have some plans to discuss for General Yarrow. This'll be a good time."

"Yes, ma'am," Jason said, and she half expected him to salute.

Once they had left the kennel building, they strolled along the sidewalk in one of the more remote areas of the base. Jason held Shadow's lead.

"So tell me," Sara said. She was horrified to hear what he described about the latest issue regarding General Yarrow's vehicle. "Can we go look at it? I want to see what you're talking about."

"Sure. I told Drew and General Yarrow before. The sentries are going to be back again, although I don't know what good they can do."

"They can at least make sure that no one uses those guns and ammo," Sara said.

"Or brings any more."

They walked in silence, taking their time as Shadow sniffed their path and occasionally stopped to lift his leg.

After one such occurrence, Sara stopped and found herself smiling into Jason's twinkling golden eyes. "No need to ask. Yes, I do such things while shifted. I've got enough of my human consciousness, though, to do it in private."

She laughed. And felt drawn in by the intensity of Jason's gaze as it turned serious. And hot.

Hot enough for her to consider tearing her clothes off on this cool Maryland morning. There were no other people around.

But that was absurd. And Sara quickly reminded herself of the silent promise she had made. She looked away, but not as fast as she'd have liked.

"Jason, I'm sorry," she said softly. "I just can't—"

"I get it. Me, neither. It's too unmilitary, and I've made my choice to stick this out for now, at least. So…let's talk about cars."

They had reached the garage where General Yarrow's damaged vehicle was housed. On their way to that area, Sara half heard Jason's description of which kinds of parked cars they passed that he knew, from working on them, were the best.

But Sara couldn't help thinking about what else they had done, in Jason's own car, in that parking facility.

Chapter 17

Danny's Delicious Café was a family-oriented restaurant with a variety of foods. Its theme was deliciousness, and its walls were covered with posters of close-ups of all kinds of food served there—from soups to desserts.

Those posters included entrées, too—and Sara was glad to note, for the sake of the Alpha Force shifters, that some were delicious-looking steaks.

She was glad she'd called the night before, since there was a separate dining room at the rear that had been reserved just for the military group. It was lunchtime, and the rest of the place was crowded.

As Sara walked in with General Yarrow, others from Ft. Lukman behind them—all in camo uniforms—she felt some curious gazes on them. She also saw some people—patrons and servers alike—stop talking to one another, then start up again quickly.

Drew, behind Sara and the general, whispered, "There are still a lot of rumors around this town about werewolves and their supposed connection with Ft. Lukman."

"I heard something about that," Sara responded softly, dropping back to talk to Drew. "But I thought it was the result of some bad guys who were caught, and the town was set straight about the…false origin of those rumors."

"Not exactly," Drew said drolly.

No one had to mention that those rumors, though supposedly dispelled by the capture of someone who'd been using them for his own benefit, just happened to be true. And Sara continued to recognize that a person from Mary Glen could be causing the turmoil at Ft. Lukman...although getting onto the base, with all its security, would be problematic.

Sara had already had a few minutes to speak with the general and Drew, along with Jason—who followed them—about what had most recently occurred with General Yarrow's destroyed car.

The federal investigators were now finally rescheduled for a day or two away. Drew had previously dispatched some trusted Alpha Force members who wouldn't join them for lunch to photograph the newly besieged vehicle then collect the weapons and ammo to be checked for fingerprints.

Not that anyone believed whoever put them there would be so careless.

Since General Yarrow had arranged for this lunch, he got to determine who would sit where. "Join up with the people on your teams from yesterday," he said. "Since these tables seat eight, each should accommodate two of those teams."

Sara consequently sat at Jason's table, seated beside him. She kept her gaze averted most of the time. But she couldn't help looking at him now and then, enjoying the view, when he ran the conversation at their table.

He started, not unexpectedly, with his teasing demeanor. "Hey, all. Did you notice that bunch of civilians gossiping about us? What if we prove to them that all those Mary Glen werewolf rumors are true?"

A collective gasp circulated through their fortunately closed-off room. Not even any servers were with them yet.

Drew, at the same table, stood as if to do something dire to silence his cousin. "Look, Jason," he said. "You—"

"You didn't let me finish, cuz—er, sir." Jason went on to elaborate in a completely joking manner. "Too bad we didn't think to bring along wolf costumes we've collected to provide cover now and then. If we did, our USFT members could wear them as they pounce on the civilian tables next door."

Outrageous. Way over the top, Sara thought. Yet it was interesting to watch the reactions. Almost everyone, from both units, laughed and bought into the fun Jason suggested so whimsically. General Yarrow scolded Jason, but General Myars guffawed over the idea—because, he said, he'd heard about those ridiculous rumors even before the Ultra Special Forces Team was deployed to Ft. Lukman, and thought the townsfolk must be the most gullible folks anywhere.

And so the discussion went.

At their own table, the ice had been broken by Jason's silliness. Jonas Truro was the other Alpha Force member. Also seated with them were Rynton Tierney, Vera Swainey, Manning Breman and Samantha Everly. The next table over accommodated both generals, Colleen Hodell, Jock Larabey and some USFT members including Cal Brown. Sara noticed that Rainey Jessop was absent and wondered if she was still ill.

Sara saw Cal glaring daggers toward Jason. Obviously, he chose not to get the Alpha Force's humor. But every once in a while that gaze went toward her. Was he resentful she hadn't joined his attempts at flirtation?

Maybe he had been attempting to hide, all along, that camaraderie with Alpha Force members was not his preference.

Did he hate the shapeshifting unit enough to try to kill its CO by setting Greg Yarrow's car on fire?

Did he exacerbate even that by planting the weapon and

aiming it at the car's remains when they were supposedly secure and out of the way?

Sara chose not to act as disturbed as she felt. Instead, she made it a point to keep talking with everyone at her table. Crack jokes designed to outdo Jason's.

Suggest that maybe she'd like to trade places with him someday—and describe to everyone that she actually had, in a way, done so that morning as she had helped to train Jason's cover dog Shadow.

Servers came and went. The conversation was edited when they were around to ensure that any eavesdropping, which would obviously be easy, wouldn't yield anything to stoke the rumors that might be circulating in the outer restaurant area.

The idea of grabbing a glass of wine intrigued Sara, but it was only lunchtime and this was, in effect, a military exercise. Instead, she chose a diet soft drink, then a Cobb salad. She also helped Jason goad the USFT members into ordering hamburgers or steaks like the shifters did—keeping the terms light and only alluding to any reason why some of the people at this luncheon might want to select meat dishes over salads.

Even so, the servers occasionally exchanged glances. Sara now felt certain they'd share their experience, and possibly their suspicions, with the restaurant's other guests and employees.

All the more reason to make it appear that they were only cracking jokes.

Sara enjoyed her salad. The others all appeared to find their meals tasty, too.

And the discussion? It turned military. Each person at the table described prior assignments and deployments—making it absolutely clear that no one described any parts of their former assignments that were classified.

Eventually, most everyone had finished. General Yarrow stood. "Okay, let's turn this into an abbreviated game of musical chairs. I want all USFT members to stay where you are, and Alpha Force, each of you replace someone else in your unit at a different table. On the count of three— one, two, three…"

The room became suddenly, and briefly, chaotic, as the Alpha Force personnel rose and complied with General Yarrow's orders.

That included Sara. And Jason. They wound up at different tables—and Sara wasn't happy with her own feelings of regret at their separation.

Given her preference, she wouldn't have sat with him in the first place, she reminded herself.

This time, Sara sat with Colleen Hodell as well as some USFT members she hadn't met before.

The cougar shifter seemed at home, asking right away for the others at the table to tell why they had decided to enlist in the military in the first place, and then why they had gravitated to an elite, demanding—and highly regarded— unit like the Ultra Special Forces Team. They all seemed pleased to talk, proud of their highly classified and uniquely skilled sight and marksmanship abilities.

Colleen herself mentioned how thrilled she had been to discover the existence of Alpha Force, and how it had made such a big difference in her life. She didn't go into detail, but Sara recalled their discussion at Colleen's apartment where she'd admitted to a difficult childhood as a shifter. Now in Alpha Force, her shifting abilities were accepted. She seemed happy to Sara.

Alpha Force looked like a good fit for a lot of people— especially shifters.

But Sara hoped that no one would turn that kind of question on her. She'd have no problem discussing why she had joined the military. It had been her goal for years. Yet she would have to be careful in the rest of her response.

She had mostly been thrilled to have been selected by General Yarrow to become his aide. But she would never be able to tell strangers, even those she was ordered to get along with, what she had originally thought of the strange yet compelling abilities of Alpha Force.

Especially some of its members…

Jason now sat at a table that included Captain Samantha Everly—again. How did that happen? Sara thought they were all supposed to find different members of the other unit from those they'd already talked to.

But she hadn't really kept track of who was with whom. The thing was…well, the usually haughty and commanding captain seemed to listen to every word Jason said. Maybe even leaning her curvaceous body toward the man that Sara was fighting her own attraction to.

If she couldn't fraternize, neither could Samantha.

But as Sara excused herself, ostensibly for a restroom break but intending first to stop at the table where Samantha flirted with Jason, she found herself confronted by Cal Brown.

"So what do you think, Sara?" he said. "Are our two units finally getting it—becoming colleagues that get along?"

"Looks that way, Cal," she responded, not liking the fact that he was blocking her progress. She was between two tables filled with gabbing troops. The only way around was to turn and wend her way in a different direction.

Cal was a large blockade.

Before she decided how best to handle this, Drew rose from the table where he now sat—which again included both generals. So maybe Samantha hadn't been completely out of line, despite General Yarrow's orders to mingle.

By then, everyone had finished their meals and had their plates bussed. It was time for coffee, iced tea and for some of them, desserts. But not Sara.

"We have something to go over before you're all dismissed," Drew said. "I wanted to let each of you know about something that was just brought to my attention before we sat down here. I don't know the origin—although my suspicions suggest that some of you particularly excellent marksmen in the USFT might have some ideas. But has anyone recently lost some weaponry and ammunition?" He described the AK-47 that had been loaded and aimed at General Yarrow's destroyed car. It certainly wasn't the kind of equipment that Alpha Force members used most often. Nor was it what the USFT shooters had used the other day. But it was undoubtedly accessible to them.

Sara heard whisperings and looked around. Most of the quiet conversations were between members of USFT.

Which suggested that Drew's question might have the effect of erasing whatever progress had been made here in the joining of forces.

But it was entirely proper, Sara thought. Get everyone off guard, then press for answers.

"What the hell are you doing, Major?" General Myars had risen, hands on his broad hips, and addressed Drew, his round face red and furious.

"Just looking for a few answers, sir," Drew said calmly. "I don't suppose you could address them?"

"If you're accusing me, or anyone reporting to me, Major, you had better retract it. Now."

Sara saw Drew exchange glances with General Yarrow, who gave a nearly imperceptible nod. "I'm sorry, sir, if you thought that was what I was doing. I would just like to find out any way I can where that weapon came from. If anyone here, from either unit, has any answers or suggestions, please let either General Yarrow or me know."

The entire group started to disperse then. Most people seemed to get back together with others in their own units.

The supposed camaraderie had been temporary, anyway, Sara figured, and Drew's comments at the end only precipitated the separation once more.

Sara didn't plan it, but she found herself walking out the door with Jason.

"So, are you best buddies now with some of those USFT guys?" he asked. "I had fun with them, myself. Although I'm not sure any of them will talk to any of us again after my cousin's comments at the end. I really liked how he did that. We're all still under orders to get along, so it'll be interesting to see how that works now, with them knowing they're each under suspicion by a bunch of—" he lowered his head to whisper into her ear. A shiver ran through her at his proximity, even though there was nothing sensual about it. Or shouldn't have been. "—a bunch of werewolves," he finished quietly. Good thing, too, since they were outside by then, in the restaurant's parking lot, and it wasn't just military members who surrounded them.

They'd come in a number of vehicles from the base, and Jason had used the opportunity of visiting town to finally exchange the tow truck for his own classic red Mustang.

"I just hope this doesn't backfire on Drew, or on General Yarrow," Sara said. She'd have loved to ride with Jason—to listen to him make light of what Drew had said, and that was all, she told herself.

But discretion was in order. Instead, she stood there with some of the others who had dined with them.

And watched as Jason drove off first.

Jason understood what Drew had done.

There would be a lot of follow-up conversation, he was

certain. He wished he was in a larger vehicle—one where he could invite USFT people on board and eavesdrop on them.

He figured that all shifting Alpha Force members who'd come in vans from the base were using their acute senses of hearing to do that.

Things were tense now. As they should be.

Until whoever had tried to harm General Yarrow, and still made silent threats, was found and stopped.

He wished he had a further opportunity to talk it over with Sara. To get the general's take on it, he told himself, but that was just an excuse.

He simply wanted to talk to her.

Oh, and if he found some way to seduce her, caress her hot body, kiss those sweet lips…well, that would be fine, too.

Maybe he'd even suggest he needed her help shifting that night.

He hadn't actually considered doing so before…but what if he hung out in wolf form near that parking garage in case whoever left those weapons decided that, now that a new threat had been discovered, it was time to do more?

And Jason, in wolf form, would be in a perfect position to catch whoever it was.

Especially with Sara as his backup.

It couldn't fail.

Chapter 18

Sara waited at the curb patiently with Greg Yarrow until the car that had brought them to Mary Glen arrived—a black military sedan driven by one of the Ft. Lukman privates.

Probably one that Jason worked on. It was shiny and had purred on their way downtown before.

She quickly moved her thoughts away from car care—and Jason.

She hadn't previously considered what she'd be doing that afternoon after lunch. But as usual, she was on call with General Yarrow.

"We're going to my office," he said as he held the rear car door open for her. "I've already invited Myars and the officers reporting to him. Contact Drew Connell and make sure he's there, too. We'll be discussing his tactics."

Sara used her cell phone to call Drew as they rode toward the base. She'd seen him get into the car that Jason drove. "We're on our way," she told him. "General Yarrow wants us to meet at his office as soon as possible."

"Got it," Drew said.

Sara hung up. She felt certain that Jason would learn about the meeting, too. But he wasn't one of those whom the general wanted to see there.

Just as well that Sara wouldn't see him, either.

* * *

The meeting took longer than Sara had anticipated. She'd figured, from what General Yarrow had said, that it would be a quick recap of what had gone on at lunch—including an explanation of why Drew had decided to push the envelope with the USFT and what, if anything, had been gained by it.

But the representatives of the USFT had a lot more to say than Sara had figured on.

They sat in General Yarrow's quaint, antiques-filled office, everyone facing the mahogany desk with Greg holding court behind it. Present were the general, Drew and her from Alpha Force, and General Myars and Captain Rynton Tierney from USFT.

Sara knew that General Yarrow intended to run the meeting. But almost as quickly as she shut the door, General Myars began a tirade.

"What the hell makes you think one of my men ambushed your Jeep, Yarrow?" demanded the tall yet flabby officer. "Why would they? And then to think any one or more of them would be stupid enough afterward to point to the USFT by leaving some of our own gear there—especially a weapon that makes them what they are—ridiculous! Someone's obviously trying to mess not only with you, but with your mind, too—and they've succeeded."

"I asked the questions I did to see the reaction." Drew was at the end of the row of ornate chairs facing General Yarrow's desk. Now he stood. "Indignation was what I expected— and mostly what I got. There were a couple of your people, though, whose expressions—and scents, by the way—were a bit off. Fear, maybe. Although one, at least, also looked smug."

"Who was that?" Tierney demanded.

"You." Drew's bland expression looked to Sara as if he tried to hide his own smugness.

Tierney denied everything. His face was flushed and his hands were fisted enough to make his muscular arms fill out his uniform sleeves. He did, however, admit to pride in his unit. He wouldn't protect anyone who resorted to attempted murder to upgrade the USFT's status at Ft. Lukman, though, if that was what had happened. And if the later game with the AK-47 was to underscore the USFT's involvement, that was sheer stupidity.

"You know what I think?" Tierney said. "Not only is someone trying to frame us, they're trying to make sure our two units never get along enough to accomplish a vital mission together."

"And who would do that?" General Yarrow was a lot calmer than Sara.

"If I knew that, it'd have been stopped by now."

Sara would have liked to believe Tierney committed the dangerous mischief they were discussing. But she doubted it.

She decided to throw out the other possibility they'd all considered, no matter how unlikely. "Who says it's someone here on base who's trying to discredit the USFT and antagonize Alpha Force? I know we've kind of eliminated that as a possibility, but what if it is, after all, one of the civilians from Mary Glen?" She looked at Drew, who'd had his own issues with some Mary Glen residents a while ago. "Could it be because you caught whoever was after Alpha Force before? Or because there are others who want the military here at Ft. Lukman to go away?"

"That's something we need to consider further," General Yarrow said. "And it's why I wanted us to have our lunch there today."

The rest of the discussion that afternoon speculated even

more about who might be conducting the nasty shenanigans to distract the military at Ft. Lukman, and how to follow up with the security staff on possibilities.

Of course they reached no conclusions.

Then General Yarrow brought up the main reason for this meeting. "Our exercises the other day came out all right, though not perfect. What I want next is to ramp them up. Perform exercises where the two units don't just show off their talents to one another, but have to work together— the way they'll need to if the mission the commander in chief has in mind for our combined troops goes forward."

Discussion on methodology and how it could be accomplished filled the rest of the afternoon. General Yarrow even had Sara call the cafeteria and get them to deliver the equivalent of a fast-food dinner as the planning continued.

Eventually, the members of both units sounded satisfied with the maneuvers to be held in two days.

The USFT members finally departed the general's office, leaving Sara there with Drew and Greg.

"What do you really think?" Greg Yarrow asked Drew a minute after the door had closed behind their visitors.

"We have to work with them, even if we're still not sure we can trust them." Drew shook his head.

Sara once more absorbed the resemblance between the major in charge of Alpha Force and his cousin, Jason. Their coloration—dark hair with silver highlights, their golden eyes—and even their muscular physiques were similar.

Why was she even thinking about Jason at that moment, in his absence? She felt irritated that Drew Connell brought Jason back into her thoughts.

She had to stop. As the two men in the room continued to discuss strategy for a while, she reminded herself that there was no way someone like Jason could have participated with them.

Eventually, General Yarrow said, "Let's meet again tomorrow—for less than an hour, I promise. Before that, Sara, please enter our proposed plans onto the computer and print them out so we can go over them one more time before the final exercise."

"Yes, sir." And then Sara said good-night and left the general's office.

Sara felt stifled. It wasn't that she didn't love what she did. And the meeting in the general's office, being his confidante and assistant—well, that was who she was these days, and she wouldn't trade it for any other post in the world.

But attacks on the general, disagreements between the two units, other issues she'd had to face lately—including her unwanted attraction to a noncommissioned officer who also happened to be a shapeshifter—she thought about these too intensely. Too often.

She needed a break.

A short one would be fine. And so, after leaving the office, Sara headed not for the BOQ but for the small openair parking lot nearby where she had left her car.

She was off duty for now. She'd hidden a civilian outfit in the trunk. She could change clothes inside the vehicle and head back to Mary Glen—for a smoothie. Or a mocha. Or something else sweet to perk up her mood.

It was sunset and only a faint glow of sunlight's residue illuminated the base. Soon artificial lights would flick on.

A few other people were on the sidewalks mostly across the street from her. She saluted or smiled, as appropriate, and kept going.

Nearby she saw the building where noncommissioned officers were housed. Was Jason inside? Or was he off somewhere getting dinner, meeting with other Alpha Force members or doing something she didn't even imagine?

Like shapeshifting? Tonight?

She wouldn't be there as his aide, though plenty of others could help. But why would he?

Making notes on a computer was far different—a lot more boring—than handing a shifter a vial of elixir, aiming a light on his naked body and watching him change from the most gorgeous specimen of male human to an amazing, feral yet somewhat tame wolf.

She closed her eyes for a moment at the recollection she tried so hard not to think of. Or to consider Colleen Hodell's shift from a female human's body to a cougar's.

Sara knew full well the old axiom: the more you don't want to think about something, the more it'll pound at your mind.

Sighing, she opened her eyes—a good thing since a car, a huge SUV, was driving out of the lot. Cal Brown was the driver. He saw her, too. He grinned and waved and stopped, rolling down his window. "Need a ride?"

"Thanks, no. I've got it covered. Have a good evening." And then she walked on.

Too bad he didn't attract her in the slightest. If she wanted to take up with someone at Ft. Lukman, Cal, at least, was also a lieutenant. A more or less by-the-book commissioned officer, unlike Jason. She allowed her thoughts to return not to Jason, but to her old college boyfriend who'd gone rogue and tried to get her to take drugs with him, too. And how fast she had dropped him.

By the book was the only way for her.

She reached the last row of cars parked along the curb in the nearly full lot and turned to walk toward hers.

And stopped—as soon as she noticed the broken glass on its far side, near the wall of the adjoining parking garage.

She walked around. On the side of her gold hybrid, deep scratches etched the side.

Some seemed random—but others formed words. Nasty words: *Die bitch. Your CO is still alive but you won't be for long.*

The headlight and taillight on that side had been smashed.

Sara bit her lips. Who could have done this?

The obvious answer was that the perpetrator had been whoever had set General Yarrow's car on fire.

Who'd also aimed the weapon at the remains of the general's Jeep?

Maybe.

But why target her, too? Because she worked with the general?

She wanted to scream. Instead, she looked around the parking lot, then stopped.

Even if she saw someone, whom could she trust?

The answer came to her immediately. There were several people here to trust.

But only one was committed to taking care of cars.

She pulled her smartphone from her pocket and pressed the buttons for the number that somehow had gotten programmed in—because she had called it before.

Jason's.

But the call went into his voice mail before he answered.

He had gotten shifting assistance from Noel Chuma.

Now Jason prowled in his wolf form.

He had first headed to the garage where the general's car slept, its remains further violated.

People around here might look for a shifter, but it was still easier for a wolfen creature to crawl low to the floor, hide in smaller crevices, be less obvious.

The place was empty except for cars.

Plus, the guard remained there.

If anyone came to further bother the Jeep, it would not likely be now.

And so, restless and not wanting to shift back yet, Jason now roamed the periphery of the base.

Spotting what—who—he wanted to, he'd stayed hidden as he watched Sara McLinder leave the office building and head toward the parking lot.

Communicate with that ass, Lieutenant Cal Brown.

Then continue toward her car.

Time for Jason to creep away, back to the garage before shifting back.

But he watched Sara a few minutes more.

Good thing he did.

For in moments, he had joined her at the far side of the car.

Even in wolfen form, he understood the desecration that had occurred.

And smelled a hint of whatever had sickened him before while investigating the destruction of the general's car.

Resisting a howl, he joined Sara at her side and rubbed his furry body against her uniform-clad legs in sympathy.

Chapter 19

Sara knelt to hug the wolf that was Jason. She needed his presence, his comfort. She would prefer it if he were in human form, but his being there for her, no matter what presence he was in, helped her deal with the horror.

"Thanks for being here, Jason," she whispered. Those tall wolf ears moved at the sound. He nuzzled her cheek, and she sighed. "Who could have done this?"

Her mind roiled, especially after the day's events—hearing about the weapon aimed at what was left of the general's Jeep. Lunch, and then the meeting. She'd sensed possible animosity from the USFT personnel toward Alpha Force.

Not against her, too…or was it?

The damage to her car couldn't have been done by a civilian from Mary Glen—could it? If the whispering and glares she had seen there translated into genuine hatred, why her? Even if someone knew who she was and hated her position as General Yarrow's aide, how could they have gotten onto the base unnoticed?

How would they know which car was hers?

In any event, how could the damage have been wreaked and not noticed while it was happening, even by someone stationed here?

She realized then that she was vocalizing some of her thoughts.

Jason's golden wolf eyes were locked on to her. He understood.

"Can you shift back?" she asked. "You know cars. Maybe you can see some clue here that I won't recognize."

He bent his head as if nodding, then turned it slightly, as if telling her to follow.

"Okay," she whispered.

As she stood, she looked around the parking lot again. It was late enough that it remained devoid of people, thank heavens. Not that most people here would be surprised to see an Alpha Force member with a wolf, or perhaps a cover dog, even if the timing seemed off.

Even so...she didn't want to talk to anyone else about shifters or her car, just now.

Instead, she followed Jason's sleek, wolfen form as he crossed the street and entered the woods at the edge of Ft. Lukman.

Maybe he shouldn't have shifted that night.

Maybe he shouldn't have assumed that any nastiness at Ft. Lukman would only center around the remains of General Yarrow's car.

But shifted or not, he couldn't have been everywhere on base. Seeing everything.

Watching everyone.

Consequently, he had missed the one thing he had needed to see: someone vandalizing Sara's car.

Now at a clearing in the woods, he was back in human form.

Naked. With Sara's eyes trying so hard not to look at him—and failing.

Under other circumstances, he'd have laughed. Teased her.

She had offered her shirt for him to tie around his waist

and drape strategically, but it would have left her clad above in only her bra. Intriguing, but he wouldn't embarrass her that way.

"Sorry," he said. "I'd intended to return to the lab area before I shifted back. I left my clothes there."

"I... We're not far from your quarters," she said. He enjoyed the flush on her face, visible even in the faint glow from the base's artificial lights. "I could go inside and get you something—if I could get in, that is."

"Maybe." But his keys remained in his uniform pants, and they were still at the lab. "Look, I shifted back now because I didn't want you to be alone. Why don't you just accompany me back to the lab? We can stay in the woods for most of the walk."

"All right." Her next words surprised him. "Or maybe we should just go deeper into the woods first."

He looked at her. Her lovely, full lips were raised into a teasing smile.

She was teasing him for a change. And he loved it.

"Like the thought behind it," he said. "But I don't think either of us would do well rolling on the ground there. Scratchy leaves, nasty bugs, the works. At the lab, though, I just happen to know where some nice, clean and unused bedding for the dogs upstairs are kept."

Her expression turned speculative. And hot. Especially when she glanced down at his exposed genital area. All the talk had spurred his interest—enough that his cock had grown hard. Really hard.

"Sounds promising," Sara said huskily. "If I can hold out that long." She was suddenly in his arms, her body pressed hard against his, especially down below.

"This isn't just because you're scared, is it?" he managed to ask. He wouldn't want her to regret what they surely were about to do—at least not for the wrong reasons.

He already figured she sometimes regretted having made love with him before.

"Yes, I'm scared," she said, "but no, that's not the reason."

He groaned with need before pressing his mouth on hers. She tasted salty, seasoned by her tears of anger and fear upon finding her car.

The thought spurred him to hold her closer. Deepen the kiss—partly out of an urge to protect her. To make her feel safe and cared for. To replace the thoughts of her car with thoughts of him...and the sex they soon would be sharing. That they now had to share.

He'd want to get back to that car soon, to check it out. To move it inside near the general's, to ensure it wasn't damaged further, especially not until he had a chance to examine it.

But the hour was late enough, the car's position in the parking lot distant enough, that it could wait.

It had to wait.

He had other things on his mind.

He ended that kiss, pulling his searching tongue from her welcoming mouth then placed one more hard kiss on her lips.

"Let's hurry." He grabbed her hand and began to lope with her through the trees.

"Sure," she said, matching his pace. "But...why not go even faster?" She started to dart ahead, still holding his hand. Now it was his turn to keep up—which he did, gladly. Grinning in anticipation.

Sara knew that Jason was aware of all aspects of the kennel and lab building, certainly a lot more than she was.

As they reached the rear entry to the low-slung building and eased into the shadows beyond its exterior lights, she asked softly, "Are you sure no one will be here at this hour?"

"Can't be sure of anything, but it's unlikely. I'd already told Noel, who helped with my shift, that I wouldn't need his help on the other end. We just arranged to leave my clothes downstairs where I changed. I'm supposed to call him later. If we see anyone else, you've already aided in my shifting before. We'll just say you helped again—and can even mention what happened to your car. That'll keep them from suspecting what we're really up to."

She shouldn't be so drawn to his teasing ways, his sexy smile. But she was. Especially now, when she needed a distraction from reality.

And what a distraction, with his hard, muscular body so close. So bare. So enticing, with his penis thick and jutting and daring her to partake in mind-blowing sex with him.

She doubted they'd be able to voice their way out of anyone's noticing that. But heck, maybe they wouldn't run into anyone.

She hoped not.

But as they entered the building, after going in through a seldom-used rear door that was left unlocked for Jason while shifted, the dogs inevitably sensed their presence and began to bark.

Sara laughed nervously. "So much for trying to sneak in here."

"It's soundproofed enough that, unless someone's already inside, no one will come to check why they're barking."

They headed for the door to the narrow stairway that led downstairs to the lab area. Sara noticed that the scratches on the door were still there.

"The general got me my own key cards for this building," Sara told Jason, but he'd already gone down the hall and into an unlocked room, where he emerged with a key card of his own. "Was that one hidden, too?" she asked.

"Yeah, but not all Alpha Force members would know where to look for it—only those with a need to get to the lab. Or their cousins." He grinned.

"But you'd have returned as a wolf," Sara reminded him. "How would you have gotten the key and gone downstairs then?"

"If I didn't have an aide with a card around, I'd have shifted first if necessary," he told her. He zipped the card along the track that opened the door.

Then Jason flicked on the lights and held her hand as they walked down the steep flight.

She held on as if she were frail and needed his help. On the contrary, she felt strong. Jazzed. Ready, really ready, for what she was anticipating below.

Jason turned on the hallway lights once they exited the stairwell. The area looked sterile—like a laboratory should, Sara figured. The doors were all closed. Each had a small window, and no lights into the lab rooms were on.

Jason led her to the last door on their right. "Here we are," he said.

Sara wondered for a moment what the room would be like inside. She'd seen some of the labs before—and they all had easily cleanable tile flooring and plenty of laboratory cabinets and surfaces.

Not the kind of place she hoped they would wind up in each other's arms.

She'd also seen the small office that Drew Connell used here.

She really didn't want to think about Drew now.

Still clasping her hand, Jason turned the knob and pushed the unlocked door open. He turned on the light.

Sara followed him inside.

And smiled.

This was an unexpected lounge area. Jason's clothes—she assumed the camo uniform that lay there—were resting on a plush, if well-worn sofa.

This must be where those hanging out in the lab went to veg out while their concoctions were brewing—or whatever.

In any event...well, given her choice Sara would have chosen something more comfortable than that sofa for what they had in mind. But it was better than so many other alternatives.

She opened her mouth to say so as Jason turned—and his erection, still taut and enticing, waved slightly in the air. She saw that before he took her into his arms and kissed her again.

And more. His hands didn't rest. She felt him immediately start to unbutton her shirt. "I'll—" she began against his mouth, but he didn't let her talk. Instead, he stripped her shirt off her, then stuck his hand immediately beneath her bra, clasping one breast gently, then the other, pushing the bra upward so he could more easily reach them—which made her moan.

Without waiting for him, she moved one of her hands from behind his back downward to push her pants off. She had to kneel to finish the act, and he moved with her. Helping her.

Then using his hand to move slowly, teasingly, sexily up the inside of her leg.

She moved so he could reach her. Touch her. Plunge a finger inside her, even as she grasped his cock and began pumping it gently.

Enjoying his deep moan of pleasure.

In moments—she wasn't sure how—she was on her back on top of that sofa. Its texture scratched at her back, but she didn't care. Her sense of touch, everywhere, was heightened by her sensual awareness of Jason.

She wanted him inside her. Instead, he kissed her once more, then moved down her body, tasting her with his lips, sucking her nipples, then farther down until his tongue lapped at her intimately and nearly made her scream. She caught herself, not wanting even the dogs to hear. "Please, Jason," she whispered huskily.

He moved away from her altogether for what seemed like eternity, but when he returned from behind her, near the end of the sofa, he had apparently fished a condom from his pocket.

He carried one all the time?

She didn't want to consider what that meant. Not now. For the moment, it only meant he was prepared, and she loved that.

And then, after he was shielded, he fulfilled her desire, plunging his hot and hard cock deep inside her. She was ready, bucking upward at his every thrust.

She didn't know how long it took, but all too soon she reached a crescendo and he levered her over the top into an orgasm unlike any she had ever experienced before, ameliorated by his own gasp of pleasure as he, too, climaxed.

Jason lay there, out of breath, on top of Sara. Lord, had that been magnificent. Earth-shaking.

And even though he had not a shred of energy left, he knew he wanted—needed—even more.

He would never get enough of this woman.

But this was not the right place.

Neither was his car.

He wanted to take her somewhere special the next time. There had to be a next time.

But at the moment, there was only now.

She was breathing just as heavily below him. He moved a bit, wishing the sofa was a little wider. He didn't want to crush her.

"You okay?" he asked.

"Oh, yes."

He smiled. Those words… They surely weren't the biggest turn-on in the whole world. But they were enough, that and her body still up against his, to lure him into touching her again. More. And as she gasped his name, in a way that suggested she, too, was ready for more, he started in once more to touch her. Everywhere.

Sara had no idea what time it was. She just lay there on the couch, Jason pushed up against her, facing her. His arm over her, just as hers twisted around him, since she had no other place to put it.

If she hadn't felt so sated, his body so close and so hot would turn her on again.

His breathing had eased up a bit, as had hers.

They couldn't stay here all night, though it was tempting. But someone might come in. Even if no one did until morning, staying here was really no option.

A thought struck her and she wound up smiling.

"What?" Jason asked in a lazy tone. His eyes had opened and now studied her face.

"I thought we were here for you to get dressed, not for me to get undressed." Despite how her respiration had quieted, she still felt her nipples touch his hard chest with each breath. It felt damned sexy—but with all that she had just experienced, she couldn't do it again…could she?

"Both," he said, and she realized he was speaking in only single syllables at a time. He must feel as exhausted as she did.

"Let's do the other part, then," she said with determination she didn't really feel. But then she considered how, and why, they had gotten together in the first place that night. "I want to get back to my car. I'd like for you to examine it while you're not shifted. And…should we move it into the same place as the general's till it's been examined? Maybe there'll be fingerprints or some other way of figuring out who vandalized it."

His body grew tense against hers. "You're right. We can't leave it there like that. Not till we at least make an attempt to figure out who did it."

He drew away and stood, and she almost sighed at the loss.

He disappeared from her view in the dim light, but she heard him beyond the end of the couch. He was undoubtedly getting dressed.

Time for her to do the same.

Odd for her to feel a little shy standing and searching the floor for her clothing. She didn't even look toward Jason—even though she felt certain she would enjoy watching him put his uniform back on.

She definitely had the other times she had seen him perform that action. Even more so when he took it off.

The light in that room remained dim, but it was bright enough for Sara to follow the brief trail they'd taken while Jason helped her remove her clothes. She took it in reverse now, picking things up. She wished there was someplace private to go to get dressed, but of course that was silly.

Even so, she drew everything back on quickly, looking down at the floor as if not watching Jason would keep him from watching her.

Which was ridiculous. And wrong. When she finished and looked up, he was back near the couch, fully dressed, his gaze on her. Smiling.

She knew she was flushing again. She felt shy suddenly.

But that was silly. "Are you ready to go?" She attempted to sound businesslike, a soldier prepared to jump back into battle.

With herself.

The fact that she had just made love with Jason— again—remained wrong, no matter how good it had felt.

But she would scold herself for it later.

Right now she needed his assistance with her car.

And she especially liked the idea that her car would give her a good reason to remain in his presence. For now.

Chapter 20

The walk back to Sara's car helped to wake Jason. No, it did more than that. It stoked the anger that he'd felt even while shifted, when he had seen the vandalism.

He liked cars. He liked them in pristine form. No one should harm them intentionally, for any reason.

Mostly, he wanted to strangle whoever had done this, since it was Sara's car. More than anything, he wanted to protect her.

Well…maybe have sex with her again. But that would come later. He hoped.

For now he just stood there with her, in the dimly lighted parking lot, staring at what someone had dared to do to her nice hybrid. Scratches were bad enough. So was the damage to her headlights and taillights.

But that threat: *Die bitch. Your CO is still alive but you won't be for long.* That begged to be avenged. Maybe even doing to the perpetrator what he had dared to suggest would happen to Sara.

And that wasn't just the wild, shifter side of him talking. No, even as a human he craved some kind of retribution.

He didn't tell Sara, though. She had waited till they got there but was now on her cell phone. "Yes, General," she said. "I know it's late but I wanted you to know what happened. I'm going to take some photos, then drive my car to store it, for now, with yours, where there's at least some security." She paused to listen. "No, sir. I'm not here alone. I called Jason Connell first since he works with cars. He came as soon as he could, and he's here with me now."

She tossed a glance at Jason, as if asking him to back her up—that he had just arrived. He nodded as if hearing her request aloud. Far as he knew, no one had seen him here before, in shifted form, when he'd first reconnoitered with Sara near her car.

Sara looked away again, staring at the car. She appeared pale in the soft light, all military in her camo uniform, all woman in the way she hunched over her phone, her short, blond hair framing her face, her blue-green eyes even more luminous than usual as she seemed to hold back tears. The outdoor parking lot remained full of cars. Sara and he stood off to the side of her car, squeezed in near the wall that had obscured the damage at first.

"Yes, sir," Sara said. "I will." She hung up and looked at Jason. "He's calling base security. We're to wait here until they arrive." Her smile was wan. "I guess till then you're under orders to help to keep me safe, notwithstanding what's written now on my car."

"Yes, ma'am." Jason saluted her, hoping his sorry attempt at levity would cheer her, even just a little.

He thought—hoped—maybe a reminder of what they'd just shared would do that, too.

He considered taking her into his arms, just for a minute, to comfort her. But he'd no idea how long security would take to get here so he stayed back.

Instead, he told her about the awful added smell that hid from him the scent of whoever had done this.

It didn't take long for a couple of guys in a marked sedan to arrive. They wore the same kind of uniforms and insignias as the guys who guarded the front gate—who hadn't been much help when General Yarrow's car had caught fire.

They exited their car and approached where Sara and Jason stood. "This the car?" one asked, the tall, skinny private named Kerry.

"Yes," Sara said.

They looked at the damage, took some pictures then said to Jason, "General Yarrow said it was okay for you to drive it to the area where his Jeep is now being stored, sir. But you're to use gloves and not touch anywhere outside the car, in case there are fingerprints."

"Fine," Jason said. "Thanks."

He was not about to let Sara stay with them. Donning the rubber gloves proffered by the guards, he gingerly opened the passenger door—careful not to touch anything other than the handle since that was the side that had been damaged.

At the guards' attempt to voice an objection, he said, "I want Lieutenant McLinder to stay with the car until I get it parked. This is the best way to let her accompany me. Her fingerprints will be on it and inside anyway, if that's what you're worried about." Then he got into the driver's seat and they drove off.

Sara had remained quiet. She didn't say anything as he drove, either. He wondered what she was thinking.

The parking garage was nearby, and they reached it quickly despite having to maneuver a bit along the roads inside the base. Jason drove Sara's hybrid to the enclosed area, behind which the remains of General Yarrow's car still sat. A lone guard stood outside. After a peek to see who they were, he opened the door and allowed Jason to drive in.

He had barely parked before he saw, in the rearview mirror, the general approaching.

"Look who's here," he told Sara. With him were the security guards they'd left behind in the outdoor lot.

She turned, then leaped out of the car. She stood beside it, waiting for the general to reach them. "I didn't realize you were coming here, too, sir."

"I wanted to see the damage." He turned to look at it then got closer. Shaking his head, he said, "This damn thing is escalating. Guess whoever it was isn't pleased I wasn't killed so he's issuing more threats—including to my personal staff. We have to catch whoever it is. Fast." He turned to the guards and began asking procedure questions.

Jason saw how Sara hung back, not offering suggestions or taking notes or acting the way she did in full general's aide mode. Instead, she seemed to just watch and listen. And study first the scratches on her car, then the ground.

He hated to see her this way. It was as though she had turned into a different person. Quiet. Sad.

As if she had also forgotten what they had just shared.

Maybe this time it had just been a respite for her. An interlude to take her mind off what was troubling her.

Something she wouldn't want to think about, let alone experience again.

That made him want to punch something—like whoever had done this to her car.

He had already determined to figure out who it was. That person had been crafty enough to spread some of whatever had make Jason ill at the site where the general's car had been sabotaged, so he hadn't been able to find the perpetrator's scent.

He'd have to think of something else...like making the person believe that little trick hadn't completely worked.

So far, though, he wasn't sure how.

While the general talked to the others, he edged closer to Sara. "I'm working on some ideas," he told her. "We can talk about them. We'll find the guy. Count on it. For now, though, we need to make sure you stay safe." He turned away before she could say anything.

He decided to present his idea to General Yarrow. As soon as the CO was done talking to the guards about how they'd better ensure things in this garage remained under scrutiny, he approached him.

"Sir," he said, "I would like to volunteer to help protect Lieutenant McLinder."

He heard a soft gasp from behind him—Sara.

"Thank you, Sergeant," she said, "but that won't be necessary."

Jason saw the frozen look on General Yarrow's aging face and groaned inwardly.

Had he made a mistake just by suggesting it?

He meant well, Sara knew. Under other circumstances she might have appreciated Jason's protective nature.

But she had already been around while he had shifted. General Yarrow knew that, and that she had seen Jason with no clothes on.

He didn't know the rest, at least. Even so, Sara worried about her position as the general's trusted aide.

She moved away from Jason, close to where Greg Yarrow stood with the base's security personnel. "I'd like to request that some members of your group be posted around the BOQ," she said to the guards. "To keep both General Yarrow and me under your protection."

"I've already got a guard contingent," the general said. "I'll have them keep an eye on your quarters, as well."

"Thank you, sir." Sara looked at her CO. She knew him well enough to recognize that he wasn't as blasé as he acted. Not with that slight lift of his dark brows, the interest shown in his unyielding light brown eyes.

"I'd like to speak with you in private, Lieutenant," he said, and those words made Sara tremble deep inside.

"Of course, sir."

She accompanied him to the area beside his car's remains.

"Sara," he began, "I don't have to tell you that I'm quite concerned about a lot of things going on here at Ft. Lukman. If I don't assign you to further TDY here—and I'm inclined not to now—then we'll be able to leave here in a few days, after the exercise the day after tomorrow where members of both units show their stuff together. But when we do, we're likely to leave some questions unanswered— like who's threatened both of us."

"That's true," she said. "Unless…well, maybe we can get further information before we go."

"Do you think Sergeant Connell can help with those answers?" He didn't let her respond before continuing, "He seems very protective of you, Sara. Maybe too protective. I don't think I have to remind you that he is a noncommissioned officer, and you're a lieutenant who in any event is here only on temporary duty."

Sara felt as if he was giving her advice, not only as her commanding officer but as a father figure. And friend.

She cared about Greg's opinion. Always wanted to stay in his good graces. Intended to keep her military career spotless so she could rise someday in rank.

"I understand, sir," she said. "And though it really wasn't necessary, I appreciate the reminder."

They returned to her car, where Drew Connell had just arrived, too, to survey the damage.

"I've called my investigative contacts again," Drew told them. "I doubt they'll be much help now but assured me they'll arrive soon to look into both cars."

While the general and Drew were talking, Sara edged

her way toward Jason. "Thank you again for all your help, Sergeant," she said. "But it won't be necessary again."

And then she walked off to stand beside the two officers in charge.

When she dared a defiant glance toward Jason, she saw him staring at her. The expression in his eyes was far different from the sexual interest he'd shown before. Or even his protective look.

Instead, he appeared disgusted and remote.

At least he apparently understood what she wasn't saying.

And Sara suddenly felt glad…yet bereft. And alone.

They all left—except for the guards stationed to watch the cars.

As if whoever had damaged them would return in the middle of the night to do more. Or gloat.

Jason felt certain that whoever it was felt delighted to cause such concern at Ft. Lukman.

And was undoubtedly planning something else.

That's why he stayed in the garage for a little longer. Or at least part of the reason.

Even more important was that he didn't want to be anywhere near Sara. He wasn't certain what General Yarrow had said to her, but her attitude, which wasn't great with everyone around previously, had gone to crap.

It was time to move on. Or go back to being who and what he'd been before she arrived here: a guy who'd joined the military because he had to, to salvage the rest of his life.

"Hey, guys," he said to the two guards on duty. "Just wanted to let you know I'll hang around a little longer. You know I work on cars for Alpha Force?"

Both sentries nodded. One appeared to reposition his rifle a bit, but not in a threatening way.

"I'll be looking over this latest damaged vehicle. Maybe I'll recognize someone's handwriting. What do you think?"

He grinned, and both guys grinned back.

Good. He still had the ability to jostle people's sense of humor.

Now if only he could feel a bit humorous, too.

Sara felt furious with herself.

She should have checked before to make sure she hadn't left anything behind in the lab, when her clothes had been strewn all over the floor.

But her keys, including those to get into her quarters in the BOQ, weren't in her pocket.

Fortunately, she'd walked back there with the general, who'd swiped his key card to get into the building then headed for his own more elite wing without walking her to her apartment. He'd obviously not been concerned, despite the threat on her car, that someone would be stupid enough to attack her here.

Neither was she.

But when she got to her unit, neither her keys nor her cell phone were in her pocket.

She could have awakened some maintenance person and gotten inside her unit. But how would she ever explain losing the keys—and her phone? She knew where they had to be: on the floor in the lab, having fallen out of her pocket in the frenzy of stripping to make love with Jason.

She didn't want anyone else to find them. Consequently, she decided to retrace her steps, return to the lab to retrieve them.

She doubted Jason would be there. He was probably a lot more sensible than she was and had headed back to his quarters to sleep for what was left of the night.

If she did happen to run into him…well, she'd made it clear to him that whatever they'd shared was over.

For now she stayed in shadows as she maneuvered toward the far end of the base, where the lab building and kennel were.

At least no living quarters were nearby, so even if she disturbed the dogs no one would be awakened by their barks.

She worried, though. Among what she was missing were her own key cards into the building and lab that the general had gotten for her. She'd seen that an upstairs door had been left unlocked so a shifted Jason could get into the building, but that was before. And she didn't know where the key card to the downstairs lab was hidden—if Jason had even left it again.

If she'd had her phone, she could call him so he could let her in.

He might misinterpret that, though. No, she'd check first to see if she could somehow get inside—no matter how unlikely that was.

In the meantime, she'd stay alert. And careful.

It was late enough that she saw no one as she returned to the low, secluded building and started walking around it, testing doors.

Fortunately, a remote door to the kennel floor—not the one Jason and she had entered—was unlocked.

Which seemed strange. But maybe upstairs security was never that good.

Downstairs was a different matter.

Sara went inside. As anticipated, the dogs heard her and began to bark.

A dim security light illuminated the area, so she could see well enough without flicking any switches. She approached the nearest lush kennel areas and began talking to the dogs, including Shadow. Presumably, most Alpha Force members on duty at Ft. Lukman had brought their dogs into their quarters for the night.

So why was Shadow still here?

Sara had to hurry. Maybe Jason hadn't yet gone to bed. If he'd left Shadow here he might return for him.

"Good night," she said to the dogs then walked rapidly to the narrow door at the top of the stairs leading down to the lab.

Unsurprisingly, it was locked.

She closed her eyes in frustration. Where had Jason gotten the hidden key card?

She doubted there was another, easier entrance but she had to look. She walked farther along the short hallway and tried additional doors. One led into an unlocked closet that contained animal supplies. Another was also locked.

Damn.

Should she contact Jason?

But how—without her phone?

The dogs started barking again. She hadn't said anything aloud. Maybe they were just frustrated.

She headed back to calm them while considering ways to contact Jason—and saw the reason the dogs were noisy once more: Jason was there.

He spotted her at the same time as she saw him. "What are you doing here?" he demanded, loud enough to be heard over the barks.

She approached and explained about her missing phone and keys. "A door to the kennel was already unlocked," she finished, describing its remote location. "The door to the lab was locked, though."

"Strange," Jason said. "And definitely against general policy. I locked the door that had been left open for me under the unusual circumstances of a shifter having to get back inside alone. No other door in this building is ever to be left unlocked."

He looked concerned as he pushed past her to the door down to the lab.

It again wouldn't open—not without his key card. He had to use it twice, though, before it worked. "Did you try to force it?" he asked her.

"Of course not."

But the skepticism on his face alarmed her. And made her feel even sadder that what they'd shared so briefly was definitely over.

He finally opened the door and they went downstairs. Sure enough, her card keys and phone had fallen beneath the sofa—the one that she would never be able to look at again without being bombarded by delightful, and now bittersweet, memories.

They left soon after. He'd gotten Shadow from his kennel, and they walked together across the base in the dark toward her quarters.

She only hoped that no one saw them and assumed they were fraternizing.

Because they weren't. Not now. Jason was just her champion. Her guard.

And this was likely to be the last time they'd ever be alone together.

Chapter 21

The designated night had arrived. Both of the major units at Ft. Lukman were to conduct a joint final exercise to ensure they could be deployed together on the anticipated mission in sync, without conflict between them.

No matter how individual members might feel about one another.

All those to take part in the exercise had met first in the assembly room. Sara stood off to the side while the two generals greeted their respective troops as they filed in. She watched intently. As she'd figured, members of the two units acted cordial yet sometimes remote toward one another. At least she saw no overt antagonism. All seemed well.

Except that, as Jason entered with Noel Chuma, he acted as if he didn't see her.

Which was probably best…although even the USFT members seemed friendlier to the Alpha Force members that evening than Jason acted toward her.

"Everyone take your seats, please," Sara called at General Yarrow's nod. Compliance seemed instantaneous.

General Myars deferred to Greg Yarrow. The Alpha Force general described, at last, what their real mission was to be: to work together to rescue some U.S. government civilians who'd been taken hostage months ago by terrorists in one of the many Middle East countries once again threatened with civil war.

Interesting, Sara thought—and probably a good assignment for such a unique, combined group of elite soldiers, since it appeared that all else had already failed. She had heard of the kidnapping, and the news was periodically full of updates about attempts to save the captives. Diplomacy had failed. Military saber rattling and even attacks had been to no avail, except that one of the hostages had been killed in retaliation. Negotiations were at a stalemate. The options for saving them had become nil—almost.

The situation clearly called for something more covert and absolutely effective. Like a combined mission using the extraordinary senses and unanticipated stealth of the shifters of Alpha Force and the lethal, perfect weaponry of the Ultra Special Forces Team.

And that, apparently, was what would happen—assuming these two units truly did find their rhythm of working in harmony.

General Yarrow explained the rationale and the current status. General Myars then described how the exercises tonight would be conducted.

Then they were all ordered to go outside to their assigned areas to get ready.

The Alpha Force shifters would all change into their animal forms, with the backup of their respective aides. They would sneak into the area on base where mock civilians were being secluded in similar conditions to the real ones overseas.

They would be followed by the USFT members who would wait until military members designated to act like the bad guys were confronted by the wild animals. In the ensuing chaos, they would shoot unloaded weapons until the pseudo-civilians were rescued.

Sounded easy. Sara was completely fascinated by the process—and hoped it worked out problem-free. Of course if it was less than perfect in this exercise, the flaws could still be dealt with.

First to leave the auditorium was the Alpha Force team. The shifters included Jason, Drew, Seth Ambers, Colleen Hodell and Jock Larabey. Their aides accompanied them, including Rainey Jessop, who'd apparently recovered from her illness.

Would five shifters be enough to stoke the distraction needed for the real mission?

Of course foreign forces confronted by wolves and a cougar would at least be unnerved—and hopefully scared enough to allow the creatures to reposition them away from their hostages…until all were rescued by the lethal, armed human forces of the USFT.

This exercise was being conducted at night, when it was easiest to hide the shifters.

Sara was there as General Yarrow's aide, extra pair of eyes and backup. And as an enthralled observer.

At the general's nod, she followed the Alpha Force members outside. They headed from the main office building into the wooded area at the periphery of Ft. Lukman.

There, in a clearing, aides removed vials of elixir and light from their respective backpacks.

After drinking elixir, the shifters repositioned themselves. One of them, Colleen, the only female, was sent off by herself for a little privacy, along with her aide.

And then the shifting began.

He felt free! Even though it hadn't been long since his last shift, Jason had been aching to prowl again.

Besides, this exercise would be vital to the United States, and he would be a part of it.

Would its success provide him the ultimate redemption in the eyes of his cousin? His country?

He hoped so.

But for now, he would just revel in his ability to leap into a staged situation and help rescue pretend hostages...and wait until he could accomplish the real thing.

And the fact that Sara would be watching this exercise? Possibly watching him?

Irrelevant.

For now.

The exercise went smoothly. Almost.

There was a bit of chaos when the USFT members arrived after the shifted Alpha Force team had done a great job of scaring the pretend kidnappers. Sara knew that the supposed victims and their captors hadn't been informed of all the details of how the rescue would be staged, so they didn't realize that many wolves and a cougar would be scaring the bad guys off till they were captured by the armed and dangerous USFT members.

But it all worked—though, for a while, the shifters in animal form were dispersed by the pseudo-captors' own use of unloaded weaponry. Sara watched them run off, glad about their caution.

She recognized, of course, which wolf was Jason. He moved away but stayed close enough to slink around to watch what was happening. So did the other wolves.

Poor Colleen, though. The cougar that was her must have been more unnerved. Sara didn't see where she went, at least not at first.

But in the end, it all worked. The "kidnappers" were all rounded up and locked in an area of the base that had been fitted out to act like a surrogate jail.

All the shifters, including Colleen, regrouped along with

the USFT members after changing back to human form. The "rescued" hostages reconvened at the "jail" area, where those who'd played kidnappers were also released. All participants soon got together to congratulate themselves. The generals, too, celebrated.

Sara saw how pleased Jason appeared. How he seemed to joke and enjoy the party. His cousin Drew patted him on the back for how well he'd done. Sara hadn't been watching at the time, but apparently one of the "captors" hadn't been fazed by the shifted animals until Jason virtually attacked him, knocking him to the floor as might happen in the real situation and keeping him under control till the human marksmen could take charge.

He was in his glory.

Sara was happy for him, but she didn't want to stay there. Not then.

She slipped away.

She considered returning to her quarters but decided she needed face time with some of the dogs in the kennel, who hadn't been invited to participate in this exercise with their humans.

She could take one for a walk. Maybe even Shadow. No problem getting inside; she'd brought her card keys along in case she was needed to help the shifters.

When she reached the building, she stopped and stared. The door was wide open.

She ran inside. The dogs remained in their kennels and started barking at her.

Sara knew that Jason had reported to Drew the other day about her having found this kennel door unlocked when no one had intentionally left it like that to help a shifter. Everyone was under orders to take special care not to allow that to happen again.

But this was even worse.

Worried, Sara went down the hallway to the door that led down to the lab.

It, too, was open.

She needed to report this. Not touch anything. Not go inside herself.

She could call the general. Or Drew. In fact, Drew was the one she probably should notify.

But Jason had been with her here the other night. They'd both talked to the major. She'd thought security would be beefed up—but on this night, with the exercise that had involved nearly everyone at Ft. Lukman, someone had either been completely careless...or had taken advantage.

Sara pulled her phone from her pocket. "Drew? It's Sara. I'm at the lab. It looks like someone else has been here, too."

"Like the other night?" he demanded.

"Maybe worse."

"Wait there. I'll join you right away."

"Please bring Jason," she said. "He also saw what went on here the other night."

"Fine," he said. "Oh, and Sara?"

"Yes?"

His words conformed with the sternness of his tone. "I hope you're armed."

Damn the woman.

Soldier or not, she shouldn't put herself into dangerous situations without backup.

Jason was furious as he accompanied Drew back to the kennel/lab building.

At least she was waiting outside—with Shadow on a leash beside her. For company? For protection?

Though they stood near the building, away from the door and in an area near the back that was sheltered, neither would be protected from being shot from a distance—

particularly if the attacker was one of the highly skilled marksmen of USFT.

That was where he and Drew found them—partly thanks to their enhanced sensory abilities. At least Sara and Shadow weren't easily visible, but Jason quickly smelled the woman's citrusy scent as well as the dog's light canine odor.

"You okay?" Jason asked Sara immediately. Bending to give Shadow a pat, he watched Drew hustle around the building toward the open door to the kennel area and slip inside.

"Yes, I'm fine." She looked better than fine—except for the paleness of her smooth skin. But there was anger in her blue-green eyes and a determined set to her mouth that told him she wasn't lying. "But this attempt to get in was more successful than the other. There was even an intrusion into the lab area. The stairway door was unlocked. But the doors along the hallway downstairs that lead into the actual laboratories were still locked. I checked."

Jason wanted to throttle her. Better yet, kiss her in relief to find that she was unharmed.

But even if he chanced Drew seeing them, Sara wouldn't appreciate his touch or even his concern. Instead, he merely snapped, "You checked? Before you called us?"

"No, after. But I wanted to—"

"What if whoever broke in was still there?"

"I'm a trained member of the military," she said slowly, as if she needed to remind him. "I also had a weapon in my pocket."

"Good." Drew was back with them. "Show me the unlocked door then we'll go downstairs."

They did. All was as Sara had described.

After locking everything again, Drew called in the base's security force to plant sentries outside.

When the security detail arrived, Sara, Drew and Jason

again began walking, in the dark, toward the area where they'd left the participants in that night's exercise.

"So who was it?" Sara asked. "Like before, with the cars, it's unlikely to be a stranger from town who snuck onto the base. With all the activity here tonight, they'd have been noticed."

"Unless they dressed like some of the others," Drew reminded her. "A lot of the people stationed here were in disguise for the roles they played tonight—pseudo-hostages, tangos who were the false enemy terrorists. Not to mention the USFT members."

"And even Alpha Force members, although a lot of us were shifted most of the time," Jason said.

Sara shot a look at him that suggested she'd seen him shifted. Maybe even shifting. But any heat in her gaze dissipated immediately into the chill of the nighttime air.

"I still think it's got to be someone in USFT," Drew said.

"Yeah," Jason agreed.

They walked on in the darkness, the silence broken by noises from the distance, including voices and cheers. Everyone was still celebrating this night's activities.

Everyone but them.

"We need to figure out—" Jason began.

At the same time, Sara said, "Let's see if we can trap whoever it is."

Drew's pace slowed as he laughed. "Great minds think alike," he said. "I was trying to come up with a plan, too, to bring this to a close—and figure out who's trying so hard, and getting so close to, breaking into the lab."

"I have an idea," Sara said as the three stood on a sidewalk facing each other under the dimness of a base streetlight. She looked gorgeous to Jason, despite the way the faint illumination cast shadows onto her face. "As you said, Drew, the most logical scenario is that it's someone from the

USFT trying to get in. Are those rumors still going around that the elixir can help regular people become shifters? If so, why don't we add to them? Suggest they're true, but because of the attempts to break into the lab, all the premixed stuff will be moved the day after tomorrow since you need time to figure out a safe enough place to take it. And then we'll watch and wait for what should be the final break-in."

Jason couldn't help it. He grinned at her. "Hey, Drew and I are the ones with the woo-woo powers around here. Are you some kind of mind reader?"

"What, you want to claim my idea as yours?" Sara demanded. Though her tone was sharp, there was a twinkle in her eyes.

Damn, but he really wanted to kiss her.

Even more, he wanted to do exactly as she'd suggested— but find a way to keep her far from the site of their trap.

Though he couldn't be near her anymore, he still wanted to keep her safe.

But he had a feeling that trying to prevent her participation would be as impossible as making love with her again...no matter how hard he strove for either.

Sara kept Shadow leashed beside her as she walked back along the darkened sidewalks of the base. Her goal was the area where she'd left the participants in that night's exercises. Then, she had departed because she didn't feel part of what had been accomplished.

Now she had another mission to accomplish.

With Jason, of course. He stayed with her on the walk. Even tried to take possession of Shadow's leash and tell Sara to disappear.

A far cry from the times they had made love, and the last thing he'd wanted—either of them wanted—was for one of them to go away.

Drew was with them, too. As he should be. He'd need to be the primary one to start—actually, add to—the rumors that would hopefully result in ending the attempts at breaking into the lab once and for all.

Because the perpetrator would be caught and appropriately dealt with.

"So how will we handle this, cuz?" Jason had walked ahead to join Drew while Sara lagged behind as Shadow did usual dog things like sniffing the ground and lifting his leg.

"I'll keep as close to the truth as seems logical," Drew said.

Sara enjoyed watching both men from behind. They were of similar height and build. They strutted in their camo uniforms as if proud of who they were and what they represented.

They looked all military, even if Jason was just pretending because he had to.

And the fact that both men—dark haired with silver highlights that glowed now and then as they walked beneath streetlights—happened to be shapeshifters? That wasn't obvious at the moment, but Sara was well aware of it.

Everyone they eventually met up with would know it, too.

"I'll tell them you went to get your cover dog Shadow to take him back to your quarters for the night, and you found evidence of an attempted break-in at the kennel. Since the lab is below, you checked there, too, and found there was an apparent attempt to break in to the refrigeration storage unit."

"Will you mention that it wasn't the first time an Alpha Force member became aware of possible tampering?" Sara had moved up, urging Shadow forward, so she wouldn't have to speak loudly to be heard.

"That's not necessary now," Drew said. "We'll hold it

back, use the knowledge when and if it makes sense for trapping our bad guy."

Jason had stayed quiet all this time. That wasn't like him. Sara expected a quip of some sort.

When he did speak, it was to Drew. "I think it's important, cuz, to make it clear I was the one who noticed the attempted break-in. If we do get our bad guy to make himself visible, he may not be happy. It'll be better if I'm the one who has the fun of fighting back."

He didn't even look at Sara, damn him. He ignored her. Pretended she wasn't even with them. What, was Shadow walking himself?

"I appreciate your attempt to protect me, Jason, if that's what you're doing," Sara said coldly. "But as you know full well by now, I can take care of myself. I'll definitely be prepared."

"Maybe so," Jason retorted, "but since when have you become a shapeshifter? Or maybe you want to buy into those rumors we're about to exaggerate—that all you gotta do is take some of the elixir. One of us is a lot more likely to be able to—"

"Enough," Drew cut in. They had reached the exterior of the sham jail area of the base. There were still a lot of voices emanating from inside, so clearly the party wasn't over. "We need to present a unified front. My orders, for now, are that Sara will be our lead since she'll represent not only Alpha Force but also the general. I'll start things off by making the announcement that hopefully will result in our capturing whoever's doing this."

"Fine," Jason snapped, but Sara was glad to see he was addressing Drew's back. She followed with Shadow. Jason was left to follow them into the concrete building usually used for storage that now represented triumph and unity in the two units' working together.

Yet they were about to be torn apart again, Sara thought.

Temporarily. But when the thief was caught, everyone else, in both units and otherwise at Ft. Lukman, would be able to cheer.

Chapter 22

"Everyone, listen up," Drew called from the front of the crowd.

If Jason had been in charge, he'd have let out a loud whistle to get the crowd's attention. But his cuz was a major in a crowd of mostly subordinates, except for the generals. So everyone listened up.

Jason did, too, although he kept a sideward gaze on Sara and Shadow, who stood just behind Drew. Like it or not, and notwithstanding Drew's outranking him, Jason would do what was needed to keep Sara out of whatever was about to explode.

Sure, she was one fine military officer, trained and all that. But despite her skills, this wasn't her war.

It was Alpha Force's, since it involved someone attempting to undermine it by stealing its best underlying weapon: the elixir.

"You all need to know what's going on," Drew continued loudly. "We've just uncovered an incident at our laboratory where apparently someone tried to break in and possibly steal some elixir. Right now we've set some guards there. We need to move the premixed elixir to a safer location, though. We'll figure out where first thing tomorrow morning, then get it done."

General Yarrow joined him at the front of the throng.

Good, Jason figured. That would give even more authority to what Drew was saying.

And most of it was true.

Except maybe the part about moving the elixir. That was just a ruse to smoke out whoever would attack the formula in motion and try to take it then.

If that didn't do it—well, they'd use wherever the stuff was theoretically taken to keep the trap set. Whoever it was would undoubtedly move soon.

Maybe thinking that all he had to do was steal some of the elixir, drink it and turn into a wolf who could be vicious enough to ward off all who would stop his theft.

Not gonna happen, you goon, Jason thought.

"If whoever tried to steal the elixir would come forward and confess, we'll make sure things go a lot easier on him," the general said calmly. "We'll need to take precautions that the elixir, and the secrecy of Alpha Force, haven't been compromised, but that person might even be able to help us. Advise us on why you did it and how we can better protect our people and our Alpha Force supplies and objectives."

That, too, wasn't reality, but Jason still felt admiration for the general. Something like that just might make the bad guy step forward to protect his own butt.

No one in the large crowd remained in disguise after the exercise. All stood watching as if they gave a damn. None leaped up and confessed.

No matter.

The bars would be lowered tomorrow. Whoever it was would be caught, confession or not.

And Jason, on behalf of Alpha Force, would be there to lay his paws all over the guy.

Sara felt exhausted.

Though she had only been part of the Ft. Lukman exercises as an observer, that had still been tiring—to make sure all seemed to go well.

And then there'd been all that had happened since.

She was back in the BOQ now. After the meeting Drew had presided over, she'd wandered through the crowd, using Shadow as her ostensible reason for walking around.

She had eavesdropped on a lot of conversations.

Some Alpha Force members sounded outraged that someone had used their primo exercise as a cover for trying to steal the elixir.

"What a jerk," Jock Larabey proclaimed. The muscular lieutenant shook his head and gritted his teeth as if he'd have liked being in wolf form to go for the perpetrator's jugular.

"The fool probably wants to become like us," Colleen Hodell said, running a hand sharply through her layered, tawny hair as if she wished it belonged to the bad guy. "Can you blame whoever it is?"

"Maybe not." Rainey Jessop sucked in her lips grimly as she looked at her Alpha Force boss. "But that isn't going to happen."

Sara had listened just as avidly to some USFT members. Captain Rynton Tierney was his nasty, confrontational self as he told his subordinates, "You'd think after a successful exercise like we had, those damned conceited Alpha Forcers would suck it up and not assume the whole world wants to be them. We don't. We just have to work with them."

Other members of that team were not as blunt, but neither did anyone she heard admit to believing the rumors that they, too, could become shapeshifters on the swig of a bottle—nor did any say they wanted to. No indication from this who'd been trying to steal the stuff.

Afterward, Jason took Shadow back with him. "He's going to stay with me in my apartment tonight," he told

Sara. "I'll enjoy his company. No need for both of us to be on our own. And you should be safe as long as you're in your own quarters—so head back there with other Alpha Forcers who're your neighbors then stay inside your apartment." He'd turned his back on Sara then and walked off with his cover dog.

Leaving her feeling hurt. And bereft.

But she made herself snap out of it—after watching Jason's sexy backside for a minute more than she should have. They were both doing what they should: staying away from one another.

But even if Jason hadn't made that jibe, Sara would have felt envious of Shadow and the fact the dog could stay, unquestioned, in the same apartment as Jason.

If Sara could have...well, she wouldn't get any sleep that way.

She might not, anyway, despite how tired she felt. Her mind might not leave her alone after all this.

She had hung around that busy area until some Alpha Force members were ready to head back to the BOQ. She'd said goodbye to them inside the main entry hall and headed toward the door to the stairs leading to her unit.

As she started walking up the steps, though, Colleen came into the stairwell behind her. "Hey, Sara?" she said. "Got a minute?"

Sara turned and looked down. Colleen had a perplexed expression on her face. "Sure," Sara said. Did she want Sara to help her shift again? But Rainey had looked fine that evening.

"Come on outside with me, would you? I thought I heard something that might help to figure out what's going on with that attempt to steal some of the elixir."

"Really?" Sara perked up slightly. That might be worth staying out of bed for a few minutes—especially if she learned something that could help catch the thief even before the planned ruse for tomorrow.

She'd love to do that, particularly if she could then show Jason she was more than just the general's assistant.

She followed Colleen back outside. Together, they stood in the shadow of the BOQ.

"I don't know if it'll help or not, but there's something I need to see in the lab before I tell you what I suspect. I know it's late, but what I heard is just so odd, and yet it might make sense. But I want to look and see if all the pieces fit together."

"I'd rather wait till morning," Sara said. "I'm tired. Aren't you? You were right there in the middle of the exercise."

"And that's why… Okay. If you don't want to come, I'll do it on my own. I can tell Drew tomorrow, or the general, if I'm right."

Sara pondered that, but only for a minute.

She wasn't about to tell anyone, even Colleen, about the ruse they would be conducting tomorrow—or about what had really happened that night with the attempt to steal the elixir.

But if she could learn something useful just by going back there…

She recalled Jason's warning, of course. He'd said she should stay in her quarters. But this was Colleen. A member of Alpha Force. Even if they weren't good friends, they were at least close enough acquaintances that Sara had helped the feline shifter before. Had no reason not to trust her. And she would stay wary.

Besides, she still had a military issue weapon in her pocket as she had earlier that evening.

"Let's hurry," she told Colleen. "I'd really like to get to bed soon."

But as it turned out, Sara realized about twenty minutes later, she wasn't going to get to see her bed that night at all.

Maybe it was exhaustion, or her belief she could solve the main Alpha Force problem before Jason or anyone else could, but despite her earlier determination to remain wary, she wasn't as careful as she should have been.

After Colleen had slipped her card for the two of them to pass through the kennel with the barking dogs, they headed for the door downstairs to the lab area.

"I just need to check my recollections about something down there," Colleen said.

She had a key card for that, which somewhat surprised Sara since not all Alpha Force members were given ready access to the labs. Maybe Colleen was working on the elixir formula without Sara knowing about it.

But when they reached the bottom of the stairway, Colleen stopped, moved swiftly behind Sara and grabbed her around the neck, jabbing the barrel of a small gun against her cheek.

"Hold very still while I pat you down," Colleen said, slightly loosening her grip around Sara's neck as she ran her hands along her sides—and pulled Sara's weapon from her pocket. "Ah, here it is. Now we're going to go into that dumb little office of Drew's down here and you're going to call him."

Sara felt dumbfounded. "It's you?" she demanded, although her words came out as a croak since Colleen once more held her neck as she propelled Sara down the hall. "But why?"

"Shut up," Colleen demanded and kicked Sara's side. "You don't need to know anything. You just need to obey me, you damned nonshifter bitch."

What the hell was she doing?

Jason had been outside giving Shadow a final walk of

the night when he saw Sara leaving the BOQ with Colleen Hodell.

Staying in deep shadows, he followed.

He realized, after they passed through most of the base, that they were heading toward the kennel/lab building. Why? Especially at this hour.

He decided it was a good thing he had Shadow with him as cover. He could say he needed to leave his dog in the kennel tonight—which wasn't true. He liked having Shadow's company whenever possible and had planned to have him around overnight.

Now, though, he drew nearer, watching as Sara and Colleen walked into the upstairs area of the kennel—causing all the dogs inside to bark. He waited for a minute, then entered with Shadow before the noise died down. Were they just going to see the dogs?

Colleen's cover feline was in her own quarters, wasn't she? This probably wasn't a middle-of-the-night visit to wish the small cougar look-alike sweet dreams.

So...were they going downstairs into the lab?

If so, why? Was Sara taking Colleen there? She had an access key. But what was this all about?

Using his own card key, Jason walked inside with Shadow and waited while his dog traded nose sniffs through the wire mesh entries to the kennels—also using his own enhanced senses to try to hear voices through the barks.

He couldn't make out any words, but he did hear something from downstairs, or so he thought.

He tied Shadow's leash to a kennel door then headed toward the stairway, where he carefully opened the door.

And listened some more.

And froze. If he had been shifted, he knew his hackles would rise.

"I don't understand," Sara was saying. She sounded as

if something was choking her. "Colleen, if there's something we should—"

"I told you to shut up, bitch! Oh, and if you're wondering what you're doing here, you're bait. And my ticket to get out of here with everything I want. Come on, we're going to see the guard who's now outside the refrigerator unit…again."

There was a gagging sound, and the shuffling of feet.

Jason almost bolted down there. Instead, he made himself wait patiently, but only for a minute.

He was glad the dogs kept barking—and that Colleen was not a wolf shifter.

He knew what he had to do. And he had to do it fast.

He drew his weapon, in case he ran into the two women, but he prayed that wouldn't happen. Colleen would undoubtedly use Sara as a shield.

No, Jason knew he needed the element of surprise to save Sara.

Slowly, but with utter determination, he sneaked his way downstairs and into the nearest lab.

"What the hell—" Kerry began. The sentry had been sitting on a chair while guarding the door to the refrigeration unit, but now he stood.

When she realized where they were heading, Sara had hoped that the guard would be able to help her.

Instead, she realized, she had become a bargaining chip.

"I know you're buddies with Lieutenant McLinder," Colleen oozed smoothly from behind her. "If you don't let me into the refrigerator this time, I'll kill her slowly in front of you, and then it'll be your turn."

"But I can't…" the guard said. "You'll be caught, anyway. Why don't you—"

Sara felt Colleen's arm tightening around her neck and

tried not to gag. Instead, she realized how lightheaded she had become. She was going to pass out.

"Do it!" Colleen snapped. She aimed the weapon she held now in her free hand at Kerry, waving it back and forth between Sara and him, even as she kept Sara close.

This time, Kerry closed his eyes briefly then nodded. He used the electronic release and soon the door snapped open.

"This way," Colleen said. "Both of you."

Sara was too weak to resist. She knew she was going to die, anyway now. How could she have been so stupid? She hadn't suspected Colleen.

She should have suspected everyone.

Now…she would at least try to save Kerry.

And if only she could see Jason just one more time…

"He's right," she managed to say to Colleen. "You'll be caught. You think I just went with you like an obedient dog? I let people know—"

"You bitch! You told someone, signaled them, whatever?" Colleen's fury spewed out—and so did the force at Sara's throat. She saw Colleen wave Kerry into the large refrigeration room, even as she was dragged inside.

She was suddenly released, and she stumbled to the floor. That was when Colleen, still holding the gun on them, pulled free a large cloth bag she'd used as a belt around her waist and started, with her free hand, to carefully stick vials of elixir from the many shelves of the unit into it. Because of their usual potentially rough handling in the backpacks of shifters' aides, Sara knew that the thick glass of the storage vials was fairly unbreakable, and the seals were secure and tight.

Shifting Alpha Force members were generally issued only enough of the elixir to help with their next change or two to keep in their possession. How much was Colleen taking? All of it that was currently being stored, apparently—enough to trigger hundreds of shifts.

"I thank you, and my family thanks you," Colleen said. "Not that you'll be around to enjoy their gratitude. But now there's something I'd better do so I can..." Her voice tapered off as she moved away from them.

Sara had no idea what Colleen meant by her family and its thanks, but she couldn't be allowed to get away with this. As Colleen backed toward the door, Sara, weak as she felt, aimed a careful glance toward Kerry. The look in his dark eyes seemed terrified, but she thought she detected a small nod.

"Now!" she cried as Colleen moved to open the door, the bulging sack attached at her shoulder.

But the distraction didn't help.

"You're going to die in here," Colleen said. "I don't even need to use this." She waved the gun toward both of them, making Kerry hesitate, Sara saw from the corner of her eye.

She didn't hesitate, though—but her strength had ebbed because of the choking she'd undergone.

She didn't reach the door before it slammed shut—leaving Kerry and her inside.

Should he have taken the time to shift?

No matter now. Jason figured that he would be better able to slink around the lab facilities—and subdue Colleen—while in wolf form.

He had stopped within the main lab and set things up for himself, drinking elixir and using the light to ensure he could shift quickly.

But not before he had used his phone to notify his cousin what was going on, and where.

Now, easing his shifted form against the wall, he moved down the hallway toward where he heard voices—clearly,

*now that he was in wolf form, despite the fact they radiated
from behind apparently closed doors.*

Sara was in trouble.

He had to get there in time....

*Suddenly, a form jumped out of a door just in front of
him.*

A growling cougar.

It leaped upon him—its fangs going for his neck.

Sara stopped talking to Kerry, who, shivering, had
ceased arguing with her and headed toward the control
panel within the refrigeration unit.

He'd been certain that Colleen would be waiting outside
to shoot them. She knew better.

Especially now, with the roaring sounds of animals
fighting to the death outside, the sound muffled by the
thickness of the door.

Jason, shifted? Some other werewolf?

And Colleen? A few minutes had passed since she had
locked them inside. Had it been a mistake to lie and claim
Sara had the foresight to secretly notify someone she was
going to the lab with Colleen?

At last, Kerry was successful. The door burst open, allowing heat to pour into the area that was just above freez-
ing. Sara no longer had her gun. Colleen had taken it. But
even if she'd had it, aiming it would have been difficult.

She had to stop shivering.

She first needed a weapon.

The best thing she could find at the moment was one of
the substantial shelves that was now emptied of elixir. She
grabbed one, wresting it away from the wall.

"You take one, too," she demanded of Kerry.

Then she hurried outside into the hall.

And stopped, horrified to see the fighting wolf and cougar. Was the cougar winning? Both were covered in blood.

Her wooden weapon was unlikely to help, but she ran forward, anyway, hoping she could get a good aim at the feline's head.

Before she could, the cougar saw her, bared its teeth and leaped away from the wolf and onto her. Sara felt its fangs on her throat—but only for an instant.

The wolf had not only knocked it off her, it shoved the cougar onto its back on the floor and stood on its chest, its own fangs sinking into the feline's neck.

The creature roared and moved—but only for a minute.

"Freeze!" shouted a human voice, and suddenly a cadre of armed military men, led by Major Drew Connell, stood down the hall, aiming their weapons at the cougar.

The wolf moved off it and loped toward Sara. It soon sat at her side, bloody but looking up at her with caring golden eyes.

"Thank you, Jason," Sara whispered throatily, bending to give the wolf a hug.

Chapter 23

It was over.

Sara sat in General Yarrow's office once again, eager to hear everything that had gone on since Lieutenant Colleen Hodell was taken into custody yesterday.

From what Sara had heard, Colleen was being flown to Fort Leavenworth, Kansas, where she would be incarcerated in a highly classified facility within the U.S. Disciplinary Barracks there, pending her court-martial trial for treason and more.

"So here's what we've learned, sir," Drew Connell was saying to General Yarrow, who scowled from behind his desk. Drew sat in a chair on Sara's left.

"One thing I hope you learned, Drew, is that your vetting process for Alpha Force members had better be beefed up." Greg leaned forward with his arms crossed.

"Yeah, like getting more shapeshifting car thieves to enlist." That was Jason, who sat at Sara's right. That comment brought a smile to the general's face and lightened the atmosphere, just a little.

"Yeah, car thieves do a good job of protecting the rest of us," Greg Yarrow agreed. "Or at least one does."

Jason's face lit up in a proud grin that managed to enhance his rugged, handsome features.

Sara felt herself begin to smile, too, but she stopped herself. She still had a lot of questions.

She also knew that her time here, around Alpha Force and Jason, was limited.

Not much to smile about…despite Jason's teasing bad-boy way breaking through the otherwise heavy atmosphere here.

"What do you mean, sir?" she asked, addressing the general. "I take it that there were things about Lieutenant Hodell that weren't known before?"

She made it a question, since she didn't want to accuse Drew, or his other Alpha Forcers, of incompetence. They had their procedures that had to be followed before a shifter could be invited to enlist and join their unit. She had to presume that those procedures were used with Colleen Hodell, too—even if they failed.

"That's right," Drew acknowledged. "She was one hell of a liar. She convinced not only me but our whole enlistment committee, too, that she was a solid shifting citizen despite an upbringing in the wilds of South Dakota that left a lot to be desired."

Hadn't she said she'd come from the Midwest? That part of what she'd said, at least, wasn't a lie—although she hadn't been specific about the state with Sara.

He described what they'd heard from Colleen about her childhood attempts to hide out from hunters and others who tried to kill them.

"She said that her family had had to fight back, and that some of her relatives had actually become more feral, even attacking humans and claiming it was self-defense. She didn't believe in what they were doing, so she fled as soon as she reached college age. We felt sorry for her."

She'd told Sara about her family and having to hide, not

that they'd fought back—nor that she had supposedly run away from them because of their actions.

"So what's the truth?" General Yarrow demanded, which was exactly what Sara was wondering.

Drew sighed. "Well, she's admitted now that she remained part of that family. Close to them. Hated nonshifting humans and vowed revenge on them. So when she heard rumors of Alpha Force and its elixir...well, she made up a story that had us believing she was one of the good guys and deserved a chance. She's been with Alpha Force for almost a year now, and we had no reason to doubt her, or consider her anything but what she claimed...till now."

The major looked ashen, his golden eyes, usually so much like Jason's, haunted and flat.

"That'll teach you to try to help someone, cuz," Jason interjected. Sara felt horrified at the criticism and prepared to chastise Jason, but then he continued, "Like me. I'll blame it on my family that I became such a loser, like them. I mean, I even had a loser of a cousin who developed an elixir that helped all shifters choose when they change and keep their human awareness. What could be worse? And—"

"That's enough," Drew snapped.

"Nope, it's not," Jason said. "I want to hear more about dear Colleen, but you've got to stop blaming yourself, cuz. She's the loser. Not you. Bad family or good, we make our own choices."

Drew stood suddenly and turned his back on the rest of them, looking out the window of the general's antiques-filled office. "She could have killed General Yarrow," he said, so low that Sara had to strain to hear him. Greg probably did, too, since neither had a shifter's enhanced hearing.

She rose and put a comforting hand on Drew's camo-clad shoulder. "Did she admit that?"

"Yeah. You know, she shoved stones into the road to

slow the general's car. Then she shot a wooden arrow that she'd set fire to, one she'd doused with an incendiary liquid that enhanced the flames but burned up so it was unidentifiable. She'd already checked out the general's Jeep and figured it would work. Hopefully kill him, or at least warn him to stay away from Ft. Lukman."

"Why did she want that?" Sara felt confused.

"She was angry that the general had brought the USFT unit here for exercises. She wanted the base to stay remote—so she could steal as much of the elixir as had already been formulated before running back to her family. But then she decided to use the USFT presence, frame its members, so she could get away with what she wanted."

"Which was?" Jason was now standing at his cousin's other side. He was touching Drew's other shoulder in sympathy, and Sara adored him for that.

"Okay, let's sit down again," Drew said. "I'll tell you what we know, or think we know, so far. Some Colleen has admitted, some is just speculation, but here goes."

They all resumed their seats. Drew explained that Colleen, instead of hating her family and its destructive attitude toward nonshifting humans, felt part of them. Wanted to help them.

Her intent, in joining Alpha Force, was to steal both the formula for the elixir and as much of the brewed formulation as she could. She'd take it all home to her family—they'd already acquired some property in the Canadian wilderness—and they'd all learn how to make elixir. They planned to take turns drinking it then going places where they could attack people while shifted and kill as many as they could.

"They surely didn't think they'd be able to destroy all regular humans that way, did they?" Sara demanded.

Drew's face looked bleak. "No, but apparently they hated

people enough to kill as many as they could possibly get away with."

"Strange. And damned nasty." General Yarrow stood behind his desk, shaking his head. "Did she manage to steal the formula? Any of the elixir?"

"No, I do keep the formula well protected in a safe down in the lab area," Drew said. "And the amount of elixir kept in the refrigerator at any time wouldn't have let her succeed in her horrible plan, either. I think that's one reason she was so frustrated. She'd stolen a little, whenever she could get her hands on it, but not much. But she did make good use of having the USFT group here."

"How?" Jason asked. Where he sat, at Drew's other side, made it harder for Sara to see him. Just as well. She needed to wean herself away from what she now considered an addiction to him.

"She started the rumor that the elixir, taken by nonshifters, would turn them into shapeshifters. She swore the few she told to secrecy, which of course meant they blabbed it to one another. She'd also 'revealed' it to her aide Rainey so she, too, would pass the lie around. The thing was, Rainey decided to try it herself."

"Oh, my," Sara exclaimed. "Is that what gave her the stomach problems she's been experiencing?"

"Exactly," Drew said.

"But did it—" General Yarrow began.

"Turn her into a shifter?" finished Drew. "Of course not."

Colleen had additionally planted the AK-47 aimed at General Yarrow's car out of anger that things weren't going exactly as she'd planned, and she blamed the Alpha Force CO.

"She also resented your attempts to protect the general and chase down what was happening here," Drew said to Sara.

"So she was the one to deface my car, too," Sara said.

"Right," Drew agreed.

"Anyone contacted her family?" General Yarrow asked.

"We've tried, but they've disappeared."

"Into the wilds of Canada?" Jason asked.

"Maybe," Drew said. "Just in case, we've notified the Royal Canadian Mounted Police. And we're still trying to figure out how she finally got a copy of the card key that let her downstairs into the lab. Like all Alpha Forcers, she had a card key to get into the upstairs kennel area, but since she wasn't working on the formula she didn't have a way to open the door to the lab stairway. She'd been the one to scratch that door out of frustration that she couldn't open it."

"I wonder..." Sara said. She told them about how she had helped Colleen shift that one night when Rainey was ill. "I don't know how she did it, but there probably wasn't anyone else around the lab building that night. Maybe she found a hidden card key then."

"She's stopped talking," Drew said, "so we may never know."

Their meeting was finally over, but Jason wished that it had gone on all day, not just the morning.

"You going to drop over to the area where the general's car and Sara's are finally being examined by the military investigating team?" Drew asked him.

"Yeah," Jason said. From the corner of his eye, he watched Sara as she conversed with her boss, the general. Drew had already said that a couple more exercises would be held here at Ft. Lukman with the USFT gang, and then both they and Alpha Force would be deployed to handle the overseas rescue of the kidnapped government civilians.

The general was apparently heading back to the Pentagon.

So, then, would Sara. Jason knew that, and it made him feel like someone had run over him with that big car-mover tow truck he'd rented. Or worse.

Well, he'd already known that things couldn't stay as they'd been. At least he'd been able to have mind-blowing sex with Sara. Twice.

He'd have to be content with the memory.

Yeah. Right.

"I think I'll head there now, in fact," he told Drew. "Are the feds there yet?"

"Yes, they arrived early this morning and I met them at the gate to the base then took them where they needed to go."

"Great. I'll be interested to hear what they have to say."

"And you can do a little prompting, if you want. See if any of the detritus found in the ashes could be remains of the arrow or ignition stuff."

"Oh, and what the hell did that bitch Colleen use to mess up my breathing, make me cough when I found where she'd been hiding to shoot her arrow?"

"That's still an unknown, too," Drew said. "She only grinned when we asked. But see if the feds can draw some samples from the earth and run tests."

Jason had become enough of a military peon to salute goodbye to General Yarrow and mention that Drew had given him the assignment of helping the fed investigation team. He nodded briefly toward Sara, whose stare, with those gorgeous blue-green eyes, remained unreadable.

And then he left.

Sara sat in the general's office for a long time after Drew and Jason walked out.

Greg and she had talked. About the situation with Colleen Hodell and Alpha Force. And the harm the angry shapeshifter had inflicted on the unit.

As well as relief it hadn't been any worse.

They also discussed Sara. And her future in the military. As Greg's aide.

So much depended on things that weren't entirely within her control. Like shapeshifters.

And yet....

Afterward, she walked into the part of the base garage where the general's Jeep, and her car, were still being stored.

"Hi," she said to Kerry, the sentry. Sweet, young guy, he flushed and saluted and waved her into the secured area.

Four guys in suits were there, wandering around the site and apparently poking here and there into the remains of General Yarrow's car. They wore rubber gloves and carried a bunch of plastic bags with ashes and more potential evidence inside them.

And there was Jason, with them. Scowling.

"How are they doing?" Sara said after reaching Jason's side.

"Fine. Probably confirming all the stuff we already know now."

"Well, that should be a good thing." She paused. "When you're done here, would you call me? There are a few things I'd like to discuss with you."

"Sure." He looked at her then. Was that a shred of hope she saw in his gold-flecked eyes? If so, it disappeared almost immediately.

"Promise you'll call," she added.

"Sure," he said again, and only then did she leave the suits to their work.

* * *

Jason watched Sara depart. How could she look so sexy in the same old shirt and pants with camo print and work shoes as everyone else around here?

Everyone but these guys he was watching. Listening to their chatter. Finding them exceedingly annoying.

So far, he had not heard anything that he hadn't suspected before.

He'd told them about the bow-and-arrow scenario. The flame accelerant. The stuff that had sickened him outside—of which they still needed to collect samples.

They'd taken pictures of these ruins and the damage to Sara's car.

Nothing new.

Now he wished they'd hurry.

He had a phone call to make.

Would he hear anything good from Sara? Maybe she just wanted to talk over more about Colleen Hodell and her treachery around here.

Sara had seemed excited. Maybe even eager to talk to him.

More debriefing about what had happened around here could excite her that way. But not him.

So could her obtaining orders from the general to return to D.C. and their usual posting. Maybe she just wanted to say goodbye.

Hell, all this speculation was doing him no good. But as much as he tried, he couldn't keep his mind off Sara.

Sara was in the cafeteria, drinking coffee with Rainey Jessop when her smartphone rang.

Poor Rainey was distraught. The pretty, young brunette with the curly hair said she'd loved being a shapeshifter's aide.

She hated that the shapeshifter she'd been assigned to was a liar and a potential killer.

She hated that she had been a fool.

"I really believed her," she had wailed a while ago. "I thought it would be so cool to drink something and turn into a shifter. Instead—" She'd groaned and clutched her stomach. "It still hurts just thinking about it."

"I'm sorry," Sara had lied. Oh, she felt bad that the young woman had suffered, but she had brought it on herself.

Not that the truth about shapeshifters was easily available on the internet. But if Rainey had just asked someone around here—someone other than the bitch whose aide she had been—she'd have had it verified that shapeshifting was strictly hereditary. Not something she could just opt into by swigging a drink.

Now she was delighted that her phone rang, a good excuse to say bye to Rainey.

And she was even more delighted to see who it was: Jason.

"Hey," she said. "Those guys through?"

"Yes," he said.

"Great. Then please meet me outside the BOQ in five minutes. There's something inside my apartment I'd like you to see."

"Aren't you afraid that'll look like fraternizing?" His tone over the phone sounded jaded and skeptical.

"No. Come on over and let me explain."

Five minutes later she was outside the BOQ door she preferred as an entrance, where she could open the door and walk up the stairs to the floor where her unit was.

She saw Jason strolling down the sidewalk toward her.

She tried not to smile but didn't succeed.

Nor did she succeed in keeping herself from melting

down below from the heat she couldn't suppress at just seeing him.

"Hi," she said as he reached her side. She looked up into his eyes, watching his gaze heat up as he observed her, too.

He was the one to pull away. "What's up?"

"Come to my apartment and I'll explain."

She could hardly keep herself from grasping his hand and pulling him up the stairs at twice his pace. No one was around in the hall to observe their entry. Probably a good thing. But at this point...

He walked behind her into her small apartment. She shut the door behind him—then reached up and pulled him down for one torrid kiss.

"Hey," he said against her mouth. "This feels like fraternizing to me. Not my problem, but you're the officer."

"Yeah, I am. But my next assignment...well, that's what I want to discuss with you."

She adjourned into the kitchenette, where she pulled a high-end beer from the fridge—a bottle for each of them. Then she led him into her living room and pointed to the small sofa.

"Please, sit down."

When he complied, she joined him, putting her beer bottle onto the coffee table.

"So...what's up?" The remote expression on his gorgeous masculine face nearly made her cry. But she understood where it came from. He probably thought she'd invited him here to beg him to fix her car.

She might do that—but not now.

"Well, I have a decision to make, and I wanted your input." She felt her throat close with emotion and took a quick swig of beer to open it again.

"Yeah?" He still sounded skeptical. Where was that teasing bad boy that she had fallen in love with?

Love? Was she willing to admit that even to herself?

Hell, yes. Wasn't that why she had brought him here?

She held her beer bottle toward her lap and watched it, not his face, as she said, "General Yarrow told me he's leaving for the Pentagon in a few days, after another exercise is held here between the two units. Both groups should be deployed for their joint mission next week, if all goes well, as it should."

She looked up to see Jason nodding. "Yeah, without the shenanigans of Colleen Hodell getting in the way." She opened her mouth to continue, but he beat her to it. "So... does that mean you're leaving, too?" There was a choking note in his voice. Dared she hope that he wanted her to stay?

"That depends," she said quietly. "Jason, do you know Lieutenant Quinn Parran and Staff Sergeant Kristine Norwood?"

"Sure. They're Alpha Force, stationed here. They're off on vacation now, but they helped to save Simon and Grace—Quinn's brother and sister-in-law—from some pretty bad stuff that happened on their honeymoon."

"That's right." Sara nodded. "They're on vacation...together. A lieutenant and a staff sergeant."

"Guess they're fraternizing," Jason said.

"Guess they are—but since they're members of Alpha Force, and things around here aren't as formal as the rest of the military, it's okay."

At that, Jason's tight expression seemed to change into something else. That hint of hope was back. So was his cocky attitude, the way he gave a half grin. "So I've heard."

"General Yarrow said he needs eyes and ears right here. Oh, he thinks your cousin and the others are doing a fine job running Alpha Force, but he suggested that I stay here on a long-term assignment and observe what's going on. Report to him often. Even offer suggestions for keeping

Alpha Force running well and interacting with other units like the USFT."

"So you might stay here?"

"Yes, but that depends on you. If you think—"

She didn't get a chance to finish. Suddenly, both bottles of beer were on the table, and she was on her back on the narrow sofa, Jason on top of her. His lips were on hers. His hands were exploring her body, first on top of her uniform, then beneath it.

"Hey, Lieutenant," Jason whispered against her mouth. "I'm all for informality around here. Aren't you?"

"Yes," she said breathlessly. "But Jason, for how long—"

She didn't get to finish before he pulled back. "If you're asking how long I'd like to fraternize, how about forever? I love you, Sara."

His tone was so serious that it brought tears to her eyes. "I love you, too, Jason."

"And if you think you could stand hanging around a mechanic, former thief and wolf shapeshifter—"

"Stand it? I'd love it!"

He kissed her again. And again. And soon his hands were tearing off her clothes.

"Can I watch you shift again tonight?" she gasped between kisses and her own efforts at undressing him.

"Count on it, Lieutenant," he said, and then he entered her.

Epilogue

Just over a month had passed since the last exercise at Ft. Lukman between Alpha Force and the USFT—and the capturing of Colleen Hodell for her attempts on the general's life as well as Sara's and others.

A lot had happened in that month, Sara thought as she sat once more at the front of the assembly room. It was filled again with people from both military units, only now there was a true camaraderie between them.

As there should be. They had joined together in the mission to rescue the government workers held captive in the Middle East—and had succeeded in liberating them.

The rumbling of voices around her sounded pleased. An aura of excitement enveloped the audience members.

This was a special event. The USFT members would be redeployed to another base as of tomorrow, their mission here accomplished.

That was why today had been chosen for the awarding of medals for bravery.

And more.

Sara sat between Melanie Harding-Connell, Drew's wife, on one side, and Captain Rynton Tierney on the other. Melanie had always been friendly, thanks to her close ties to Alpha Force. Rynton not so much—before.

Now he was chatting with her on and off as though they were best friends.

"I still wish I'd been more than an on-site observer during the rescue," he was telling her. "Things happened so fast—and all to the good."

"Your real-time reports back here were definitely appreciated," Sara assured him. She had been on the radio with him a lot of the time, giving up-to-the moment updates to General Yarrow and General Myars, who had remained here.

"You've heard, haven't you, that the terrorists we rounded up in the raid—those who survived—are being sneered at by their fellow countrymen for claiming that they were attacked by a bunch of dogs as well as snipers."

Sara laughed. "Yes, I heard that."

A hush suddenly befell the room. Sara quickly looked up. Speaking of the generals… There they were. Behind them stood the members of Alpha Force and the Ultra Special Forces Team who had been deployed on this mission.

That included Jason. Sara couldn't help smiling at how proud he looked, all smiles up there in his camo uniform just like all the rest—but somehow he stood out.

"Thank you all for coming," General Yarrow said to the crowd. "This is a very special day."

"It sure is. For all of us." That was General Myars who, for once, didn't appear to be playing one-upmanship with the CO of Alpha Force.

They told everyone to stand, and the entire room pledged allegiance to the American flag.

And then it was time.

More than a dozen troops had been sent to perform the overseas mission, most of them from the units stationed here.

"I want to read the commendation from the commander

in chief first," General Yarrow said, and he did. The president of the United States expressed his pride in the soldiers who had participated and those who had helped to train them.

Next both generals pulled out the medals of bravery and each awarded them to the members of their units who had performed so honorably in rescuing the captive American citizens.

That was when Sara couldn't help really smiling. Oh, it felt good to see the commendations given to Alpha Force members Drew Connell, Seth Ambers, Jock Larabey, Marshall Vincenzo and Simon Parran.

Their shifting aides, too, were commended.

She even appreciated the medals given to the USFT members: Cal Brown, Samantha Everly, Manning Breman and Vera Swainey.

But mostly she waited.

And then it was time. "We've saved the best for last," Greg Yarrow said. "Sergeant Jason Connell, please step forward."

Jason did, approaching the general.

"Jason, thanks to our camera equipment used on this mission, we both heard and saw your actions in combat, when two tangos attempted to flee with a couple of the hostages. You were in wolf form then, and despite the gunfire around you, you attacked the enemy, brought them both down and maintained domination over them until the USFT members were able to approach and take control. I hereby award you this medal for your bravery." The general took a box from the table near him, pulled out a medal and pinned it onto Jason's uniform."

"Thank you, sir," Jason said.

"And in addition," the general continued, "that special bravery both then and here at Ft. Lukman during our recent issues has earned you more, Sergeant. You have earned the right to be equals with the other shifters in Alpha Force. You are hereby promoted to Second Lieutenant." And General Yarrow pinned those bars onto Jason's uniform, as well.

Jason beamed. "I really appreciate this, sir." He saluted the general, then turned and saluted General Myars and the others. "We all did a damned good job, didn't we?" he asked his fellow soldiers.

They mostly laughed and shook his hand.

Sara couldn't get close to him. Not just then. But she would congratulate him later.

Damn it all, Jason thought a while later. Who'd have thought that he'd actually be proud to be in the military?

But heck, he was a real officer now.

Which meant...

The crowd was dispersing.

And there she was. Sara.

She hurried up to him. Saluted. "Good afternoon, Lieutenant," she said.

"Good afternoon, Lieutenant," he repeated.

They had been told of his promotion in advance, and she had already expressed her pride to him. But now...

"Hey. Come here. I want to show you my new...stuff. And prove to you how brave I really am."

She laughed. "I already know how brave you are. But I do want to see that medal more closely."

Lord, was she beautiful. And she looked at him so proudly that he couldn't help grinning back.

He hurried with her into Drew's office and closed the door behind them. His cuz had been primed to stay away for now.

"What's—" Sara began, and then she gasped. He saw

the tears in her gorgeous blue-green eyes as she watched him go down on one knee.

He was about to do something he'd never have dared—before this moment.

"Lieutenant Sara McLinder, would you do me the honor of fraternizing with me for the rest of your life—I mean, becoming my wife?"

"Oh, Jason. Oh, yes, yes, yes."

He pulled out the box containing the ring he'd bought a few days earlier on a trip to D.C. He'd kept it in the glove compartment of his Mustang until a short while ago, just before the awards ceremony was to begin.

He stood and slipped the ring onto Sara's finger.

And this time, when they kissed, he knew it would be the first of forever.

* * * * *

A sneaky peek at next month...

NOCTURNE™

BEYOND DARKNESS...BEYOND DESIRE

My wish list for next month's titles...

In stores from 16th April 2014:

☐ Demon Wolf — Bonnie Vanak

☐ Possessed by an Immortal — Sharon Ashwood

In stores from 6th June 2014:

☐ Night of the Shifter — Caridad Piñeiro,
   Megan Hart, Linda O. Johnston,
   Doranna Durgin & Katie Reus

Available at WHSmith, Tesco, Asda, Eason, Amazon and Apple

Just can't wait?

Visit us Online

You can buy our books online a month before they hit the shops! **www.millsandboon.co.uk**

0514/89

THE
CHATSFIELD®

Collect all 8!

Buy now at
www.millsandboon.co.uk/thechatsfield

MILLS & BOON
Book Club

Join the Mills & Boon Book Club

Subscribe to **Nocturne**™ today for 3, 6 or 12 months and you could **save over £50!**

We'll also treat you to these fabulous extras:

- **FREE L'Occitane gift set worth £10**

- **FREE home delivery**

- **Rewards scheme, exclusive offers…and much more!**

Subscribe now and save over £50
www.millsandboon.co.uk/subscribeme